The Magellan Chronicles

Quest for Glory
(Book 1)

A biographical novel series of Ferdinand Magellan

By

Brett Stortroen

The Magellan Chronicles: Quest for Glory (Book 1)

Treasure Hill Publishing
Dunedin, Fl, USA

Copyright © 2022 by Brett Stortroen

Library of Congress Cataloging-in-Publication Data

ISBN 978-1-957612-01-0

Cover art by Mark Daehlin

For inquiries, please email the author at
bstortroen@protonmail.com

Brett Stortroen

Mecca, Muhammad & the Moon-God: A Candid Investigation into the Origins of Islam

Night of the Dragon: The Saga of Saint George

The Magellan Chronicles Series (Books 1-3)

Dedication

A special thanks to Thomas Nowaczyk for editorial assistance. His insightful comments were invaluable, much appreciated, and instrumental to the project.

Another thanks to my wife Iris for having patience during the many years of research for this book.

Maps

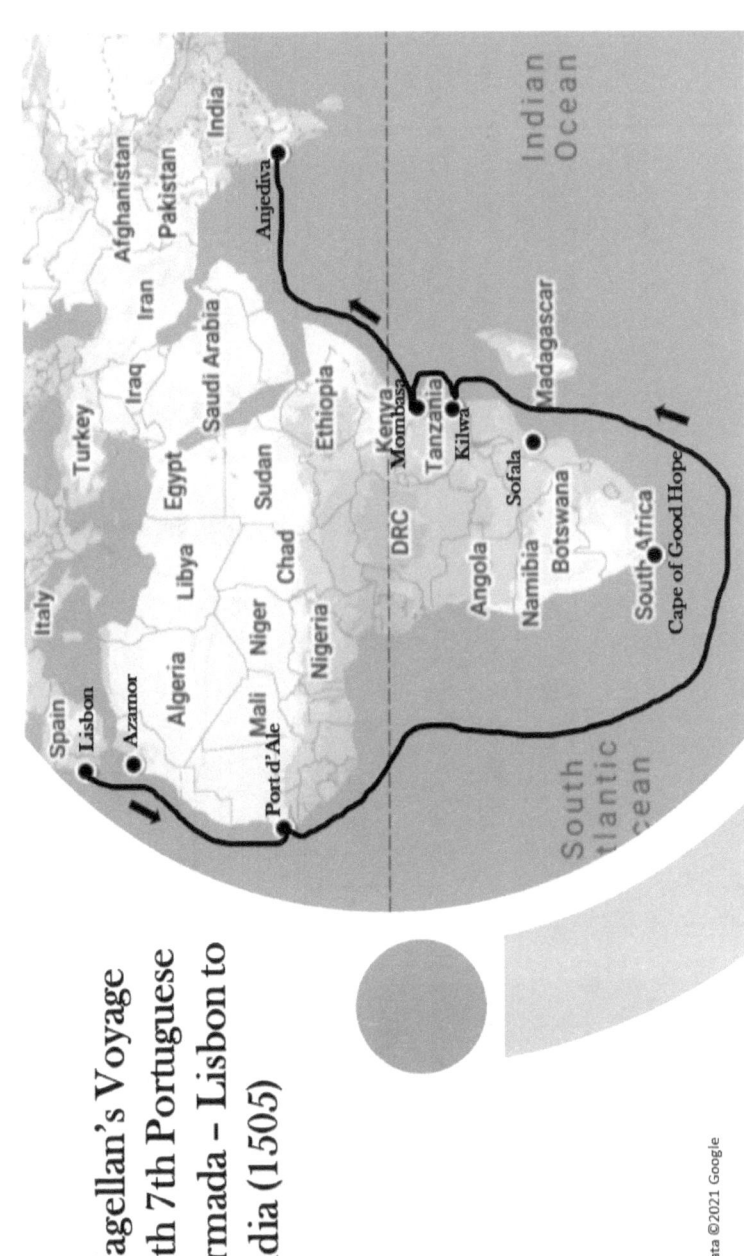

Magellan's Voyage with 7th Portuguese Armada – Lisbon to India (1505)

Map Data ©2021 Google

7th Portuguese Armada Sailing Route – Mombasa to India (Aug 16 to Oct 30, 1505)

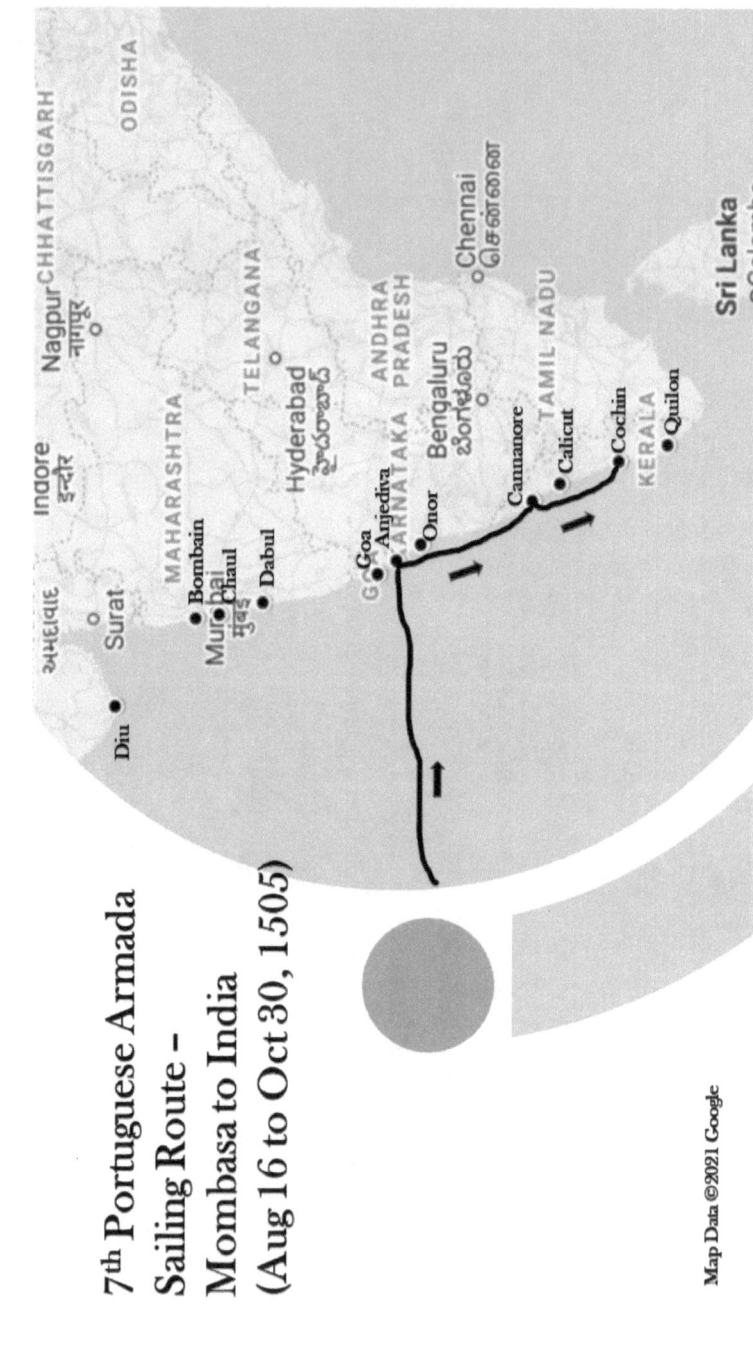

Map Data ©2021 Google

1

Lisbon, Portugal

With daring naval exploits, by men such as Amerigo Vespucci and Vasco da Gama, the tiny impoverished nation of Portugal had arisen from obscurity to become the first global maritime superpower. By December 1504, the seafaring industry in Lisbon was booming, and not even the winter chill was able to deflect the king's mandate to expand the fleet. Cold winds stirred up the mighty Tejo River. Enormous swells crashed against the docks as laborers struggled to maintain their footing on the slippery pavement while loading supplies for refitting: nails for the planks, lead to fill seams and various caulking pastes. Another large ship lay tilted on its side as sailors careened it by scouring off various barnacles and other organisms from the wooden planking. Another crew followed behind to apply pitch and tar imported from northern Germany, to seal the hull watertight. The ominous black-hued tone of the Portuguese warships anchored in port instilled admiration and awe to townsfolk and visitors alike.

Fernão de Magalhães, short, swarthy and 24 years of age, pulled at rigging on the deck of an anchored vessel. His rippled arm muscles flexed taut as he tied the last knot to secure the mast. Wind gusts splashed icy water across his exposed skin, but with an intense focus to the task at hand, he remained oblivious to the raging elements. From the dockside, Diogo de Sousa, dressed in a heavy black and furred overcoat called to Fernão, then pointed to the gangway. As he disembarked, Diogo tossed him an identical coat.

'You need to maintain your health,' Diogo said.

Fernão grinned and slipped on his overcoat. 'Brother, you know I never get sick.'

Diogo de Sousa, almost an identical twin, just slightly taller and older, was indeed Fernão de Magalhães' legitimate brother by birth. Their family lines traced back to a French crusader who fought under Duke Odo I of Burgundy during the Iberian Reconquista of the late eleventh century. Their paternal grandmother was a de Sousa, a family of nobility much respected by the Royal House of Aviz, the power behind the Portuguese throne. Their father, Rodrigo de Magalhães was appointed sheriff to the Port of Aveiro in the northwest coast of Portugal. Since Diogo was the eldest, the family decided he would change his surname from Magalhães to de Sousa in order to inherit the family estate and preserve their noble status. However, their nobility was only fourth in ranking out of five. The Magalhães brothers were indeed *fidalgos*, but they would never be guaranteed vast wealth or prestige, they would have to earn their livelihoods. Globally, the Portuguese surname 'Magalhães' would eventually evolve to the Spanish 'Magellanes' and in English, 'Magellan.'

Fernão slipped on his overcoat as he took particular notice of some men loading empty rectangular coffin-like crates onto ships. The two brothers crossed their arms and observed. Fernão pointed. 'There lies our future. One liberty chest full of pepper will free us from four years of labor, if loaded with cinnamon, eight.'

Diogo's eyebrows furrowed and released. 'Indeed, but many never return.'

Fernão tugged at his beard. 'I hear a captain can bring home up to seven times the sailor rate, a prize of 6,000 cruzados for pepper and double for cinnamon.'

'It sounds tempting,' Diogo said. 'I would only risk such a voyage to secure an early retirement . . . enough to manage our farm.'

Fernão tilted his head to Diogo and said with a twinkle in his eye, 'I hear it is all tax-free.'

The two brothers grinned. A commotion broke out across the dockyard. A resolute middle-aged man attired in a regal black, gold, and red overcoat strutted with a brisk pace toward several sailors warming themselves near an open firepit. His signatory thick black beard, long nose and thin lips identified him as the king's admiral. He barked orders, 'Get back to work! Now!'

The startled sailors scurried away to their assigned tasks.

The admiral noticed the Magalhães brother's idle posture and hurried toward them. No other man in Portugal simultaneously instilled such dread and endearing respect as did Vasco da Gama. His epic voyages from 1497-1499 and 1502-1503 opened a new Portuguese trade route around the Horn of Africa to the Indies. Before his second voyage, King Manuel commissioned him with the title "Admiral of the Seas of Arabia, Persia, India and all the Orient."

Da Gama glared at the petrified young men. 'Well, why are you two standing around? The king has given me command to outfit the armada by March, not April!'

'Pardon our break,' Diogo said. 'My brother just finished the rigging . . . the weather has been difficult—'

'Ha! You think you know foul weather?' Da Gama barked. He looked over the brothers. 'Yes, yes. I remember you both now, pages at court. You are now appointed to our marine department?'

'Yes admiral,' Fernão said.

'You must know the winds, men. It was 8 years ago when I led a fleet of 4 ships and a fine crew of 170 men to India. We set out from Malindi across the Indian Ocean, and with the summer monsoon winds at our backs, we made landing in Calicut after 23 days. But the return . . . against the winds . . . a fatal mistake. After 132 days, half our remaining men had died, most from exposure and disease. Timing of the winds is, so important.' Da Gama turned toward the Tejo's crashing waves with an empty stare. 'We made it to Lisbon with only 55 men. My brother Paulo died in my arms from disease on our return . . . I buried him in Terceira. We were so close to home—so close!'

Fernão fixated upon a dagger in the shape of a red cross dangling from a thick-gold chain around Da Gama's neck. Like all honorable noblemen, Fernão had respected and strived to achieve status by acceptance into one of three current military orders forged during the crusades of the Reconquista. A red dagger cross signified the Order of Santiago, a squared cross to the Order of Christ and a green standard ornate cross to the Order of Aviz. All three Orders had their own political aspirations.

King João II's family lineage was under the House of Aviz. Yet, the king also became master of the Order of Santiago. Those who were knights of the Order of Santiago and the Order of Aviz were strongly aligned with the former King João II.

In contrast, the current reigning King Manuel followed the Order of Christ. Manuel had become a legitimate heir to the throne after a long string of deaths in the royal line. But his predecessor, King João II, did not trust him due to his family lineage to the Braganza family. João II conspired to replace Manuel with his own illegitimate son, Jorge. The court split its allegiances, with Queen Leonora siding with her brother, Manuel. A few years of intrigue ensued until King João II died in 1495 thus crushing Magellan's aspirations for advancement. As the new king, Manuel replaced many of João II's counselors with his own, and elevated the Order of Christ as dominant.

Da Gama noticed Fernão's transfixed gaze upon his red dagger cross. 'Your father was loyal to our great King João II.' His fingers rolled over his cross. 'You know the Order of Santiago was also aligned to serve him?'

Fernão nodded.

'On my first voyage, the king gave me a white pennant with the Order of Christ emblazoned upon it. We sailed under that commission. But I never disavowed my allegiance to our family's Order of Santiago.'

'What do you think of our chances to sail with the next fleet?' Fernão's asked excitedly.

'You realize favoritism in the courts wins the prized commissions,' Da Gama replied. 'Your family's past allegiances will make it very difficult.'

Diogo took a cautious step forward. 'How did you manage a command if your family was of the Order of Santiago?'

Da Gama bellowed a hearty laugh. 'My boy, I fought in the Moor crusades—I have experience in war, and the sea.' He paused and contemplated the insightful inquiry. 'Maybe you have a point. The King has pressured me often to join his Order of Christ.

Da Gama noticed the two brothers attention upon the empty liberty chests ready to be loaded onto their assigned vessels. 'Glory, riches, adventure—above all—bringing salvation to all lands.' That's why they do it, why we all do it.'

Diogo blurted out, 'What of the treasures?'

'Indeed. Last year we brought home 13 shiploads full of pepper, valued like gold,' Da Gama reveled.

The brothers looked at one another, awestruck.

'We sought out new trade routes but not everyone welcomed this. In many lands, men roam like wild beasts, ever guarding their territories, especially the Muslims. They met our arrival with a jealous fury.'

The two brothers hung upon every word, as if the elder mariner was an oracle of God.

Da Gama continued, 'During one conflict we captured one of the Mopla ships and found an idol weighing 30 pounds in gold, it had 2 emeralds for eyes, a cloak of fashioned gold, and a large ruby embedded on its chest.'

Fernão de Magalhães had heard of these encounters with the Moplas; Arab Muslims who had settled the Malabar Coast and intermarried with the Indian women.

Da Gama revealed further details. 'Our ships carried back 2,000 *mitkals* of gold from Sofala, tribute paid from Kilwa. King Manuel handed the gold to our esteemed goldsmith and playwright, Gil Vicente to fashion the monstrance of Belém.'

Fernão had recently walked the shoreline of the Tejo and observed the initial construction of the new monastery of Belém. In 1497, just before his inaugural voyage, Da Gama had prayed with his men in the exact same site, the old chapel dedicated to Santa Maria of Belém. Fernão and Diogo were both devout and understood the importance of Gil Vicente's task to create a display casing of precious jeweled craftsmanship to house the Host of the Eucharist and worthy of such an important new monastery.

Da Gama declared, 'Vast treasures await those who dare—,' when something crashed from across the stone yard. A mast had crashed dockside, and carpenters and caulkers argued over who let the rigging slip. Vasco da Gama tipped his head to the brothers then bolted off to settle the construction dispute.

In the early evening, Fernão and Diogo meandered along the cobble stone streets of cosmopolitan Lisbon. Candles and torches flickered from windows along the city hillside. They halted near a white stucco two level edifice with large wooden doors. Revelry and laughter reverberated from within. Diogo rapped his fist hard three times against the wood. A brief moment later, the door creaked open and an attendant stared blankly at the two young men. 'Francisco Serrão,' Fernão said. 'Is he here?'

'Back table with the blue silk cover.' The man pointed toward the back of the room.

The brothers maneuvered their way through the tight confines of clustered card tables. Ladies and gentlemen played cards in teams of two, four persons per table. From commoner to royal courts, the card-gaming craze had swept across Europe. Imported wood block engraved cards from France, Italy, Spain, and Germany appeared all over Lisbon. The Portuguese had their own variations and the card suits represented medieval classes: cups the church, swords the military, coins the merchants, and clubs the peasants. In addition, dragons represented Aces and the Jacks were female.

Francisco Serrão, clad in flamboyant red and silver, sat closely with a beautiful and scandalously buxom lady. Across the table from him, a proper well-dressed middle-aged couple appeared anxious. Small beads of sweat gathered on the gentleman's forehead. Francisco tapped his fingers on the table with a smirk across his face. 'Well then,' he said calmly. 'Shall we continue our final wager?'

Fernão and Diogo leaned against a balustrade staircase and watched unnoticed. The nervous couple glanced at one another, and then at their low score scribbled on a piece of paper. Francisco tossed 20 gold cruzados onto the table. The other couple fumbled through their pockets and purse in search of coins. They could only retrieve 2 cruzados.

The gentleman pleaded, 'We are short, but maybe you will take a note for one quintal of pepper, fresh from the Indies?'

Francisco continued tapping his fingers, staring quizzically. 'Hmm, pepper you say? Sure, why not.'

The man retrieved a note from his pocket, signed the bottom and placed it near the pot of cruzados.

'Let's deal,' Francisco answered with a grin.

Fernão and Diogo approached the gaming table and caught Francisco's attention. 'Fernão and Diogo,' he exclaimed. 'Perfect! Just in time for a new game.'

Fernão scowled.

'Ha ha! Still playing the monks are you? Francisco asked? 'Relax, it's only cards and a few wagers.' He continued dealing.

'We like to earn our living with hard work,' Diogo said.

Francisco scoffed, 'Can't you see I am working hard?'

After a few more hands the odds tilted. Francisco's fingers fidgeted and his mouth opened wide. 'This cannot be.' He carefully tabulated the scores again. 'Madre di Dios!'

Fernão shot a stern look toward Francisco. The older couple embraced, kissed and scooped up their gold cruzados. Francisco stared dumbfounded at his sudden turn of luck.

Fernão smirked. 'Looks like I will have to buy your dinner tonight.'

An hour later, the Magalhães brothers and their friend Francisco found an open table a few doors down. A waitress served them dishes of dried cod along with green olives and rice. Francisco took a small bite and shook his head. 'Hmm. Imported salted cod from lands in the far north. Nice fish but too bland. Let me show you something.' He rushed to the kitchen and two cooks turned in astonishment at the flamboyant intruder. 'Spices, we need spiced dishes. Give me just a brief moment and I will show you a secret.'

The Magalhães brothers peeked around the kitchen door. Francisco studied the counter and shelves. He found a plain glass jar and poured a cup of olive oil into it. 'Chili peppers,' he said to the cook. 'Where are they?'

The cook meekly pointed to the far end of the counter.

'Thank you,' Francisco said. He chopped up two garlic cloves and a quarter cup of chili peppers. Next, he poured all contents into the jar along with a dash of salt and stirred the mixture. 'Nice, very nice,' he grinned, taking a little celebratory step on his way back to their table.

'You're crazy,' Fernão chuckled. 'Absolutely crazy.'

Francisco spooned out some spicy liquid onto Fernão's rice and cod. 'This will clean you out.' He gestured for the waitress to bring them a jug. 'Best to have some wine ready.'

The men added the spicy concoction into their food. After taking some bites the brothers' faces flushed red.

'Hot,' Fernão gasped as he wiped perspiration from his brow. 'But very good.'

'Chili peppers are much cheaper than black pepper,' Francisco said, spicing his own food.

Fernão and Diogo nodded. Chili peppers had been imported from the Americas since Admiral Cristoforo Colombo's expeditions. Now they were cultivated all over the Iberian Peninsula and anywhere the Portuguese trade network spread.

'Precisely,' Fernão said. 'Black pepper is the new gold. And there are many other spices and jewels worth much more, most from the Indies. Speaking of which, Diogo and I plan to ask the king for leave to join the next armada. Will you join us?'

Francisco took another gulp of wine and considered the brothers for a moment. 'You are aware of course that many do not return.'

Fernão merely nodded. Diogo continued to eat without looking up.

Francisco grinned. 'My friends, you are gambling men after all.

The three chuckled at this.

'But you also realize the king can be moody,' Francisco said. 'There are no assurances he will grant any of us leave.'

Fernão smirked at him. 'If we do not ask, the answer is most surely no.'

2

A dreary morning, misty with drizzle engulfed the Alfama district hillside. Francisco and the Magalhães brothers trudged the damp earth upward along the steep winding path toward the Royal Palace. It was also known as the alcáçova, built upon the highest peak of Lisbon's seven main hills. The imposing military towers and high walls of Saint George Castle grew larger as the trio approached.

It was once a tenth century Moorish fortification and strategic outpost, liberated during the *Reconquista*. Due to adverse weather, European forces headed to the Holy Lands had anchored off the Portuguese coast in the northern city of Porto. These included knights of a Second Crusader army. D. Afonso Henriques, warrior of the Iberian *Reconquista* and Portugal's first king, had persuaded these crusaders to join forces with him and liberate Lisbon from the entrenched Moors.

Diogo looked over to Fernão who seemed transfixed in thought, 'So much history here, eh brother? So many glorious battles and noble victories.'

'Indeed,' Fernào remarked with a grin. 'I was just thinking of the sacrifice of Martim Moniz, using his body as a wedge of bone and flesh as the Moors tried to close the north gate. It allowed the crusader knights time to break through, finally ending the siege after 17 grueling months.'

'I can't imagine, Diogo said.

Fernào halted for a moment. 'That was 1147, in the year of our Lord. But walking near the fortress, it does not seem like 350 years ago.'

'Three hundred fifty seven,' Diogo said.

Francisco picked up his step as they approached a guard stationed in front of the eastern palace gate. 'Beautiful day, is it not, Rodrigo?'

'Very funny,' the guard said. 'Serrão, always the jester. Why don't you take my watch and I will go back to bed.'

'I could not deprive you of the pleasure,' Francisco said.

'What's so important to visit in this foul weather?' a guard perched high upon the gate ledge asked.

'We wish to join the next armada to the Indies,' Francisco replied.

Rodrigo laughed at them. 'You are serious,' he said. He looked at Francisco, at Fernão, and Diogo. 'What an idea, we should all ask the king for leave to go find some treasures and cease our employment to the crown. I am sure he will not care.'

Rodrigo gestured them and waved them entry through the gate.

Once inside the royal property they continued west toward the palace courtyard. One of several royal court guards stepped forward. 'Fernão, good to see you.'

'And you, Estevão. Can you escort us to the king?'

Estevão hesitated a moment in thought. 'May I suggest you first speak with our lady, Leonora?'

'I did not think we should concern her,' Fernão said.

'Nonsense. It would be more diplomatic if nothing else.'

'I see your point. This is a good idea then, my friend.'

They followed him to the palace, home of the royal family and court. King Manuel's passion for architecture permeated the entire complex, along with multiple structures throughout Lisbon. Along the palace walls, numerous scenes of nature were chiseled out; corals, seaweed, parrots, turtles, seabirds, elephants and lions.

'I will bring her to the chapel,' Estevão said. 'Wait there.' He hurried off toward a different door.

Fernão entered the atrium of the domed chapel. His eyes were immediately drawn to a large hollow armillary sphere, or astrolabe, perched upon a six-foot black forged iron stand. This sphere, or astrolabe, was a virtual model of the sky; constructed with multiple rings positioned around the earth, representing celestial longitude, latitude and the ecliptic. King Manuel made this armillary sphere his personal emblem. He dedicated it as his symbol of the quest to circumnavigate the globe.

Diogo walked next to Fernão, staring. 'One day someone will sail the entire world, one day soon.'

'With God all things are possible,' Fernão said.

Leonora, sister of King Manuel and former widowed queen to King João II, entered the chapel. Her long strawberry blonde hair draped over her fur-lined red cloak. An exquisite embroidered golden gown with red sash over a white undergarment, and with an enclosed neckline, provided her a layered warmth in the chilly winter season. Leonora's fair complexion had aged gracefully. Her gentle green eyes twinkled and focused upon the young men.

'Boys, I miss your presence in the palace. I wish you had decided to stay with us here, not those cold damp quarters in the marine department.' She turned her gaze back to the armillary sphere. 'Yet, I know you have worked hard as our court apprentices. Your mastery of literature, martial skills, mathematics, astronomy, and navigation have not gone unnoticed. I am so proud of you both. Now you are working with our great men of science and exploration.'

Fernão bowed. 'You are the king's sister and confidant. Could you persuade the king to give us leave to join the next armada?'

'My late husband João dreamt of great accomplishments; advancement of science and navigation, new trade and finding the great Christian King of the East—Prester John,' Leonora said as she stepped around the sphere. 'Your family was loyal to my dear João. I will see what I can do, but the king, as you know, may have reservations.'

Fernão knew they at least stood a good chance with Leonora, for she had always regarded Diogo and himself like adopted sons ever since their arrival to the court as young pages.

The men followed the royal guard Estevão and Leonora along a stone walkway lined with porticos of brilliant blue and gold mosaic in elaborate geometric designs. Music wafted from behind an ornate door. The guard rapped hard at the door. When no answer came, he pounded harder. The music stopped and a servant opened the door. Behind the servant a trio of musicians held their instruments in mid-note. A young lady held a lute, an odd looking guitar-like instrument with a bent upper neck. A young man strummed a small guitar, a *viola de mão*, and another held his flute aloft in dexterous fingers and a quizzical expression on his face.

The servant beckoned them to enter. Bookshelves lined the entire perimeter of the office. In front of a desk stacked high with books sat an impeccably dressed man in a blue velvet vest over a white shirt with puffy sleeves. He was hunched over an open book writing notes in a frantic pace with ink and quill. Abruptly, he straightened his back and exclaimed: 'Music, where is my music!'

He rose from his chair and turned, towering in height over the musicians nearby. King Manuel's well-built physique, fair complexion, chestnut hair, long face with pointed chin impressed those who saw him. Yet, one physical oddity distinguished him: his arms were disproportionately long, fingers dangling to his knees. 'Ah, the Magalhães brothers! And Francisco Serrão. I was revising my uncle Afonso's law code. Such an important task for our nation—not so good to be interrupted.'

Fernão, Diogo and Francsico averted their gaze to the floor.

Manuel glanced to the musicians. 'You may continue.' Sounds of lute, guitar and flute once again filled the chamber with melody.

Manuel stretched and arched his back. 'Well, what brings your unexpected appearance?'

Fernão raised his head, 'We all wish leave to join the next armada for the Indies.'

Manuel's eyes narrowed as he crossed his arms. 'Not possible. You were all appointed to our marine department for a reason, to conduct research for our naval operations. You know we are in a race against the Spanish crown for new lands and resources. I need you right where you are, keeping us in the advantage in navigation.'

'But your majesty,' Serrão interjected. 'We have been trained for all aspects of exploration. Should we not sail with the armada?'

'Have you not already met our great explorers in our India House and allowed access to our valuable secrets? Charts from Cabral, Da Gama, Dias, Vespucci, Corte-Real, and the others? Manuel's face reddened as he continued. 'Remember my decree? Anyone who divulges any of our classified information from the marine department will be executed immediately. What if you are captured and talk under torture?' Manuel was clearly evading their requests.

'We have always honored any pledge we took,' Fernão said. 'Have we not earned the right to sail?'

Manuel glared at such impudence. Fernão never had much tact.

Leonora heard the elevated and agitated voices from outside the office and entered with her usual quiet grace.

'Manuel,' she said. 'Would you seek your courtiers? You already have a council meeting this afternoon. Maybe they have an opinion?'

Manuel looked at her, inhaled deeply, and exhaled slowly. 'Very well, let us consult my advisors. We convene in the royal hall in one hour.'

Half and hour later, the Magalhães brothers and Francisco Serrao sauntered along the perimeter of the steep castle walls overlooking the mighty Tejo estuary. From this strategic lookout point they could see numerous carracks and caravels anchoring in harbor while others sailed out to sea. Francisco stared along the distance of the Tejo. 'Trade is good, sailors and nobles return rich—.'

'With fantastic tales of glorious deeds and honor,' Fernão added. Both young men breathed in the fresh sea breeze.

'We must join the next expedition, Lisbon is no place for me.'

'It will be, if we do not get going,' Diogo said.

The royal ceremonial hall of the alcáçova was built of stone and used to entertain guests, hold official councils, and celebrate religious festivals. They entered the chambered hall and mingled in with the king's inner circle of courtiers and guests. The hall was rectangular with curved support pillars along the middle, with large windows to let in daylight.

Fernão, Diogo and Francisco stood near the perimeter and midpoint of the chamber. Metal fire pits were stationed along the walls and pillars which provided agreeable warmth during winter months. A few minutes passed before King Manuel emerged from a lower chamber stepped entrance. He moved with his royal guards through the chamber greeting courtiers one by one. Manuel climbed some short steps along the perimeter which led to a royal platform overlooking the guests below. He stared over the chamber for a moment then seated himself upon a regal purple throne.

Fernao noticed the former queen, Leonora, standing near a pillar with Gil Vicente, the famous playwright, dramatist, and court goldsmith. He nodded. She nodded, smiled briefly, and then looked at the king.

Manuel raised his right arm. Whispers, coughs, and small rustles of the crowd in the hall abated to absolute silence. 'I have called you here today concerning our trade in the east. Just three years ago, I decided to help defend our Christian brothers of Venice against the Turks. We sent out our best 30 ships, manned with 3,500 troops. Yet, once the Ottoman Sultan heard of our crusade he called off his attack fleet—.'

A priest in a black robe cleared his throat, catching the king's attention.

'Frei Henrique, what concerns you?' Manuel asked.

Fernão and everyone in the court knew of the personal confessor to the king, Frei Henrique of Coimbra; a zealous Franciscan missionary who had sailed west with Cabral to Brazil in the year 1500 and celebrated the first mass in this new land, then sailing east to the bustling port city of Calicut in India, he preached the gospel. Later, he escaped the massacre of Calicut and sailed back to Lisbon with Cabral. Manuel always listened carefully to his well-traveled priest.

Frei Henrique's eyes scanned over the hall. 'We cannot trust Venice. They have spies in our midst.'

'Indeed. I do suspect,' the king said. 'Which is another reason for my decree of death to anyone sharing our charts, navigation science or secrets of the crown's business.' Manuel rose from his throne, then ambled over to a hearth situated upon the royal platform and warmed his hands near the glowing embers. 'But now, we have another task. The Mamluke sultan of Egypt has dared to threaten our Christian brothers, even sent a letter to Pope Julius.'

Fernão knew of the Mamluke warriors through his frequent contacts with explorers at the India House; a military caste which arose from the ranks of slave soldiers controlled by Muslim rulers. The ruthless Sultan Al-Ashraf Qansuh al-Ghawri was a Mamluke from a Turkish dynasty of the royal bodyguard who arose to become Potentate of Egypt. He was loosely allied with the Venetians, due only to their trade agreements. He controlled a monopoly of trade via the key market ports of Damascus, Beirut and Alexandria. Heavy tariffs were levied upon any products moving through these ports, especially pepper. The Venetians bought the goods at inflated prices and in turn sold for yet higher cost to the European markets. But now, with the new Portuguese free trade routes around the Horn of Africa and blockades in the Red Sea, trade only trickled in for Venice and Egypt. Venice sent ambassadors to Egypt to persuade them to take action. The Sultan responded with blackmail and threats against Portugal while Venice feigned their own neutrality.

'The Sultan has been busy stirring up the rulers in Africa and India to fight our trade expeditions.' The usually even-tempered Manuel riled with indignation. 'Who gave him authority to control all trade? Has not our Lord given us authority to take dominion over his creation . . . to take a part of his great and plentiful bounty?'

Frei Henrique nodded in approval and boldly exclaimed: 'It has been reported that Venice has supplied the Mamlukes with weapons and ship masters. They have betrayed your majesty.'

The Palace Hall murmured with comments of treachery and revenge.

The King held his long arms high, then lowered them, as a que for silence. 'A few months ago, a letter from the Sultan to the Pope was delivered demanding we cease all trade in the Indies. The Sultan threatens to put to death every Christian in his domains, level all Christian churches, and even destroy the Holy Sepulchre! The Pope sent me the letter to know my answer.'

The courtiers felt conviction and energy in the king's speech as he railed on.

The king continued, 'Let the Sultan wait for the day when our armies, as by God's mercy we trust will be soon, have reached the House of Mecca where lies the false prophet, and will have taken it by force of arms. After that he may complain!'

The Palace Hall erupted in cheers of support.

Manuel added, 'And we will send our greatest fleet thus far to the Indies and appoint a Viceroy to govern and protect our interests!'

Manuel basked in the courtiers' cheers of support. Fernão took a short, yet bold step forward, hoping to catch the king's attention while he remained in good spirits.

'Oh yes, I almost forgot,' Manuel said. 'I have our former pages here, eager to join this mighty fleet.'

The courtiers snickered and whispered. Fernão's short stature, with dark swarthy complexion and coarse face conveyed to the courtiers the unstereotypical low-class country boy, working in the fields. Fernão knew well how the king's courtier sycophants had always clambered for prestige and advancement. He understood how they viewed their upper-class status against his crude appearance and simple roots. The courtiers held the king's will in check by convincing him of the merits and values of his own interests.

'Surely the king has some reservations to send such untested recruits?' a courtier remarked.

'Are they really capable of such responsibility as mere fourth level nobility?' another member of the council chided.

A third courtier with a dark moustache and pointed beard said loudly, 'Would the king trust simple farm boys from the north backwoods for such an important expedition?'

Gil Vicente who had been in the north, was about to speak when Leonora grabbed his arm. She whispered something to him.

'I hear your words, Dom Alvaro,' Manuel said. 'Well then, how shall we determine if they are ready?'

Another courtier stepped forward, 'May we suggest a duel with the canes? *Jogo do Pau.*'

Manuel smiled. 'Hmm, so that we may be entertained while witnessing what skills they may have. Yes, a duel with Fernão Magalhães, then. The duel shall take place in the courtyard, tomorrow, at four in the afternoon.

Cheers and applause erupted among the courtiers. The entire entourage of spectators dispersed.

The following day, according to the king's orders, servants with whips escorted lions pulling at their leashes from the royal menagerie toward the courtyard. Musicians pounded a rhythm on kettledrums. The entire palace complex stirred with excitement. Current visitors of the court—ambassadors, ship captains, trade agents, students, and servants from around the known world—gathered among the courtiers in eager anticipation.

An African man in his mid-thirties, garbed in priest vestments with a gold crucifix dangling around his neck read from a book as he paced slowly across the courtyard. He glanced up and noticed Fernão. 'My friend, good to see you again,' the priest greeted him with a smile.

'And you also, Ndeke,' Fernão answered. As a court page, he had befriended many young students from far off lands. He fell in beside him as he walked along. 'Your studies almost complete?'

'Like yourself, I can read and write the Latin and Portuguese texts, but I prefer to wait another year so I can perfect my Greek and Hebrew,' Ndeke said. His pace slowed as he said thoughtfully, 'Spend a little extra time on it, then I can teach our priesthood in the Congo with greater clarity.'

West African princes sent their young sons for instruction in the Christian faith, ambassadors were often exchanged, and other worthy youth were often sent for training into the priesthood.

Ndeke frowned at him. 'I hear you agreed to a cane match with the king. Have you not had enough punishment when you were a page?'

Fernão remembered his frequent combat training sessions with Manuel, who had once been captain of the pages at court. Dom Manuel always had an advantage due to his extraordinary long reach against Fernão's own shorter stature. Fernão grimaced, thinking of his bloody and bruised past contests as a youth.

'It is worth the pain,' Fernão replied. 'Besides, we are both older now. If I win, the king grants me leave for the next armada.' Fernão leaned toward Ndeke and confided, 'I have learned a few tricks since then.'

'But is not the king one of Portugal's great champions?'

'I promise it shall be an interesting duel,' Fernão said confidently.

Ndeke placed his hand on Fernão's shoulder and gave his short blessing, 'May our Lord guide your path then. No matter where it may lead you.'

Fernão clasped his long time friend's arm with some emotion. 'Thank you my friend. And may he illuminate your studies.'

'May you be blessed in your contest.'

'I shall not doubt it,' Fernão said, then continued off alone toward the center of the courtyard.

As he approached the king, Manuel grinned mischievously. 'Remember your training, Magalhães?'

Fernão stood silent.

The king gestured with upturned palms toward the musicians on kettledrums as a signal to commence. A warlike beat filled the courtyard as Manuel swirled around to face the crowd. 'If Fernão Magalhães can best me—' Manuel held the people in suspense.

Jeers of mockery resounded throughout the crowd against Fernão.

Manuel continued, '—which I doubt. But if so, he and his cohorts are granted leave to join the armada.'

Royal guards delivered each contestant five-foot-long wood staffs weighing one and a half pounds each and narrowed on one end. Courtiers pointed fingers and mocked Fernão with giddy jibes and insults. The two circled one another in battle ready stance. Fernão bent his lead leg to hover just over his lead foot for increased speed upon striking. His dominant right hand gripped hard at the far narrow end of his staff while the other hand was placed a little further up, at shoulder distance. The pounding kettledrums escalated into a feverish war tempo.

An official attired in gold vestments bellowed: 'Commence!'

King Manuel took the offensive, driving forward with an oblique descending strike. Fernão parried the blow and stepped back to maintain his distance. Fernão followed with a side step and powerful horizontal swing. Manuel countered with an aggressive repelling parry by pushing through his staff, releasing a powerful upward strike to Fernão's midsection. Pain shot over Fernão's rib cage, he thought he heard a crack. It hurt to breathe. Fernão turned as another strike by Manuel landed across his shoulder—scraping both ear and face—blood ran down his dark beard. Manuel's relentless onslaught continued for several minutes, blow after blow. The crowd cringed as each strike landed. Fernão seemed hurt, and somewhat dazed. Through blurred vision Fernão was still able to spot Diogo and Francisco in the crowd. Fernão, realizing their future lay with this battle, here and now, summoned his will. He reminded himself that there was no room for retreat, to those seeking true honor.

'Had enough Fernão? Ready to concede?' Manuel asked.

Fernão stumbled forward, blood dripping onto the ground from his beard. 'I will not concede,' he replied.

'You seem used to pain,' Manuel said. 'Prepare yourself for more.'

Fernão knew he had to overcome the long reach of Manuel soon or suffer another painful barrage of blows. He thought to attempt a risky approach, parrying through Manuel's strikes to get within grappling distance, or land an inner thrusting blow. Fernão implemented his plan, pushing forward, receiving more blows. Yet he persisted, finally arriving within reach to thrust the blunt edge of his staff into Manuel's stomach. The king doubled over. Taking advantage of the momentum, he drove an upward strike into Manuel's shoulder. Fernão had a glimmer of hope, but for just a moment. Manuel quickly countered with a powerful oblique downward blow to his head. Fernão's mind went blank and he crumpled to the floor. The courtiers cheered. Others in the crowd gaped in respect to Fernão's courage in the face of the superior advantage of the king. Manuel stared over Fernão's still body. His face was covered in blood.

'A noble effort,' Manuel said in a subdued quiet voice.

3

Sunlight pierced through the glass windows of the All Saints Royal Hospital of Lisbon. Fernão awoke from the light passing through a linen curtain surrounding his straw mattress cot. Although resting comfortably on two feathered pillows, pain throbbed at his temples. He groaned. A nurse rushed over just as he struggled to sit up. The nurse slid open the linen curtain. Fernão's vision was blurry so all he noticed was a female figure.

'Please, lay down. You have many injuries,' the nurse said.

'I will be fine, just need to stand up, walk around,' Fernão replied. He braced himself against the pain, placed his feet on the floor and slowly rose. His vision began to clear. A beautiful young woman with a shapely figure, dark hair and piercing green eyes stood before him. 'You see, all better now,' Fernão bragged, hoping to gain admiration from the young nurse.

Adjacent to his bed, a grizzled old man with rough facial scars watched.

Fernão took a few steps. Suddenly his head began to spin causing him to stumble against a wall. The nurse caught him. 'You have a concussion,' said the nurse, holding him up as best she could.

'You are so beaut—' Fernão felt suddenly nauseous. He heaved and vomited, splashing chunks and bile all over himself, the nurse, and the floor.

'Lay down please. I will get someone to help clean,' the nurse said, then scurried off with vomit dripping off her white uniform. Fernão laid back down upon his cot, his right leg covered with vomit.

The old man laughed from his cot. 'Well, well. I never tried to impress a young lady with that approach,' he said. 'Maybe she gives you another chance. Or maybe not.'

Fernão glanced toward the old man, then turned his head in embarrassment.

'Don't mind me, I was just joking. Take a rest and we speak later,' the old man said.

Fernão thought of trying to get up again and clean himself, but suddenly sleepy, he laid back and dozed off.

Fernão awoke to a ringing bell which echoed throughout the hospital corridors. To his surprise, his clothes had been changed, floor mopped to a glowing shine, and fresh sheets fitted. He wondered—who had changed his clothes—was it the beautiful nurse? His face flushed as he thought of the possibility.

Three hospital staff members approached through an opening in his curtain. They were two middle-aged men and an elder woman. 'Fernão Magalhães, I am Doctor Estevão and this is our pharmacist and head nurse.' The doctor stood over Fernão. 'You have a concussion, one broken rib, and severe bruises.'

'Where am I?'

'The new hospital completed this year, All Saints Royal Hospital,' the doctor said.

Fernão had watched the construction of this modern hospital whenever he looked west from the royal palace walls. The hospital's main facade had encompassed the complete eastern side of Rossio Square. King João II had commissioned the project but Fernão was certain that it was his wife, Queen Leonora, who was the real inspiration behind the charitable institution. He was momentarily amused that he was now a patient in it.

'What time is it? How long have I been here?' Fernão asked.

'Two in the afternoon. You have been here almost two days now. The first day you never awoke,' said the doctor.

'Who changed my clothes?' Fernão asked with slight embarrassment.

'Pedro, our staff assistant for this upper floor,' the head nurse replied.

'Oh, I see,' Fernão said.

The doctor glanced to the pharmacist. 'Give him some opiate to relieve the pain.'

The pharmacist jotted down a prescription on his small writing pad.

'Two days! I am ready to go now.'

'I believe you mentioned that earlier this morning,' the doctor said with a smirk to his colleagues. 'Let us take it one day at a time. Plenty of rest with supervised care will ensure your recovery is complete.'

Fernão grabbed the arm of the pharmacist. 'Forget the opiate. It weakens the will. I will live with the pain.'

The pharmacist looked bewildered, unsure of what to do. The doctor gave a nod of his approval to obey Fernão's request.

'Pedro?' the grizzled old man asked. He laughed so hard it caused him to cough up some spittle of blood. 'I suppose you were thinking your vomit pants were changed by that fine beauty you so kindly introduced yourself to.' The old man could not help himself from adding the punch line, laughed, then clutched his chest in pain.

Fernão stared at the glossy white ceiling. The crazy old man was right, he was hoping for another encounter with the young nurse. Of course, one embarrassing moment was enough for the day.

'Hey son, you brought me some joy. Not sure how many more good laughs I will . . .' The old man coughed.

'Mind me asking? What are you here for?' Fernão asked.

'Here for stupidity, unbelievable stupidity.'

'Huh.'

'We were testing the heavy cannon mid-deck for prepping the next armada. We were also reckless, trying to finish early, only two of us manned the big gun. A rogue wave hit us on port side just as we fired a shot. I stumbled forward into the recoiling cannon. The blow crushed my lung.' The old man reflected. 'Safety and caution, so vital at sea. One mistake, and it's injury or death.'

Fernão rolled his fingers across his own broken rib, pushed in a little until he winced. He wondered how the force of a heavy cannon recoil would feel, and how much damage it could inflict.

'Funny thing,' the old man said. 'I have been on several dangerous expeditions and survived without a scratch until this costly blunder. In July I returned from India, served as a gunner for the fifth armada under Afonso de Albuquerque.'

Fernão looked at the old man. 'You sailed under Albuquerque?'

'Indeed. Also fought in this same expedition with Captain General—Duarte Pacheco Pereira. He is a valiant warrior with cunning genius, skilled as pilot, explorer, shipmaster, cartographer, and scientist. You know he was even an advisor at the Treaty of Tordesillas.'

Fernão had heard of Pacheco's exploits, a man of honor and courage. 'Yes, I know of him. This is impressive. Was it as dangerous as the stories say?

'I survived the trip back home, but we lost so many ships. Albuquerque's cousin, Francisco, who commanded the second squadron was lost at sea, all three ships under his command vanished.' The old man shook his head. 'Will we ever master the seas? I do not know.'

'Perhaps with better ships, better navigation tools,' Fernão conjectured.

'Perhaps, but do you know the sea my young friend? Have you sailed the Horn? Faced a monsoon squall? A hurricane? Or weathered the slow debilitating doldrums with no wind at the sails when the heat is unmerciful? Or had to eat rank food with foul water? So many perils at sea, so many.'

'Not yet, but I will,' Fernão said.

'You may think twice about finding a young wife if you are serious. You know well the odds of returning?'

Fernão knew he was right. Why should he even try to find a wife? It would only be selfish.

'What of the treasure, the spices?' Fernão asked, hoping to change the mood.

'Treasures? Spices? The old man said. 'Oh yes! We brought the king 40 pounds of pearls and 400 pounds of seed pearl. Even a giant diamond, shining so bright. The king was ecstatic and full of joy when we presented him with two horses—a Persian and an Arabian. The royal palace hosted such a beautiful and splendid feast on that momentous occasion.' The old man reflected upon his cherished memories.

'What else did you see?' Fernão asked.

'So many goods. Calicut must be the world's largest trading hub. It is incredible! But other ports; Cochin, Cannanore, and Quilon also bustle with trade.' The old man coughed up some blood and struggled a moment to catch his breath.

'Are you all right?'

'Thanks for the concern but no need to worry yourself,' said the old man. 'Where was I? Oh, yes, the goods. Let me recall. I already mentioned pearls. One can also trade in fine silks and porcelain from China.

There are metals of all sorts: gold, silver, and copper. Also treasures of timber, myrrh, incense, musk, amber, carpets, quicksilver, alum, coral, cotton, rubies, and diamonds. So many goods.'

'And the spices?' Fernão asked, barely containing his excitement.

'I am sure you know the most sought after: pepper, cinnamon, and ginger. But the world also craves for the delicious nutmeg and cloves, sourced much further to the east, in the Spice Islands.'

'That's why nutmeg and cloves are so costly? The distance?'

'Exactly, the distance requires another trader in the middle,' the old man said.

Fernão thought for a moment. 'Why not sail all the way to the Spice Islands, eliminate the middle traders, take the whole prize?'

The old man grunted. 'Easy to say, but those are uncharted waters. How far is it? Nobody knows for sure, there are only questionable accounts from merchants and adventurers. No trusted charts, which means much danger, making it difficult to find financial backers.'

'Someone should try,' Fernão said. 'From what you say, it seems to be there for the taking, waiting for those who dare.'

'I like your spirit my friend. Maybe you will get your chance.' The old man coughed and wheezed for breath. His face turned slightly pale.

'You better rest some,' Fernão said. But the old man had already drifted off.

Fernão felt renewed from his conversation. He struggled out of bed, taking tender care with his ribs; one hand steadied upon the edge of the cot to make sure his balance was stable. Only one attendant was on duty, sleeping in his chair. Fernão quietly made his way past the many cots of the second-floor patient wing and then down the stairway to the ground floor.

He saw the hospital layout; three infirmaries in the upper level and the ground level had the staff offices and kitchen. He walked further, looked around corners and doorways, careful not to catch attention by any staff. He saw a room called *expostos,* a place for abandoned babies. Fernão peered around the corner into a partially opened doorway and his heart raced. A beautiful young nurse had her blouse open with a baby suckling at her bosom. Fernão reasoned she must have doubled as a wet nurse for unwanted infants. Youthful passions stirred in young Fernão. Tensions of choice between seeking after a wife in Lisbon or adventurous exotic travel played in his mind. He knew having both would prove futile and painful. Fernão moved past the doorway. The nurse turned her head just as he slipped past, not knowing if she heard something or not. She continued her attention to the infant.

Fernão could view the square-shaped wings of the hospital and courtyards which surrounded the massive hospital chapel. He moved closer toward the main hospital on the west end. Fernão admired the gothic chapel rising above a massive stairway. He climbed each step with caution, his head not quite clear. He entered the chapel and stood in amazement at the architecture, and especially the nave on the east end with its ascending tower. Several worshippers prayed on the other side of the chapel.

Fernão stood in front of a large statue of the crucified Christ and a weeping Mary. He knelt in reverence, bowed his head and prayed, *'Lord, what are your plans for me? Will I have my leave to explore? Will I achieve respect and honor as a low ranked nobleman?* Fernão looked upward, hoping for a sign, but nothing happened. *'I will be your humble servant and teach your words to foreign people, if you will send me,'* Fernão said with conviction. He seated himself on a bench and meditated.

Hours later, someone tapped him lightly on the shoulder. Fernão awoke. He turned to see the head nurse looking at him with reproach. 'You must stay and rest in your bed. It is the rules. Let me escort you back.'

Fernão nodded and walked back to his bed. It was dark now and he felt drained. Sleep again engulfed him.

The next morning, he looked over and saw the old man's cot was empty.

'Nurse, nurse,' Fernão called.

A nurse in her forties wandered over to his bed. 'Yes? Are you all right?'

'Where is the old man next to me? Fernão asked. 'His bed is empty.'

'I am sorry. He did not make it through the night. We took his body away this morning.'

'I was just talking with him yesterday.'

'He left this for you.' She handed him a piece of paper.

Fernão held the note and read silently: *Do not give up your vision. Go to the Indies my friend. My time has come, and I have had my share of adventure. Now it is your turn. Farewell.*

Conviction and resolve flooded over Fernão's mind. He knew now he must forge ahead no matter what the obstacles. He rose from his bed. 'Where are my clothes? I must leave now,' he insisted emphatically.

'You must ask the doctor. I will find him,' the nurse said.

Fernão watched the nurse descend the stairs and then he limped down a side stairway to an exit and escaped down an alley.

4

It was late morning when Fernão awoke with a lingering headache. He rose from his cot in the rear living quarters of the India House. Fernão had been allowed to reside here during his internship in the maritime sciences. This edifice was first called the Mining House founded by Duarte, the brother of Prince Henry the Navigator. It was the centralized headquarters for Portuguese cartography and navigation. The Mining House also dealt in the trade of Guinea including gold, slaves, horses, iron, and fabrics of many kinds. After trade had expanded with Vasco da Gama's voyage of 1497-1498, beyond Africa to the west coast of India, the Mining House was re-named—the India House. The newly named organization oversaw the construction and repairs of ships for naval operations. Items for export were loaded for outgoing missions and imported cargoes were offloaded: pepper, cinnamon, silk, porcelain, silver, and precious stones. With so many returning voyages the India House was a hive of activity. Cartographers and scientists revised naval charts based on new discoveries, modified navigational instruments, and improved astronomical tables. All work was performed under the utmost secrecy.

Fernão snatched his daily wardrobe from a hook on the wall and hurriedly changed. He walked through an adjoining covered walkway to the main working section of the India House. Two muscular guards with six-foot long halberds gave Fernão an inquisitorial stare. From his inner pocket, Fernão retrieved a four-inch square-shaped silver medallion engraved with the king's seal and held it high. One of the guards stared over the India House badge and nodded his permission to continue. He entered a large copper doorway end emerged into a large chamber bustling full of activity. Men in the far corner of the room perused through file cabinets and huddled in deep conversation over nautical charts strewn about over round wood tables. In the center of the chamber, a middle-aged man of 45 years, Martin Behaim, huddled over several charts and an odd-looking, bronze-colored device—an astrolabe. His long brown hair draped over an exquisite gold doublet, stitched with red ornamentation and puffy upper sleeves. He wore elaborate hose; colored in red and white, with silver stripes. The heavy door slammed shut behind Fernão.

Behaim turned and with a German accent, he asked, 'Fernão, where have you been? I have new charts for you to compile.'

A despondent Fernão stared vacantly.

'What is the matter my friend?' Behaim asked.

Fernão stammered, 'I was delayed at the court. It was not a good day. I was hoping to sail with the next armada for the Indies. But the king rejected my request to join.'

'Ah Fernão, you are not the only one rejected by the king. Once our dear King João had departed this world, all those close to him were treated with scorn and suspicion. You know Manuel has many courtiers who clamor for power and manipulate his mind.'

'How can you know what it is like?' Fernão replied. 'You are still working for the India House.'

'Indeed, but now working for a small fraction of what I was formerly paid. I was demoted for my service and loyalty to King João.'

Fernão pondered. Maybe Behaim was right. Perhaps this was the reason he was denied sailing with the next armada. The courtiers had always ridiculed his country roots and they especially distrusted anyone's family loyalties to the Orders of Aviz and Santiago. The Magalhães family lineage had followed these Orders as did the former king, João II. Now, King Dom Manuel reigned under the Order of Christ and all those who aspired to flourish in his court aligned their allegiance accordingly.

Martin wrapped his arm around Fernão's shoulder. 'Do not worry my friend. You will have your time at sea. You will have fantastic adventures and glorious victories.'

Fernão smiled, 'Like your voyage with Diogo Cão up the Congo River and your later travels to the Azores?'

'Yes. But you will have better instruments and charts to sail further—speaking of which—you need to look at my latest astrolabe modification based upon our latest star chart readings. I have compared these new findings with our esteemed astronomer Abraham Zacuto's Perpetual Almanac and Johannes Müller's astronomical tables.'

Fernão knew of these great astronomers. Zacuto was a learned Jew who had fled from Spain during the great expulsion of 1492 and sought asylum in Lisbon. The Portuguese King João II welcomed Zacuto into his court and appointed him Royal Astronomer and Historian. Before Zacuto, pilots had to calculate the compass difference between true north and magnetic north by the Pole Star and a navigational tool called a quadrant. However, once voyages moved south toward the equator, the Pole Star began to wane below the horizon. Abraham Zacuto's improved tables of solar declination, along with Behaim's improved bronze mariner's astrolabe, allowed the Portuguese to use the sun as a guide and take accurate measurements anywhere they sailed.

Fernão had also heard many stories from Behaim concerning his apprenticeship in Nürnberg under his former Bavarian master, Johannes Müller von Königsberg. As was common among learned scholars of the day, Müller used a Latin pseudonym, Regiomontanus, based upon his birthplace Königsberg (Regismons). He was considered the greatest astronomer and mathematician of his era. Even Pope Sixtus IV acknowledged Müller's achievements, appointed him bishop of Ratisbon, and summoned him to Rome to improve the calendar.

'We have received word from Spain concerning the return of Admiral Cristoforo Colombo from his fourth expedition to the New World,' Behaim paused for drama, '—an incredible account of survival.'

Fernão leaned forward in suspense.

'We have been informed that Colombo and his surviving crew had been marooned in Jamaica for an entire year. In the beginning, the Cacique Indians had agreed to trade with his men. However, after some months, trade dwindled to a halt and starvation set in. Colombo was desperate for a miracle,' Behaim spoke as he stared into Fernão's inquisitive eyes. 'In a flash of divine illumination, Colombo remembered he had my master Regiomontanus' printed copy of *Ephemerides,* the astronomical tables which predicted eclipses 30 years ahead.'

'How would that help him?' Fernão asked.

'Colombo was clever, he gathered the leadership of the Caciques on board the shipwrecked *Capitana.* He preached how the Christians worshipped the true God of Heaven who rewarded goodness and punished wickedness. He also said the Indians had ceased bringing food to the Christians and had angered God. Now they were to be punished by famine and plagues. A sign in the heavens would appear as a seal of proof from Heaven in which the moon would rise bloody and in flame. Colombo relied upon my master's tables and staked his life upon them.'

'Did the eclipse occur as he said?' Fernão asked with anticipation.

'Some Indians balked while others walked away in dreadful fear. Indeed, the eclipse appeared just as Colombo said it would. The Indians cried out in great sorrow and remorse. They brought food from all directions and pleaded for the admiral to petition to intercede for them while promising to always bring food every day. Colombo agreed to pray for them and retired to his cabin. Once he knew the eclipse was about to end, he summoned the Caciques again. Colombo told them they were forgiven, and the moon would again appear normal. His words proved true, and he saved his men from starvation until their eventual rescue.' Behaim handed Fernào a printed copy of Regiomantanus' *Ephemerides*. 'Astronomical knowledge is so important my friend. It may also one day save your life.'

Fernão's head swirled with excitement as he considered the opportunity to further acquire valuable navigational skills under the tutelage of Martin Behaim, who himself was tutored under the great masters in the fields of mathematics and astronomy.

'Fernão, you have come far in your training. You have excelled in advanced geometry and mathematics. But you must remember, we have so much more to discover and need to continue refining our instruments and charts. For instance, this land-based astrolabe now has more accurate tympans added based on our latest ship logs.'

Behaim held up a bronze circular plate-like device. The main body or mater was hollowed out to house the rete and several tympans. The rete or star map depicted the brightest stars and was indicated by pointers; the sun and planets along the ecliptic circle were also displayed. A center pivot in the rete marked the North Celestial Pole. The tympan consisted of main coordinates in relation to the observer which included: azimuths, meridian, horizon, zenith, lines of equal altitude or almucantars and direction lines. Often several tympans were employed, each one configured for a specific latitude.

Fernão took hold of the astrolabe by its ring and shackle and lifted it in the air. He looked over the tympans in awe. 'Very impressive. Can we give it a test?'

Behaim pulled out a pocket watch and checked the time. 'Yes, perfect, midday exact. Best time to take a reading and avoid any errors.'

Both men walked across the room to a stairway. They climbed two floors and found an open loft used for experiments. Fernão fastened the ring of the astrolabe to a sturdy mounted steel tripod and chain with a leveling device. The backside of the astrolabe was used for observation with the outer edge divided into degrees and an alidade, or sighting bar mounted at center. In addition, two calendars were inscribed, zodiac and civil. Fernão set the date and time on the astrolabe, then adjusted the movable pinhole sight to line up with the sun. He looked at the front of the astrolabe to see the computed coordinates.

'Excellent workmanship,' Fernão said. 'The device works perfect.'

'The most advanced measuring device of our age,' Behaim beamed with pride. 'But you know, at sea—it is useless. You must use the basic mariner's astrolabe when sailing; along with the tables, quadrant, compass and good charts for verification.'

Fernão frowned. 'Useless?'

'As you know, the mariner's astrolabe I developed for use at sea has a ring to hang from deck, heavy weight to keep its stability and a spoke shape to avoid wind effects. But its main use is observation for the altitude of the sun or stars.' Behaim explained in detail, but he noticed Fernão's frustration. He pointed to his modified astrolabe. 'Of course, I would recommend any pilot bring this advanced astrolabe for any voyage. You see, one can take land-based measurements when in port to confirm or rectify any errors from the other instruments.'

'Then I shall bring all instruments,' Fernão responded with determination.

A loud thud echoed across the chamber as the heavy copper door once again slammed shut. All eyes turned toward a man with a determined gaze as he rushed toward a movable- type printer machine. Fernão reflected on how the influence of German innovation such as advanced printers had revolutionized Portugal. King Manuel loved these new technologies. Foreigners, like the Germans, were esteemed so highly that he granted them rights equal to the Royal House. Likewise, manufacturers of navigation instruments were also in high demand with the chief center of compass production located in Nürnberg, Germany—also home of Martin Behaim and Regiomantanus. In addition, valued German gunpowder and artillery were admitted duty-free into Portugal in vast quantities.

Now, here entered another foreign visitor. Everyone in the India House knew, Amerigo Vespucci. He was 53 years of age, stocky, average height, had an odd-shaped head with a low retreating forehead of great size and width, aquiline nose, large dark eyes, a slight sickly yellowish dark complexion, and a thick salt and pepper colored beard. His voyages to the New World were legendary.

'Where are my charts?' Vespucci inquired with an Italian-Portuguese accent to one of the men working a printer.

'Charts sir?' the printer operator asked.

'Yes, my charts I ordered two days ago,' Vespucci replied with a raised voice.

Martin Behaim and Fernão Magalhães looked at one another. The two walked over toward the printers.

'Amerigo my friend.'

'Behaim,' Vespucci responded with courtesy.

'Your charts—well you see—we took an early look. We have them over here.' Behaim led Vespucci and Fernão back to his table with his modified astrolabe perched upon a freshly printed navigational chart.

'Ah, quality printing,' Vespucci said, and then glanced at Fernão. 'And who is this young man?'

'Fernão Magalhães, one of my top pupils and eager to travel.'

'Travel and discovery, the real spice of life my young friend. Where do you wish to go?' Vespucci asked.

'To the Indies with the next armada, same route as Da Gama, around the Horn of Africa. But . . .' Fernão responded dejected.

'Why the long face?' Vespucci inquired.

'The king refused my request to join the armada.'

'I see,' Vespucci said. 'But have we all not been slighted? I delivered a detailed report of my last expedition to the New World, but the king has decided to keep it for himself. Perhaps he does not trust me, even after all my faithful years of service. And I assume Martin has told you of his own considerable reduction in wages for his loyal service to the crown?'

'I see.' Fernão said.

'Do not worry, your time will come. Never give up. Only a fool would give up,' Vespucci exclaimed.

Behaim moved his modified astrolabe off the new marine chart.

Vespucci stretched his arm toward the astrolabe while looking at Behaim. 'May I?' Vespucci asked.

Behaim nodded.

Vespucci held the astrolabe by its shackle and studied its features. 'Ah, interesting . . . new tympans and the fourth . . . with multiple horizons! Very clever, Behaim.'

'Now we have improved our latitude measurements for world navigation,' Behaim said.

'But the longitude—we must gain progress on longitude,' Vespucci railed. 'The pilots and captains of our missions are so ignorant of navigational tools. They rely upon outdated useless methods. I have spent many sleepless nights on deck watching the movement of the moon to positions of stars to ascertain precise longitudinal position.' He held a corner of the marine chart lying on the table. 'And that brings me to why I have come here. Is this chart plotted with all the recent voyages, including my own?'

'Yes, printed yesterday as you requested,' Behaim answered.

'Excellent, we must compare my latest computations. I have made my own estimates of the earth's circumference at the equator. Sir João Mandeville had estimated the spherical earth as 31,500 English miles and Regiomantanus 26,509. I believe these figures too high. Others such as Ptolemy estimated 20,710 and Colombo 18,777. These are much too low. I calculate 24,852 miles.' Vespucci reflected a moment. 'Too bad I could not convince my friend Colombo. The New World he discovered cannot be Cathay or the Spice Islands, but they must lie further beyond.'

'Sir João Mandeville?' Fernão inquired.

Vespucci glanced to Behaim. 'You have not shown him the writings of Mandeville?'

'I assumed he had read these at court.' Behaim replied, then looked to Fernão. 'This should have been required reading for any young page, especially one focused on exploration.'

Fernão shrugged his shoulders in ignorance.

'One of our great travel writers of the past, like Marco Polo,' Behaim said.

'Indeed,' Vespucci said. 'Mandeville told of a man—perhaps himself—who traveled from England by land and sea to India, then further east visiting 5,000 islands. Eventually he came upon a land where the people spoke his own language, even with the exact same accent.' He placed his two hands upon the table and stared at the navigational chart. He seemed deep in thought. His head turned up slowly and locked eyes with Fernão and Behaim. 'Mandeville claimed to have actually circumnavigated the entire globe.'

Fernão's mind churned with the possibility of accomplishing such a feat.

Behaim cleared his throat. 'Quite possible, but unfortunately he had no witness. Someone will have to perform such a quest with substantial evidence to make the claim of circumnavigation.'

'Agreed,' Vespucci said. 'Both Colombo and I, have tried to navigate to the Spice Islands by a western route as advised by one of our esteemed Florentine scholars, Toscanelli. Others, like Da Gama have ventured to sail the eastern route.'

'I still plan to join the next armada,' Fernão said.

'If you travel the Da Gama path eastward, perhaps you will find Prester John and seek his aid,' Vespucci added.

Fernão had learned of the famous Prester John legend from many circles. In England he was called Prester John. Crusaders had heard rumors of a great and powerful Christian king in the east. Some believed this ruler was a descendant of one of the three magi who brought offerings of gold, frankincense, and myrrh to the baby Jesus. It could be said that Prester John was an emperor for he had seven kings at his court, each of which served for one-month duty. These kings always had 72 dukes, 30 earls and many other knights and nobles. Each day 12 archbishops and 20 bishops would dine at his palace. Prester John's army was believed to number 100,000, all armed with solid iron weapons with gold engravings. He could bring a million men from his reserves to the field if needed. In his kingdom all sorts of wonders existed: a mirror in which the entire world was reflected, a massive emerald table that was brilliantly illuminated by numerous balsam-burning lamps for entertaining up to 30,000 guests, and a fountain of youth which kept the king alive for centuries. In addition, the Prester's kingdom included all sorts of bizarre creatures: centaurs, fauns, satyrs, cyclops, giants, pygmies, horned men, a phoenix, and griffins. His lands were abundant in all sorts of wealth—gold, diamonds, rubies, emeralds, sapphires, topaz, and countless other precious gems.

It was during the pioneering maritime explorations of the early fifteenth century initiated and sponsored by Prince Henry, later to be dubbed—the Navigator, when the Portuguese rulers became obsessed with discovering the location of Prester John and seek his aid against the Islamic armies. In Da Gama's voyage to the east, King Manuel gave his fleet a dual mission.

The first task was to open a sea route of trade between Europe and Asia. The second was to find Prester John and forge an alliance.

'Where is his kingdom?' Fernão asked. 'Is it located in Middle India, as some claim?'

'In the past yes,' Vespucci replied. 'Many believed India or even further east. But Da Gama had confirmation from sources in his last expedition claiming a large territory to the south of Egypt, likely Abyssinia.'

'I was at court recently. The Muslim armies threaten our people in their domains. The Sultan of Egypt said he would destroy the Holy Sepulcher,' Fernão responded with righteous indignation.

'Well then, even greater urgency to find Prester John is it not?' Vespucci asked.

'With an alliance with the great king of the east, we would crush the Islamic empire, and bring about a new age of trade and commerce,' Fernão said.

Martin Behaim stared down upon the marine chart and traced his fingers across a route around the horn of Africa then up toward Abyssinia. 'Fernão, I hope you will find Prester John and confirm Mandeville's account.' As a scientist, Behaim remained more attentive to scientific pursuits rather than a renewed holy war.

Vespucci curiously reviewed the marine chart. 'Charts have always been a life-long passion of mine. Since I was a young merchant, I have collected any map or chart I could afford; even paid 130 ducats for a detailed map made in Mallorca by Gabriel de Velasca. Such a beautiful map and so costly, but worth every ducat.' Vespucci turned toward Behaim. 'I heard about the globe you constructed in Nürnberg. I am curious. How was it constructed?'

Behaim paused a moment in reflective thought. 'Hmm, that was about 12 years ago. It was a rather simple design, a wooden frame of pasteboard two feet in diameter coated with gypsum and parchment drawings stretched over it. An iron axis ran through the center, the horizon was brass and meridian, composed of iron. I had the entire globe supported by an iron tripod.'

Fernão pictured the globe in his mind. He asked, 'Parchment drawings? What did they depict?'

'I assume you refer to the topography,' Behaim said. 'The sea was painted an aqua marine, the lands were brown and green, mountain peaks white, inscriptions and names lettered in gold, silver, white and yellow.'

'Did you bring it to Lisbon?' Fernão asked.

Behaim hesitated as if holding something back. He averted his eyes from Vespucci. 'I left it in Nürnberg.'

'Too bad,' Vespucci said. 'I would have loved to look it over, perhaps offer a good price and add it to my collection. A few years ago. I fashioned a globe for the monarchs of Spain. They seem to have enjoyed it very much.'

Fernão relished every moment of this exchange of information between the two great geographical explorers.

'Fernão has been assigned with outfitting the new armada,' Martin Behaim said.

Vespucci's raised his eyebrows. He looked over Fernão 'Excellent, nothing better to prepare oneself for a career in nautical exploration. Martin and I were merchants long before we set sail. You see, merchants must oversee the inventory so vital to any mission. Keeping strict discipline in records of money spent, so important. Loyalty to your financiers is crucial. And

56

never forget, every item in the ship's stores matters; it can be life or death on the high seas.'

'Of course, even the best preparations never eliminate all disaster,' Behaim added.

'True,' Vespucci said. 'My friend Gianetto Berardi and I outfitted the fleets for the great Admiral Colombo, but still there was calamity during his voyages. But, with the right knowledge one can refit fleets in distant lands and save many lives.'

Vespucci gestured toward Behaim. 'But you must learn from the best. I see Martin has taught you well, one of Lisbon's finest scholars. I too had a mentor, my uncle Giorgio Antonio Vespucci, a Dominican friar and one of the leading scholars in my home of Florence. He frequented the revived Platonic Academy, discussed themes of Latin, Greek, science, and geography. It was he who prepared me for scientific exploration.'

'Florence? You grew up there?' Fernão asked.

'Oh yes, such new talent in my city, a real renaissance of art and science. I remember as a youth, our famed artist, Ghirlandaio, had painted portraits of my uncle Giorgio Antonio and myself. Another talent, Botticelli, lived near our home. But one young man I met in Ghirlandaio's art studio had exceptional talent. Ghirlandaio never outwardly admitted the youth's talent, but I knew he was aware,' Vespucci said.

'Who was the youth?' Fernão asked.

'Michelangelo di Lodovico Buonarroti Simoni. I have had letters from friends in Florence informing me of a contract awarded to Michelangelo to sculpt a colossal marble statue of David.' Vespucci stared upward as if looking at the new statue. 'Well, enough about my home. We are here to discuss exploration and navigation. Martin, you know what these journeys involve. Tell him.'

Behaim paused a moment to consider how to reply. 'I remember King João had dispatched me on a secret diplomatic mission to the Netherlands. Along the way our ship was captured by English pirates. I was a prisoner for three months. But, during this time I suffered fever to near death. I will never forget the fevers, ever.'

'Yes, fever. I had the quartan ague after my second voyage. Perhaps it was from the West Indies climate. About every fourth day I had an intense fever, like malaria. I will never forget it,' Vespucci said.

Fernão stared in rapt attention.

'Disease, rot, starvation, fevers, shipwreck, mutiny. So many more perils await those who dare. And what of the eaters of men? Oh my,' Vespucci warned with suspense.

'Eaters of men?' Fernão asked.

'Oh yes. The great Admiral Colombo encountered them on his second voyage when he landed on the island, he named Guadalupe.' Vespucci paused for dramatic suspense. 'I would have named it Devil's Island. The eaters of men are of the Carib tribe. We call them cannibals, fierce warriors, experts with the bow and arrow. When Colombo's men entered their villages, many vomited from the stench of rotting flesh. Human limbs hung on wooden beams—a young man's severed head with blood dripping out—body parts roasting on a spit.'

Fernão's eyes widened. He stepped back into a table and knocked over a pile of charts onto the floor.

A sly grin crossed Vespucci's face as he continued his gory account of Colombo's expedition. 'The Caribs capture the most young and beautiful women and keep them as slave concubines. They eat the children born to them.'

Vespucci noticed Fernão's apprehension. He grinned mischievously, and then escalated his foreboding account. 'I have seen these cannibals in my second and third voyages to the New World. Out at sea, near the Island of Trinidad, we captured a canoe with two cannibals and four of their prisoners. The men were disturbed by the freshly scarred prisoners. They had been castrated, to be fattened and later eaten.'

Fernão swallowed hard. He could picture in his mind the horrific ordeal of those young boy prisoners.

'The Caribs love the taste of human flesh. It excites their appetite. They say it produces an exquisite, sweet flavor. They salt and season the limbs, hang them from the timbers of their homes, and then cure them by smoking or drying in the sun, just as we prepare our animal game.' Vespucci looked over Fernão. 'They claim the young taste much better.'

Fernão looked pale.

'On my journey to the northern coast of Brazil I met a man who boasted to have eaten over 200 humans. I believed him,' Vespucci said.

Both Fernão Magalhães and Martin Behaim's jaws dropped.

'In these lands of the New World we found other natives and wished to communicate with them. But they kept their distance. We agreed with one of their leaders to send them two of our scouts for trading goods. They were ordered to return after five days. But they never returned so we returned with our ships.'

'What happened to them?' Fernão asked in suspense.

'We were not certain why our men had not yet returned and naively thought they were only lost or had found something of value. On the seventh day, the men of the island sent their women out to meet us.

They would not trust a large contingent, so we sent one of our best in a skiff to shore, a handsome and brawny young Portuguese youth, to give them more assurance. The women touched and groped the young man in great amazement.' Vespucci continued his account, with Fernão and Behaim hanging on every word. 'Meanwhile, we saw a woman emerge from a hill, carrying a great club in her hand and moved with stealth toward our young soldier, who was now distracted with the other young women. She slammed the mighty stick into our compatriot and rendered him unconscious. They dragged him away while the men rushed to the beach and shot arrows at us in great numbers. We fired four rounds of our bombards at them to force them back to the hills where the women were tearing our man to pieces.' Vespucci paused in somber reflection. 'They roasted alive our friend upon a great fire, showing us many pieces of flesh and then eating them. The native men gave us signs showing how they had also killed our two scouts and had eaten them. We watched in horror, helpless to intervene.'

All three men reflected upon this morbid tale of woe.

'It takes strong fortitude and will to forge ahead into unknown lands full of great peril. Cannibals abound! And giants also exist,' Vespucci warned.

'Giants?' Fernão asked.

'It's true! We came across giants in the Island of Curaçao. One village had 12 houses and we found 7 women. They were so large that we considered them a great wonder and worthy of bringing back some young ones as a gift to the king. These women led us by signs into their dwelling to have some drinks. We debated among ourselves if we should bring some of these women to the ships as unique gifts for the queen. But suddenly . . .' Vespucci paused for effect, and then continued, 'we beheld 36 massive men enter the house. I would calculate they were about seven and a half foot tall, and all with well-proportioned muscular bodies. Some of our men were so frightened when they saw their size and their weapons that they did not consider it a safe mission. The giants carried bows and arrows along with massive clubs carved in the shape of swords. We prudently decided to forgo any rash plans to capture any of them, made signs of peace, and left for the ships in measured retreat. I suspect there may be even larger tribes of giants in the far-off lands of the New World.' Vespucci paced the floor with excitement. 'Perhaps . . . one day, you—Fernão—will see some great wonders.'

Fernão marveled at Vespucci's amazing accounts of exotic travel and dangerous adventure. Vespucci was indeed the quintessential nobleman, a man of clarity and purpose. 'I hope to sir,' Fernão said.

'You mentioned you sailed far to the south along the great southern mainland. How far did you sail? What were your coordinates?' Behaim asked.

'We ventured into the region where the South Pole had a height above our horizon of 52 degrees. We could no longer view the stars of Ursa Minor or Ursa Major. It was April and the nights were long, nearly 15 hours. The cold was so severe that the men could barely endure it. One storm was so intense that it blew away our sails, leaving us with bare poles and a violent tumultuous sea,' Vespucci said.

'You were not able to push further south?' Behaim asked.

Vespucci scratched his beard. 'We had to turn back. The storms and cold were too much. But one of our daring men climbed the bare mast for one last look. He swears there was a wide channel to the west.'

'What do you think?' Behaim asked.

'I believe he saw something,' Vespucci replied. 'Perhaps it was a strait, maybe a path to the Moluccas of the east.'

'Someone should send a fleet to find out for sure,' Fernão said.

'Portugal did. We were sent on a new mission. But the expedition was a disaster. Poor judgement by the captains and their faulty navigation cut short our chances. We were scarce of men and our vital gear was lost,' Vespucci said with remorse and disgust. 'I wanted to find if this strait truly existed.'

'If I ever have the chance, I will find it for you,' Fernão replied with resolve.

Vespucci looked at Behaim. 'This young man seems determined. Perhaps one day—'

'One day he will find the path to the east,' Behaim affirmed with a wink at Fernão.

'Well, I must depart for Seville,' Vespucci said. 'I wish to join my wife, Donna Maria and nephew Giovanni for Christmas. It has been a pleasure.'

Vespucci exited the India House. Martin Behaim put his arm around Fernão's shoulder. 'Keep up your navigational studies, you need to stay sharp. You will have your chance to explore,' Behaim said.

Fernão nodded and vacated the premises. His mind was in a daze. The tales of adventure and science from two of the great men of exploration continued to permeate his thoughts.

5

Near sunset, from the second level of the palace bedroom window, Leonora watched King Manuel strut briskly across the courtyard toward the royal armory. Her eyebrows raised in curiosity since the king rarely visited those premises. Manuel stood in front of a heavy brass door with hands upon his waist looking imperious. A nervous guard fumbled for a key then opened a giant metal lock that secured a massive metal brace across the armory entrance. Manuel slid the bar horizontal and opened the heavy door. Meanwhile, Leonora turned away from the window and rushed through the palace and across the courtyard.

Manuel entered the armory. Barred windows from an adjacent room let in fading sunlight that reflected off numerous weapons neatly stationed in racks across the room. 'I need more light,' Manuel said.

The guard hurried to light the torches mounted along the rounded brick walls. Manuel carefully examined the armory's tools of warfare: bows, spears, halberds, daggers, long spears, iron bludgeons, hand cannons, arquebuses, chain mail shirts, and numerous armor pieces. He grabbed a crossbow and fiddled with the release mechanism to verify its functionality. He used his leg as a counter-resistance to pull back the loading lever. Manuel snatched up a triangular-tipped bolt, loaded the weapon and scanned the armory looking for a target. 'Nothing here, quarters too close,' Manuel murmured. He bolted out the door and almost jabbed Leonora with the loaded crossbow bolt. She fell backwards, but he was able to keep her upright with his free arm.

'Ay, brother,' Leonora cried out, stunned.

'Sister, what are you doing here?'

Leonora pulled away. 'I was going to ask you the same.'

Manuel scanned the palace courtyard while speaking to his sister. 'Going on a hunt . . . found out the hunting is good now, just up the Tejo, near Santarém.'

'When?' Leonora asked.

'Tomorrow, early,' Manuel replied as he raised his crossbow and aimed through the iron sites.

Leonora turned slightly away from him and focused upon the courtyard, where Fernão Magalhães had fought King Manuel for his right to sail with the armada. Her face tightened as she remembered the prior confrontation. She always considered Fernão like an adopted son and was not pleased with how her brother had berated him. Manuel pulled the iron trigger. The bolt launched 60 feet across the courtyard into a joint between two timbers near the horse stables.

'Perfect! Such a marvelous invention. I shall use this one.' Manuel smiled with pride at his shot.

'What will you hunt?' Leonora asked.

'Wild Boar. Of course, there will be other game, but we need to train ourselves for battle, nothing better than the chase of dangerous game.'

'Do you have a good tracker?'

'We always bring good hunters, some can track well,' Manuel replied.

'What about bringing Fernão and his brother Diogo? They have hunted in the backwoods of the rugged north. They have much experience in—'

'Why? We have men who can track.' Manuel's face tensed in annoyance.

'Do you have men who can quarter and skin the game? They are experts—hunted before they arrived as pages to court—and after. And their friend, Francisco, is a skilled chef.'

Manuel's countenance eased. 'Yes. I do remember Francisco as a page at court. An exquisite master of spice.

Leonora held back her smile. She knew her brother's passion of good food would turn his decision.

'If they arrive at the port by sunrise, they may join the party,' Manuel said.

The Magalhães brothers and Francisco Serrão counted their recent catch of fish along the pier and divided out the spoils in three baskets. 'So, you think Vespucci's crew actually saw a strait at 52 degrees south?' Francisco asked.

'That is what he claimed.' Fernão replied.

'What if it is true, and there really is a westward shortcut to the famous Spice Islands of the east?' Diogo asked.

'Even so, the king's armada sails east in the path of Da Gama. And there lies our future—If only we were given permission to sail.' Fernão stared out across the Tejo estuary.

A royal messenger walked across the dockyard toward them. He called to them as he neared. 'I was dispatched by Leonora. The king has granted you permission to join his hunting party up the Tagus.'

The three young men leaned forward in anticipation.

'But on condition,' the messenger said. 'You will quarter and skin the game. Then make sure Francisco Serrão prepares a fine meal.'

'And when is this supposed to take place?' Francisco asked.

'At sunrise you must be ready at port to board the king's galley.'

The three looked at one another and nodded in agreement. 'We will be there,' Fernão said.

The messenger nodded and walked off.

'Leonora must have convinced the king,' Francisco said.

'But why?' Diogo asked. 'We still have no permission to join the armada.'

'Maybe not. But having access to the king could bring opportunity,' Fernão replied as he flung another fish into a bucket. 'At least we can join the hunt. Fresh game sounds good to me.'

Diogo and Francisco nodded in agreement.

Fernão, Diogo and Francisco arrived at port just before sunrise to join the hunting expedition. Diogo rubbed his tired eyes. 'A little early for you brother?' Fernão chided.

'It's early for me, and cold.' Francisco shivered, then stretched his arms, and yawned. 'I hope this venture will be worth the effort.'

'Have a little faith my friend,' Fernão said.

It was now sunrise and the light reflected off the polished wood of the royal galley already docked in the harbor. Crewmen arrived and began to load supplies for the trip. Wine caskets and crates of food were delivered into the ship's cargo hold. Noblemen began to arrive in small groups. Several musicians carried their instruments on board and took strategic positions near the gangway. As the sun rose further, beams of light shot across the Tagus and reflected off the two massive galley's sails, both white and emblazoned with a red cross.

Finally, the king and his entourage of courtiers arrived. 'A spectacular day for sailing up north is it not,' King Manuel remarked to one of his attending courtiers.

'Exquisite day my lord,' the courtier said with a feigned political smile.

Three leashed Grande Podengos were led up the wooden plank. Their owners strained to guide the yelping hounds toward the bow of the galley. 'Fine hunting breed,' Diogo whispered to Fernão as they stood near the gangway.

'They should help us track well,' Fernão replied.

Manuel approached the 40-foot-long galley. Pipers began to play a tune and drummers thumped upon kettledrums in a grand celebratory entrance. Two of the four-manned contingent of royal servants wheeled a large crate behind the entourage. Manuel smiled at his noble guests as he passed them on the dock.

Before entering the galley, Manuel noticed Fernão and his smile turned to a subdued scowl. Fernão, Diogo, and Francisco lowered their eyes to the paved dockyard. Manuel entered the ship and took his royal seat in a semi-enclosed structure at the stern of the vessel. An awning of upholstered silk covered the area as protection against the elements: sun, rain, and gusty winds. The courtiers and officials of business followed suit. They positioned near the king while servants brought the large crate and set it near the royal seat. Oarsmen took their places along the rowing benches to bring them out of the harbor. Francisco and the Magalhães brothers mingled in with the remaining crew boarding the ship. They took seats close to the bow alongside the Podengos. Fernão stroked the coat of one of the hunting dogs and caused its tail to swirl. The king's musicians took their places at the stern, just outside of the canopied enclosure. Lutes, guitars, and flutes brought a harmonious melody for the day's journey upriver. All four servants brought out dishes of fruit, bread, and cheese of various sorts for an early breakfast.

Fernão peeled a fresh orange and took a bite. 'Ah, so good.' Fernão tilted his head toward Francisco. 'Another reason to sail with the armada. Bring back orange seeds from the Indies like Da Gama.'

Francisco grinned. 'I go for the spice my friend, not much money in fruit.'

Once they all had a hearty meal and the galley was with full sail, Manuel signaled for quiet and made an announcement. 'I have brought gifts.'

Two servants pried open the cover of the large crate. Manuel stood and retrieved items of fine clothing from the crate. He walked among the many nobles and handed them articles of fine embroidered silk vests, puffy sleeved shirts, coats, hats, and other precious items from his own collection. Fernão knew that King Manuel had used his vast new wealth to annually purchase complete sets of clothing for every day of the year and would distribute his used items to his favored nobles and courtiers. If the clothing did not fit, they could take it to a tailor, give it to another family member, or trade it in the markets of Lisbon. King Manuel continued to hand out his gifts, working his way past midship, then to the bow. Fernão smiled in anticipation of receiving some fine clothes. But once Manuel caught sight of Fernão, he scowled and immediately turned back toward the stern. Fernão turned toward Francisco and rolled his eyes.

'No clothes for you,' Francisco said in jest.

'And none for you either,' Fernão retorted with a chuckle.

By midmorning, the galley had transitioned from the wide Tejo estuary into a narrow river meandering to the northeast. The royal musicians played on some lutes while one strummed a guitar. Fernão reminisced upon his childhood home in the northwestern territory of Portugal, for it resembled the lush greenery along the river's edge, replete with bird species and deer. With bellies full and a gentle tune from the musicians, Fernão and others reclined to take a nap.

At noon, the king signaled with a hand gesture for servants to distribute a lunch of breads and cheese. He also ordered the wine caskets to be opened and the servants to distribute with their jugs. The Magalhães brothers and Francisco filled their glasses with wine. Once all had been served, the king raised a glass of water for a toast. Manuel was extraordinarily strict in his diet. He abstained from wine, never consumed any oily foods, and ate in moderate portions. 'I salute you my esteemed noblemen and members of the court. Enjoy this fine day and may we have good fortune on the hunt.'

All the guests carried their Carracks black swords and left-handed daggers. The dark swords were a recent invention. They absorbed any sunlight and was a vital weapon for stealth missions when approaching enemy territory along the coast or in sea battle. The paint prevented rusting, useful when employed near salt-water. Each sword had two protective rings which gave protection to the fingers. Two guard terminals facing toward the tip of the blade were formed as large round plates but sharpened so they could be used as extra blades in close combat. The protective rings could trap an enemy blade and were designed for close combat. By placing the index finger in front of the guard, the fighting angle increased from 130 degrees to 160 degrees. Due to the round shaped terminal plates along the two sides of the blade, many viewed the ensemble as a warrior's testicles on a phallic-shaped sword.

By midafternoon, several of the young nobles were feeling the wine. Two of them began to boast and twirl their black swords in simulated combat bravado. They both wore colored sashes signifying their high nobility. One had long black hair, a goatee beard, and scarred right cheek. A red sash—of the Order of Christ was draped over his shoulder. He skillfully maneuvered his sword in the air. A brawny noble wearing a violet sash—of the Order of Saint Santiago, took notice and grinned. He stripped off his puffy-sleeved white shirt. His muscled right arm unhooked his sword from his belt and drew it forward. The two engaged in a simulated combat joust, their swords clanged back and forth, and they used their left-handed daggers as shields. They moved dangerously close to Diogo. Fernão stiffened and stared down the two duelists. The scar-faced man halted the fight, his face reddened as he glared back at Fernão. 'You have a problem?'

'You are reckless, drinking and engaged in sword play,' Fernão said. He held his elbows outward from his body with chest pushed forward.

The other muscled noble tapped the round testicle-shaped guard plates on his sword and growled deep. 'What is the matter, no balls?'

King Manuel rose quickly at the escalation. A royal guard nearby attempted to quell the tension. Manuel waved his hand downward as signal for the guard to wait. He continued to observe in keen interest.

'I have balls, my friend,' Francisco replied as he emerged from behind the mast. He likewise tapped the round guard plates on his own black sword. All the noblemen knew Francisco Serrão was an excellent young swordsman as a page of the court and now a master.

'We, we don't have a quarrel with you, Dom Serrão,' the muscled noble said.

'Endanger my friends and you indeed have a quarrel with me,' Francisco replied.

All eyes on board focused upon the scene, for all knew once a fidalgo was challenged, a duel was inevitable. Francisco moved two steps to his side for a strategic defensive position. The muscled guard's right arm flexed taught as he brought his sword to combat readiness and stepped directly toward Francisco. Meanwhile, the scar-faced noble with the red sash maneuvered toward his right side. Fernão drew his sword mid-level and stepped in front to block his movement toward his friend, Francisco Serrão. The scar-faced man sneered and positioned his sword for a strike against Fernão. Everyone on board placed their hands upon their own swords and daggers, unsure how far the fight would escalate.

Manuel signaled for the royal guard to halt the drama. He rose and bellowed out a command. 'Save your fight for the hunt men. King's orders, stand down!'

Once the king's royal guard gave an order everyone must obey. Disobedience equaled certain execution. The two factions glared at one another then returned to their benches and stared out to the riverbank.

It was an hour before sunset as the galley approached a port along the Tejo River. 'I can see Santarém in the distance,' Diogo said.

Ship crewmen struck the galley sails and oars were manned to steer the ship into a dock on the edge of Santarém. Pent-up Podengos yelped, in anticipation of the hunt, for they had been used on these trips often. The hunting party disembarked, and servants carried supplies to a dozen small hunting cabins. The party gathered in the main hunting lodge. It had a vaulted ceiling, a firepit in the corner, and six rough-surfaced wood tables. Manuel's musicians struck an upbeat tune and servants distributed more wine, cheese, and bread.

The king stood for an announcement. 'Enjoy the evening. But remember, we rise to hunt before sunrise.' He looked over the reveling crowd and raised his voice in jest. 'Those who actually do rise—' The king knew many would imbibe too much and never rise for the hunt, even though he set his own example of sobriety.

The men bellowed with raucous laughter and replied in unison. '—Shall feast with fresh boar.'

Nobles and courtiers cheered in response. Many continued to drink and feast in the lodge. Others dispersed in various clusters. Francisco and the Magalhães brothers strolled to the riverbank. They tied fishing string to tree branches, attached some worms on the end for bait and dropped their lines. 'Maybe we get lucky and cook some fresh fish before we turn in,' Diogo said.

'I brought spice for fish,' Francisco added.

After sunset, campfires blazed near the lodges in the cool December air. Men warmed themselves near the open flames. Francisco found a metal pan and seasoned fresh trout from his homemade stash of spices. 'Always good to be prepared,' he remarked with a grin.

The spiced aroma of pan seared fresh trout invoked a jealous fervor in camp. Other groups had not come prepared for the first night's meal, and thus had to settle for leftovers of bread and cheese. Several sneered with envy as they passed by Francisco's campfire. Others continued to drink their wine regardless of the king's warning to be ready to hunt early.

73

'Those fools drinking into the night risk their lives in the hunt,' Fernão warned. 'One's vision must be clear, reflexes quick.'

'And the aim exact,' Diogo added. 'Need to strike behind the shoulder blade into the heart and lungs. A tight target of mere inches. Not easy if the boar charges.'

'You brothers are hunters of wild game' Francisco said. 'I was trained to fight men.'

'Same thing in the end,' Fernão replied. 'All our kings have always encouraged the hunt for training in war. Like men, a wild boar can be unpredictable. It may flee to the covered woods, a hole, or a riverbank to avoid attack.'

'What's your preferred weapon for boar?' Francisco asked Fernão.

'A spear as primary. A sword as backup.'

After they finished their fine meal of seasoned trout cooked over the flames, the three retired into one of the communal hunting cabins for the evening.

Wild boars foraged for food at sunrise. The pack hunting Podengos picked up their scent and with their large prick ears heard their rustling in the distance. A yelping spread throughout the camp. Fernão awoke and shoved Diogo and Francisco inside their cabin. 'It's time. We need to split up as trackers. Remember, the Podengos will triangulate with their calls when tracking the boar.'

The camp stirred to life. Noblemen who behaved by turning in early were dressed for the hunt. Others who continued their drinking bouts until late stumbled out of their cabins and urinated in the brush. The scar-faced noble was passed out near some burning campfire embers. The smoke roused him semi-conscious. He coughed hard, heaved up vomit into the

74

now smoking embers. The Magalhães brothers watched the display of a hangover in play and shook their heads in disgust. The dog owners strapped thick leather protective armor around the chests of the three Podengos. King Manuel was always an early riser. He had already performed his daily exercise routine before the others arose. Manuel stood near the wood line ready for the hunt. His sword was strapped to his side, and he had a long spear in his hand.

Francisco caught up to the Magalhães brothers and said, 'I will follow behind. You know the pack dogs best.'

The brothers nodded.

The royal retinue of kettledrum players thumped a rhythmed beat in perfect unison, much like the nation's battle songs.

Francisco giggled. 'I know the king has a passion for music . . . but on a hunt?'

The Magalhães brothers chuckled.

'Seriously, why here?' Francisco said.

King Manuel raised his long arm then lowered it as a signal for the hunt to commence. Podengos trotted ahead, their bodies built for a combination of endurance, speed, and agility. Hunters roamed throughout the brush near the river while dogs sniffed out their targets. Manuel's two Podengos picked up a scent and increased their speed to a fast trot. He followed them alone into a brushy swamp-like meadow, a perfect lair for boars. The large Podengos yelped as they rushed to surround a focal point, it was a heavy rustling in thick brush. Manuel adjusted his grip to the center of a six-foot long spear. An upper crossbar was attached below the head for checking the thrust depth and avoiding the sharp boar tusks. The Podengos flushed out a large wild boar of nearly 180 pounds. They continued to harass it. The boar whirled around in a circle. Once it stood still, Manuel crouched down and positioned himself to the boar's side. Now in perfect striking range he thrust the spear with all his weight behind the boar's shoulder blade, then into the heart. The crossbar stopped at the hard-shelled shoulder blade. The boar writhed, squealed, and thrashed about to free itself. Manuel held the spear firm knowing that he must not lose his grip to avoid the sharp tusks. He twisted the spear to quicken the kill.

Meanwhile, Fernão's Podengo had sniffed out the same boar enclave near Manuel and was closing in from the opposite direction. Behind Manuel, a massive wild boar pawed at the dirt and foamed from its mouth. Fernão could see the king was engaged with the other boar and did not notice the danger lurking behind. Fernão rushed forward. The mighty boar snorted and then charged. The king turned and gasped as the wild behemoth, over 300 pounds of muscled flesh, closed in . . . 20 yards . . . 10 yards. Fernão rushed parallel to the king and boar, soon positioned himself between king and beast. He planted his leg into the muddy ground, gripped his spear with both fists and braced for impact. The aggressive and powerful wild boar continued its charge. Fernão did not flinch but grit his teeth as he held his spear tight. The boar rammed into the sharpened pole shaft and flung Fernão back six feet. The wild boar suffered only a slight flesh wound, for the spear had only penetrated the surface skin over its armor plating of bone. It whirled around, snorting and foaming, enraged.

It charged again at the king. The king drew his sword, but both men realized it was a useless defense in a frontal attack. Fernão unfastened his sword and dove at the charging boar. In midair, he shoved the sword deep into the flesh . . . too deep. His arm jerked forward from the momentum and was gashed by a sharp tusk as the wild beast flailed about. Fernão had still retained a firm grip on his sword. He pulled it back some, then twisted the blade to penetrate the vital organs. Blood and innards splattered all over him as he continued to fight on. Manuel looked on, but was immobile to act, for he suffered a momentary shock. Fernão's blade maneuvers finally dropped the massive wild boar as it gasped out its last breath. From within cover of the wood line, Francisco watched the events unfold, unnoticed.

Manuel raised himself and dusted the dirt and mud from his clothing. 'I suppose you will think you have saved me from injury. Well, let us refrain from such speculation and keep this incident to ourselves.'

Fernão's mouth slackened. He had just saved the king's life and given no thanks, and with only a warning to remain silent.

'I expect you will quarter and skin the game like agreed upon.' Manuel said, then turned and trudged back across the meadow, leaving Fernão stuck with finding assistance to lug back the two heavy boars.

Once the king had left Francisco emerged from the wood line. 'A fine kill my friend,' Francisco said.

'Lot of meat but no honor,' Fernao replied.

Francisco eyes opened wide. 'I saw you save the king from injury, perhaps even death.'

'Yes, but nobody will know that . . . at least nobody but you, me, and the king.'

'I see—The king's courtiers—they never cease their influence on him. News that a country boy rescued the mighty-hunter king would certainly bring consternation in the court.'

'In saving his life, he would be obliged to give us leave to join the armada,' Fernão said. 'But a king does not wish to look weak by vacillating in his decisions.

He already broke with his courtiers once when he gave me the chance in the cane duel.'

Francisco scratched his beard in thought. 'We will have to find another way then, another compelling reason for the king to change his mind and give us our leave to join the mission.'

6

On the morning of Christmas Eve, Manuel was reclined in a plush bourbon and gold-colored couch facing a window. He watched the sun rise and shine across the hills of Lisbon. Manuel was an early riser, no matter how late he was up the previous night. A harpist plucked a note. The king twirled his long arms in the air as if conducting a symphony and softly sung a tune.

Oh Portugal, how fine you are.
All the world will wonder at your deeds.
Oh, what men of courage to sail the seas.
And what a noble king does lead.

Manuel smiled as the lyrist praised him with his song. A knock on the door interrupted the harmonious scene and Manuel ceased with his musical arm gestures. A servant opened the door and Leonora entered gracefully. 'You called?'

'Yes, yes. I did request. Please sit down.' Manuel waved his arms at the servant and the harpist. 'You may leave us.'

Leonora seated herself in a soft purple chair.

'How are the preparations for the Christmas Eve dinner?'

'Everything is set,' Leonora replied.

'The food and drinks?'

'Yes. All will be ready.'

'Very good. One other thing. I need to ask your thoughts on a matter.' Manuel stared out the window. 'I want Fernão Magalhães out of Lisbon. Send him away to sea, away from here.'

'What are you talking about?'

'I am not sure how to present this to the court. Once a king has made his decision, he must keep to it, or some may think a weak mind rules the land.'

'I see.'

'In public, I have already denied Fernão participation in the next armada and to stay at his post in the India House. How can I reverse my own royal edict? I must have a credible reason to overturn my order.'

'But you need Fernão gone?' Leonora asked, puzzled.

'Yes, well, I have my reasons.' Manuel could not reveal to anyone the truth of the hunting episode. Nobody could know the powerful hunter king was rescued by an inexperienced youth from the country. But if Fernão was deployed on a voyage, the chances of perishing at sea were favorable, a perfect remedy.

Leonora's mind raced for a solution for his odd request. 'Fernão works in the India House. Has he not studied with some of our great minds like Behaim and others?' Leonora responded.

'Yes.'

'He would know of our nation's latest inventions.'

'Yes, and?' Manuel asked impatiently.

'Perhaps have Fernão present the latest studies for the event tonight, in front of the courtiers.'

Manuel's eyes opened wide, and he sat upright. 'Of course! Perfect. I have heard that he knows the modified astrolabe. Perhaps his knowledge will convince the court we need to send him on the mission.'

'And your change of mind will appear acceptable.'

Manuel stood up. His countenance was beaming with satisfaction of the newfound plan. 'Send word to Magalhães, for his attendance at the dinner.'

'Very well,' Leonora said. She arose and left the king's office.

In the main chamber of the India House, the Magalhães brothers and Francisco Serrão stood around a wooden table. Fernão held Behaim's modified astrolabe and carefully placed it inside a velvet black bag. 'I am not sure why the king suddenly asked us to represent the India House tonight,' Fernão said. 'But we do not have much time before the Christmas party begins. Diogo. Find some good charts to use.'

'What else do we need?' Francisco asked.

'Ephemerides tables,' Fernão replied.

Diogo gathered several marine charts and placed them on the table. Fernão looked them over and began to sort out the ones he needed. Meanwhile, Francisco retrieved a copy of Regiomontanus' ephemerides tables.

'I believe this is all we need,' Fernão said. 'Let's go.'

The Magalhães brothers and Francisco Serrão had rushed up the long hill to the royal palace. Fernão presented an invitation card to one of the two stationed guards at the main gate. The guard nodded and gestured with his arm to pass. The three young men stood a moment near the cobbled stone palace wall overlooking Lisbon. It was Christmas Eve and the residents had placed lanterns in their doorways and windows bringing the city to life.

They proceeded onward and entered the ceremonial hall which bustled with activity. Torches were set along the walls and candle chandeliers illuminated the room with a glowing ambiance. Servants escorted courtiers and nobles to their seats. Celebrated men of arms such as Vasco da Gama and others had been invited with great honor. A long wooden table was covered with a finely embroidered cloth with elegant settings of porcelain imported from the Indies. King Manuel and his wife Maria of Aragon took their places at the end of the table. Then Leonora and Gil Vicente took their places near the king. As customary for Christmas Eve, the entire dinner was simply fresh fruit distributed in numerous wicker baskets along with confections of sugar and sweet candies organized neatly in flat porcelain dishes. Christmas day would be more lavish with assorted meats and vegetables as a main course. Servants filled glasses of wine and water for the guests. An orchestra lined the perimeter walls. They played lively dinner music with an accompaniment of cornets, harps, fiddles, and various pipes. Francisco and the Magalhães brothers stood among the servants at the far end of the hall.

King Manuel raised a glass of water for a toast. 'On this great evening we begin to celebrate the birth of our Lord and Savior. Enjoy our bountiful blessings and rejoice for our good fortune.'

The guests drank their wine and selected sugared treats.

An obese courtier on the far end of the table, opposite the king and queen, twirled a fork in his hand as he examined its features. 'What a fine invention the Manuel family has brought to the court.'

The king and queen nodded in gracious acceptance of their guest's compliment. Indeed, King Manuel's parents had begun the tradition of using forks at the court dinners.

The fat courtier then stabbed into a juicy sugar candy and took a bite. 'Exquisite! Simply exquisite!'

'Most of our sugars are imported from our plantations in Madeira Island,' Queen Maria said. 'I am pleased you like the candies, Dom Silva.'

King Manuel waved the orchestra to disperse. As they filed out, a new ensemble formed; a choir of singers arranged themselves into a semicircle, an accompaniment of a flute, lute and tambourine played in the background. The crowd whispered in pleasant anticipation of the renowned group. The king nodded and the choir sang an elegant nativity song.

Francisco whispered into Fernao's ear. 'Fantastic. The king has hired the greatest talent in Europe. No country can compare with his choir.'

Fernão nodded in agreement.

After two beautiful songs, the king waved off the choir and signaled for the orchestra to return. Musicians played softly as Manuel rose to speak. 'I have a new feature for this year's event. Our talented fellows from the Marine Department will demonstrate our latest innovation in navigation, the modified astrolabe. With this marvelous device we will dominate the seas and bring back further bounty for Portugal!'

Nobles and courtiers raised their wine glasses in a spontaneous toast of approval to the proposal. Manuel pointed to Fernão and gestured for him to commence. The Magalhães brothers and Francisco stepped away from the servant's area and near the center of the great table. Fernão held up the new astrolabe, while Diogo referred to a marine chart, and Francisco held up the ephemerides book. Fernão gave a detailed lecture, demonstrating how to operate the astrolabe in conjunction with the tables and chart. Many of the nobility were engrossed in the new device and Fernão's skill in its usage. Several courtiers looked at one another with jealous angst.

Upon completion of the display of navigational scientific innovation Manuel interjected. 'So now you see what our captains will have at their disposal. But we also need skilled men like Fernão Magalhães to assist our captains in the field.'

Dom Silva coughed and then glanced to another courtier seated next to him—the noble, Dom Alvaro—who tugged on his pointed beard in annoyance. 'Is this not the same country boy who lost the cane duel and the same one ordered to be stationed at the India House?' He asked. 'Surely the king does not change his mind?'

'Sending farmers on the king's mission?' Dom Silva added with a smirk. 'Can we not do better?'

Gil Vicente grimaced at the snobbish insult against Fernão Magalhães, a fellow country brother from the northern woodlands of Portugal.

Manuel realized his new proposal was perceived as weakness and indecision. The king pondered a moment, thinking of a suitable distraction. 'Let us take up this matter later,' he said, then turned to his audience and smiled. 'Let us have some fun. Bring in the jesters.'

All attention shifted to the colorfully dressed court jesters, some of the greatest wits in Europe. Manuel was particularly fond of his group of three Castilian buffoons who were adept at entertaining as well as launching clever rebukes and jibes at courtier guests. Each one of the three jesters wore an absurd puffy outfit with dual colors, one with red and gold, the two others with purple and gold. They all wore flexible cone-shaped velvet caps. One of the jesters with a purple and gold outfit grinned and leapt forward with sideways body flips. Courtiers fell back in their seats as the clown passed, gliding his leg over them in rapid movements. The jester shouted and laughed as he displayed his skillful acrobatic moves. The other jester, also in purple and gold, gestured toward a bowl of apples. A guest understood the silent request and threw an apple at the clown, then another. The jester began to juggle the two apples in the air and called for more. A third apple was tossed into the mix. The jester grinned and gestured for another. One of the courtiers appeared annoyed at the whole routine and snatched a fourth apple. With purpose he tossed it four feet to the side of the clown. The jester quickly shifted his body to catch the stray apple without losing control of the other apples. The courtier sneered as the jester made the spectacular catch. The room full of guests roared, cheering, and clapping as the clowns awed them with skill and entertainment.

Meanwhile, Dom Silva whispered into Dom Alvaro's ear as the two chuckled and caught the attention of Manuel. He sensed they were mocking his decision to give the young men of the marine department an audience at their exclusive dinner. The king made a slow gestured nod to his court poet, playwright, and goldsmith—Gil Vicente—who had so impressed Leonora and the entire royal household with his skills in the arts. He had worked his way up to premier status as royal scholar and considered a sophisticated court jester. News of his legendary wit had spread from Portugal to other nations. Gil Vicente rose from his seat near the king and ambled slowly around the royal chamber. Guests shrunk in their seats in fear he would expose their secret sins. Manuel often employed Vicente to keep his courtiers in place, often in public critique, but not to the point where he would make lifelong foes. Finally, Vicente stood in front of Dom Alvaro and stared into his eyes, penetrating his dark soul. He wanted to unveil Alvaro's dark secrets but knew one must refrain from creating powerful enemies in the court. Vicente gave a final stare at Dom Alvaro and then locked into his associate, the plump and sweaty courtier seated to his right, Dom Silva.

Vicente cleared his throat as he peered into his bulging eyes. 'You sir are amazing. I wonder how such a man of your *stature* would survive in the northern wilderness of our dear Portugal. Maybe a week? No, I think maybe three days and you would be done for.'

Many of the guests chuckled.

Vicente prodded him further. 'For instance, you mock these young men as simple country people. But they are fit and well trained. They can hunt and skin any quarry, survive extreme weather, and navigate by the stars in any location. Why sir, you are the one to be mocked and jeered.'

Gil Vicente took a brief bow and took his seat. Manuel looked on with an approving nod to his beloved court poet. After this display by the esteemed court jester none dared challenge, for they knew Vicente could embarrass anyone if he so chose.

Meanwhile, Francisco Serrão had found an opportunity to sneak close enough to Vasco Da Gama, who was seated at the royal table, to briefly whisper in his ear. 'Please remember us, just like you remember my brother, Captain Serrão.'

Da Gama cleared his throat, straightened his back, and placed both hands on the table to muster attention.

'Something you wish to add, Da Gama?' the king asked.

Da Gama stood up to address the guests. 'If I may be so bold to speak candid.'

'I would not expect otherwise.'

Da Gama continued. 'Two years ago, in our nation's fourth armada to the Indies, I had an excellent captain under my command—João Serrão—brother to Francisco Serrão, one of our three marine students here. He served me well with great abilities.' Da Gama stared at Dom Alvaro and Dom Silva. 'Some may mock those from humble backgrounds. But I judge by proven actions. I have observed these young men of late and deem them worthy to sail in the next armada. We train as specialized units and sail in these teams when possible. I recommend they are given leave to sail in the next armada to India and placed under João Serrao's command as supernumeraries.'

King Manuel scanned the audience of guests. 'I hear your words Da Gama. I concur with your advice. Are there any objections?'

Manuel could see the courtiers had forced themselves to withdraw their emotional antipathy against the decision. Fernão stared in disbelief at the twist of fate. Diogo turned to face Fernão and they both beamed with excitement. When the court adjourned for the evening, Francisco joined the Magalhães brothers outside the palace.

Fernão gave a big hug to Francisco and asked. 'I saw you whisper to Da Gama. What did you say?'

'I only reminded him of my brother's service in the armada. Da Gama honors loyalty and despises traitors.' Francisco answered.

7

Lisbon, Portugal – February, 1505

Fernão rushed across a cobbled brick road near the dockyard toward the India House. As he rounded the building he nearly collided with Vasco da Gama. Fernão noticed Da Gama's hunched shoulders and his vacant stare.

'Ah, Magalhães! In haste to your duties I see,' Da Gama said.

'Sir, I heard the—'

'King's edict?' Da Gama interrupted.

'I was hoping you would take over Da Cunha's command of the fleet after his sudden incident of blindness,' Fernão said.

Da Gama shifted his eyes to the sea. 'Indeed. I respect Tristan da Cunha. He is a capable commander. He is also cousin to Afonso de Albuquerque, our fellow brother under the Order of Santiago. I should have been next in line to command, but the courtiers and the king do not take kind of my steady refusal to switch allegiance to the Order of Christ. They still whisper misleading opinions to the king.'

Fernão knew the rivalries and history of the different Orders. During the launch for the 1497 voyage to the Indies, King Manuel presented Da Gama his royal banner, that of the Order of Christ. But once Da Gama left sight of Lisbon, he had the banner pulled down. Ties to the different Orders ran deep and personal.

Da Gama's face turned red, and his veins bulged. 'Last month, with calculated political ambition, the nobleman—Almeida, switched his allegiance from

Santiago to the Order of Christ! Now he is not only captain-major, but viceroy!'

Fernão had heard the Almeida family were loyal to King João II and his Order of Santiago. However, Francisco de Almeida was a rebel, twice conspiring against the former king, and he was even exiled. Manuel had found a potential new political ally in Francisco de Almeida and the king proposed he swear allegiance to his Order of Christ. Almeida took the bait; he swore allegiance and was soon given full authority as viceroy with executive power to make decisions in the king's stead. He was now the first member of the upper nobility to lead an expedition to India.

Da Gama sighed. 'Loyalty is fickle these days. Maybe you will still fare well under this new command. Just remember, courtiers will always conspire and manipulate the king, as they have already done to you.'

Fernão knew this was all true. But still, he had reason to believe Francisco de Almeida could indeed be a capable commander. At 55 years of age Almeida was considered well experienced in martial, nautical and diplomatic skills. He was a widower, pious and giving, with good judgement. Above all, he was incorruptible and not swayed by the lure of riches.

Da Gama gave a slight nod and continued onward.

Fernão breathed heavy as he rushed up to the India House. In haste, he flashed his square-shaped silver badge to the guard for access. Fernão was known for his punctualness but today he woke up late and had been delayed further by his encounter with Da Gama. Fernão knew he must remain vigilant in his daily tasks to keep his place among the crews for the next voyage. Entering the main chamber, he saw Martin Behaim on the far end and hunched over some charts covering a table. Fernão approached. 'Sorry I am late sir. It will not happen again.'

Behaim slowly turned, his face was pale and sweat beaded upon his forehead. 'Fernão, good to see you,' he said with a conspicuous German accent. He coughed hard and wiped a bit of bloody spittle into his white handkerchief.

Fernão's eyes narrowed in concern, for this was the first time Behaim appeared sick.

'I need to show you something but you must promise to keep it between us.' Behaim braced his weight upon the table as he rose with effort. 'Come, follow me.'

Fernão followed his mentor down a corridor. Behaim retrieved from his pocket a jagged metal key and unlocked a heavy copper door. As it swung open, Fernão's jaw dropped at the massive store of nautical devices and documents in the room. Behaim retrieved another key and unlocked a wide desk drawer. It creaked as he opened it slowly. Behaim sifted through its contents, a stack of old marine charts. 'Ah, yes. Here it is.' He carefully unfurled a brittle sea chart.

Fernão's eyes widened as he noticed odd looking writings along the margins. 'What are those symbols? What language?'

'Language of Cathay, the land Colombo sought. I suspect this chart was one of many that Prince Dom Pedro brought back from his trip to Venice back in 1428,' Behaim said.

Fernão's heart pounded with excitement as his curious eyes scanned over a complete world map.

Behaim's finger traced over the continent of Europe and down to the tip of Africa, the Cape of Good Hope which Bartolomeu Dias first sailed around. He moved his finger to the west across the Atlantic sea and found two large continents vertically positioned one upon another. Fernão looked up at Behaim and the two men stared at one another.

'Look here,' Behaim said, while moving his finger to a channel running near the lower continent's southern tip. From the Atlantic Ocean it meandered through the land mass into another unknown western ocean. He then traced his finger further below the lower continent's tip, to another land mass situated at the bottom of the world.

'What the—' Fernão's mouth gaped.

'Amazing, is it not? Mariners from Cathay have been here and mapped it in detail.'

Fernão then traced his own finger across the strait and then across a great western ocean until he found another continent nearly the same latitude as the lower continent. He found numerous islands as he moved his finger northward and finally to another huge land mass. 'What is this place?' Fernão asked.

'Cathay,' Behaim said. 'It was much further west than Colombo had believed. But it *is* Cathay.'

Fernão continued tracing his finger until he came to the shape of the Indian continent, then back around the cape of Africa and back to Portugal. 'Someone has circumnavigated the entire world?'

'Not sure,' Behaim said. 'Perhaps it was indeed a complete world map based upon a Cathay expeditionary mission or maybe it was pieced together from several independent voyages. Nobody in the India House knows for certain, for our mariners have brought back many source maps for nearly a hundred years. We archived the most important in this room.'

Behaim retrieved another chart and unfurled it. It had no Cathay writings but depicted curious animal figures in various geographical regions. Behaim pointed to Portuguese writing near the channel running

across the lower continent's tip. It was named—
Dragon's Tail.

Fernão looked up at Behaim. 'Then this strait may
have been discovered *before* 1428?—Over a century
ago?

Behaim smiled and nodded.

'And here clearly marked, a path to the Spice
Islands,' Fernão conjectured with excitement.

'Indeed.'

'Then Vespucci was very close to finding the strait
near 52 degrees S. Why not share these charts with
him?'

'He is not Portuguese. The king has decided to
keep the most valuable under extra security.'

'So how did Dom Pedro acquire these charts?'
Fernão asked.

'From several sources, but a good part originated
from a certain Niccolò da Conti. He sailed the seas for
over 20 years.' Behaim retrieved a freshly printed
Portuguese manuscript and handed it to Fernão. 'Here
is his account recently translated from the Latin.'

Fernão thumbed through the pages, fascinated.

'Da Conti divulged information to the
cartographers Fra Mauro and Paolo Toscannelli.'

'Toscannelli? The one who gave Colombo his
idea to sail west to the Spice Islands and Cathay?

'Indeed. Toscannelli sent Colombo a letter with a
chart showing the western route,' Behaim replied.

'And this Cathay chart is an even older source?'

'Yes. And there are so many more secrets.'
Behaim grinned. 'Da Conti relayed what we have
heard from other sources. In 1421 he was in Calicut
and found a massive armada of Cathay treasure vessels.
It was their foreward base for exploration and trade.
Merchants in Calicut claimed all these ships were

under the command of a powerful grand eunuch, Zheng He.'

'A eunuch as their admiral?'

'Merchants say he was a mongol youth captured and castrated to serve in the emperor's household. Many living in the royal palace were made eunuchs so they could not seduce the emperor's concubines. They claim he keeps his manhood within a casket inside a temple. He expects in the afterlife he will once again become a whole man. Anyway, I digress. You should know that Admiral Zheng He was a soldier of great skill—rose to great power, and was a devout Muslim.'

Fernão's eyes narrowed with concern. 'A Moor led their armada?'

'Yes. But there were many faiths in their fleets. Their emperor had sent him on a mission with 800 ships to map the entire world and bring back tribute from the nations. He also commanded his armada to teach a doctrine of ordered harmony. It was based in part on the teachings of a philosopher named Confucius.'

'I never heard of this Confucius. Did he believe in God?'

'From what I have heard, his teachings eliminate any concept of God.'

Fernão shook his head. 'Not sure the purpose of such a philosophy.'

'Neither do I. But a fleet of 800 ships sent to map the entire world? Now, that is an audacious plan we both can respect.' Behaim winked at Fernão. 'Is it not?'

Both men nodded their heads in wonder.

'Ships, what were the ships like?' Fernão asked.

'Well, they had many ships, but their largest treasure ships were said to be 480 feet long and 180 feet wide. Some of their rudders 36 foot tall, as long as Colombo's entire ship, the *Niña*.'

'Amazing!' Fernão exclaimed.

'It is. The greatest galleys from Venice are mere dwarfs by comparison, only 150 feet long. The Venetian galleys can hold 50 tons. Those of Cathay 2,000 tons!'

'And their construction?' Fernao asked. 'Same as ours?'

'The armada kept tight security around their vessels. Da Conti could only relay a partial account, all based upon knowledge he acquired from paid informants. Many of the ships were made of teakwood and large square bows with serpent heads. Strong red silk sails were attached to the masts and some larger vessels had up to 12 masts.' Behaim took up a sketch pad and outlined a ship with all its components. 'Look here. They had 16 watertight compartments and could flood 2 without sinking the ship.' Behaim sketched more detail on the bow. 'And look here. Their bows were sturdy with channels leading into compartments. In high seas the water would flow inside and as it resurfaced the water drained back out. With such a design, any pitching motion would be minimized. Ingenious people. We really need to modify our own fleets with these concepts.'

'It appears they could sail for long distances based upon such construction,' Fernão said.

'Definitely. Fra Mauro was working for our kingdom and reported that in the year 1420 one of these ships rounded the Cape of Good Hope and sailed for 40 days with nothing but sea and sky. They made it back to the cape after 70 days and claimed to have traveled 2,000 miles.'

Fernão pondered. 'If they can sail such distances then what if there were—'

'Others?' Behaim said. 'Of course. We have records of many seafaring peoples of antiquity; Egyptians, Phoenicians, Greeks, and many more. Our explorers have found evidence—wrecks, stories, artifacts.'

Behaim walked over to a chest and retrieved a pottery shard with heiroglyphic markings. 'From Egypt, but nobody can decipher it. It was found in the Azores.'

'What? How?' Fernão asked, bewildered.

'Who knows? Maybe a ship caught in a storm off Africa or perhaps an exploration mission.'

'If people have done these great voyages in the past then there is nothing to stop us from exceeding them,' Fernão said. 'But with these charts and accounts why does the king not pursue the western route?'

'He must fortify his forts in India by the proven sailing route, and to continue the spice trade. The path west to the Spice Islands has been a failed venture with much loss.' Behaim placed his hand on Fernão's shoulder. 'But I agree, it can be done.'

'I will do it,' Fernão boldly said. 'I will find a western route.'

'Maybe you will. But you are to *first* sail east with the armada. Put your knowledge and skills to work.' Behaim's face suddenly turned pale and his forehead began to sweat again.

'Are you all right?'

'Do not worry for me. I have had my adventures.' Behaim coughed hard. 'Listen—learn from the captains and crew. Then when you are ready, use this chart.' Behaim rolled up the world chart with Cathay characters and handed it to Fernão. 'Keep this hidden well. Nobody must know. Do not divulge to anyone. Promise me.'

Fernão held the chart to his chest. 'I promise.'

Behaim looked with pride over Fernão as if he were his own son. 'I expect great deeds from you. Never give up. But, now you need to help outfit the fleet and we must part ways.'

Fernão knew Behaim was dying, perhaps meeting for their last time. The two hugged a moment before parting ways.

8

Lisbon, Portugal - March, 1505

An air of good fortune circulated throughout Portugal, hastened by a recent discovery of three ancient pillars of stone unearthed along the west coast: in particular, a windswept beach near the fabled "Moon Hill" of Sintra. Celtic settlers and Romans had revered this mystical mountain. Lush forest and frequent fog lent an aura of the supernatural to the land. Despite the constant waves and passage of time, the stones survived. A Latin declaration read: *Sibilie vaticinium occiduis decretu.* It was a declaration of prophecy to the West. It read:

The stone will be turned over and the letters set in order
When thou, O West, shalt behold the treasures of the Orient.
It will be wonderful to see the Ganges, Indus, and Tagus,
For each will exchange merchandise with the other!

The revealed prophecy induced a fervor of divine approval that coursed through the heart of the nation and its rulers. "Manuel—the Fortunate"—born on the feast day of Corpus Christi and named after Emmanuel, "God is with us," had been enthroned by such an uncanny twist of fate that most accepted the prophecy was ordained from above, as did Manuel and his courtiers. The king's messianic mandate to bring Christianity to the heathen nations opened new trade routes and steered the nation along its course. A new armada was now set to sail, and proper consecration was called for.

It was a partly sunny day in late March with a pleasant breeze flowing across the Lisbon hills. A magnificent structure dominated the city, positioned midway between the royal palace above it, and the dockyards on the waterfront below. The Lisbon Cathedral, often called the Sé, was built as both a fortress and sanctuary. Two monolithic towers flanked the entrance and loomed high above the city. It was an edifice built as a product of the Reconquista era. It provided a formidable and strategically positioned frontal base to protect the city during enemy siege.

Fernão, Diogo, and Francisco were all dressed in their finest attire, velvet suits of black and purple with white puffy sleeved shirts. With chins held high, they marched toward the cathedral to join the service. Fernão had always been amazed at this architectural wonder, but today its grandeur was heightened by the events about to unfold. They filed in with the crowd of men bound for the sea and entered the sanctuary. Fernão stared in awe at the marvelous gothic interior. Light beamed from the rose windows installed in the transept and west facade.

Francisco tapped Fernão's shoulder. 'Remember our instructions? We have our assigned positions.'

'I know. But we have a choice, seats in rear of the main chapel or stand in one of the aisles to the side,' Fernão said.

'Maybe near a column,'Diogo suggested. 'Better view.'

Fernão smiled at his brother. Both were devout and wanted the best angle possible during this momentous ceremony. Captains, pilots, fidalgos, and anyone with rank or command took their seats in the front section of the main chapel. Supernumeraries such as Fernão and those with particularly valued skills took positions in seats near the middle or rear of the main chapel and along the front aisles. Those lowest of status stood in the very rear. The entire cathedral was jammed full. Cool breezes entered through open doors and windows. The archbishop of Lisbon, Martinho da Costa, entered from a side cloister entrance into the circular ambulatory that surrounded the altar of the host. Fernão stared at the chapels along the perimeter of the ambulatory with their tombs adorned above with uniquely sculpted effigies. Many fine works of art, such as the 12 panels painted by Nuno Gonçalves, were displayed in the chapel of St. Vincent located within the Lisbon Cathedral. Fernão looked above the ambulatory to the gothic-vaulted ceiling and second story windows that emanated radiant light. Clergy went about the sanctuary and lit bowls of incense. The entire room of men bowed their heads in unison and silent confession. After the communion of bread and wine was complete, the archbishop completed the mass.

All eyes now turned to their new commander and viceroy to the Indies, Francisco de Almeida, a war veteran of distinction, who fought in the Battle of Toro and the siege of Granada. From all over the kingdom, men of war, and people of distinction, flocked to join him. They loved him much, as he was perceived to be a man blameless in action, and without any hint of deceit. Almeida was of medium height, a little bald but with a distinguished presence and authority. He raised his head and looked past the altar to the cloister entrance.

King Manuel entered with the king-at-arms carrying the royal standard. They stood near the altar. The banner from the king's Order of Christ was of white damask emblazoned with a red cross outlined in gold. The king gave a long benediction followed by a moving speech urging his men to perform great deeds and to convert the nations to the teachings of Christ. It was an inspired speech, of great power. Fernão's eyes watered up. He knew how the king had treated him—but still—the king was speaking with sincere devotion. The king asked all to raise their hands and swear allegiance to the mission and to their Lord. Those seated arose and all made vows of fealty. The king-at-arms then passed the banner to Dom Manuel. Almeida moved from his seat and knelt before the king. A ray of light beamed through one of the second story ambulatory windows. The light mingled with the incense-smoked sanctuary and expanded. As Almeida received the king's standard the light appeared as a mystical halo. Everyone took notice with great reverence. With the standard in his arms Almeida arose.

Afterward, one by one, commanders and those of distinction knelt before the king and kissed his hand. Finally, Almeida turned from the altar to face the crowd with the banner in his arm.

A herald proclaimed with a booming voice, 'Dom Francisco de Almeida, governor, viceroy of India for our Lord the King!' With the announcement great cheers echoed across the chambers.

After the consecration ceremony a solemn procession formed and wound its way down toward the port. Almeida wore a black satin tunic and frilled sleeveless coat with a magnificent chain of gold and silver around his shoulders. He rode a mule outfitted in velvet with gold fringes. Eighty of his viceregal bodyguards marched along in front; all had caps of satin with white plumes, black-velvet jackets and purple sleeves, slashed breeches with colored stripes, white shoes and carried gilded halberds. Along Almeida's side, the captain of the guard rode upon a horse. Trailing behind the royal guards and Almeida, marched captains and fidalgos dressed in splendor. Next, followed the supernumeraries and skilled craftsmen such as Fernão, Diogo, and Francisco. Those of lower status trailed further behind.

Fernão pushed his finger into Francisco's arm. 'Look! Dom Lourenço, second in command, son of the viceroy, a real ladies' man.' Francisco turned with an innocent puzzled look as Fernão jibed further. 'We all know Dom Lourenço is Almeida's only child, but I would swear, you could be his brother.'

Diogo and Fernão chuckled.

Francisco just grinned. 'Who? Me? I am too good looking to be his brother.'

Diogo tapped his brother Fernão on the shoulder. 'I heard he was born the same year as you.'

The dashing young Lourenço rode upon a white stallion through the winding cobbled streets of Lisbon. Ladies waved handkerchiefs from the windows. He wore a French silk tunic of wide sleeves lined in red satin, slashed, and designed with golden roses. A gold-flaked red sash of the Order of Christ was tied around his waist and his white breeches had raised patterns of gold and silver. A red-satin hat with golden brooches and a white feather hung loosely behind his neck from a blue taffeta band and swayed across his shoulders.

Young Dom Lourenço carried the king's standard high as he guided his steed to the lead position of the procession. A great cheer arose from all. Almeida looked on with pride at his beloved son. The national armada of ships were anchored in port and their flags flapped in the breeze. The viceroy's vessel, *São Jerônimo*, stood out among all others, with awnings of purple velvet, fringed in gold and red damask banners. Almeida's crew rowed a small boat to escort him on board, with Lourenço carrying the royal standard aboard.

'Where is our ship?' Diogo asked.

Francisco pointed. 'There. As promised, my brother arranged for us to sail with him on the *Botafogo.*'

Excited, Francisco and the Magalhães brothers went off to join their assigned ship. Once they stored their gear on board, the three moved to the top deck of their carrack or *nau* as they often called this type of vessel. They gazed upon the powerful armada in its entire array. 'Amazing, our largest fleet ever to sail, seven times that of Da Gama's first voyage,' Diogo said.

'How many ships?' Francisco asked.

'There are 22 vessels; 6 large carracks of 400 tons designed for cargo, like our vessel *Botafogo,* and the flagship. Then 5 smaller carracks of 300 ton, 4 *navetas* almost 200 ton, and 6 caravels under 100 ton.' Diogo paused to count in his head. 'Oh yes, and we brought wood to assemble 2 galleys when we arrive to India.'

'And crew?' Francisco asked.

'We have 1,500 armed men, 200 gunners, 400 skilled seamen, and hundreds of—'

Diogo's count was interrupted by a thunderous artillery salvo.

Fernão grinned. 'Time to weigh anchor gentlemen, off to Restelo.'

Ships caught the current and began to drift downstream. Fernão knew it would not be long until they reached their destination, barely four nautical miles away.

Late in the afternoon, the armada dropped anchor at Restelo near the mouth of the Tagus. They had come for one last pilgrimage to the shrine of Santa

Maria de Belem. It was here where Prince Henry the Navigator had sailed with a powerful armada to oust the Moors from Cueta on the North African Coast. He built a chapel on these grounds. Mariners have ever since prayed here for divine guidance, success, and a safe return. Fernão stared at the gothic chapel. Near sunset, the sun's rays angled directly on its white surface and emanated a warm glow. He remembered Da Gama once told him of what transpired here in the summer of 1497 before departing on his epic passage to the Indies. Da Gama, his brother, and officers had kept an overnight vigil until sunrise. As the light rose over the Tagus the remainder of the crew rowed over to join them. Families and loved ones crowded into the small chapel to celebrate a final mass. Bells from the church rang and Da Gama led a procession to the shoreline. Monks and priests assisted the worshipping throng by chanting a litany while the crowd called in response. Each sailor wore sleeveless tunics and carried lighted candles and crowds thronged to join them. The entire entourage wept as they went, for they were uncertain if any would return. Once they arrived at the water's edge, they made a general confession before embarking upon their daring voyage.

Fernão's trance was interrupted as the crews began to flock to the little chapel. This armada was seven times that of Da Gama's pioneer voyage and Almeida had decided there must be an ordered worship. Officers were commanded to enter the chapel, make their confessions and petitions before the altar, and then move along. Until late evening sailors filed in and out of the small chapel overlooking the sea. All knew that many would never return, and the levity of their situation bore heavy upon them. Thousands of families and friends joined their beloved voyagers on the lawns of the church grounds. Fernão had made his own silent petition for grace to perform his duties as a loyal subject of the crown with honor and to proclaim the teachings of the church to the nations.

Francisco Serrão sat cross-legged on the lawn as he looked out over the Tagus. He glanced over at the Magalhães brothers seated next to him who were also reclined with their legs outstretched. 'Your family come to send you off?'

'No, our parents died when we were young,' Fernão said. 'My father is the reason we studied as pages in the court. He was much respected for his outstanding service as sheriff of the Port of Aveiro. But we wrote to our sister Isabel.'

'You never mentioned you had a sister. Is she pretty?' Francisco grinned. 'Wait, looking at you two—never mind.'

'Very funny. And what about your family?' Diogo asked.

'My brother João is all the family I need,' Francisco said. The Magalhães brothers did not press for further details. All three stared solemnly toward the sea. Soon they would fulfill their destinies, whatever lay ahead.

Early the next morning, the crews scrambled into rowboats to join their assigned vessels. It had been decided by the king and his council they would sail on the feast of the annunciation, March 25, 1505. The Tagus was calm. Sailors made final checks onboard. Fernão fastened a knot to secure a loose rope. A bearded officer roamed the deck. He stopped behind Fernão and observed. 'A good knot,' he said.

Fernão turned around. 'Captain Serrão, thank you for allowing me to join your vessel.'

'My brother Francisco speaks well of you. You will have your chance to prove your worth.'

Fernão was a man of careful and precise words. 'Yes sir. I will.' He respected João Serrão, who had sailed with Da Gama as one of his commanders and returned in glory and honor.

Serrão smacked Fernão on the back. 'I like your confidence.' He laughed. 'If you survive, you may indeed witness fantastic wonders and perilous adventures.'

Along the shore a gallant procession drew near. The king had come down with a large retinue of nobles and townsfolk. Rowboats escorted the king to Almeida's flagship. Manuel greeted Almeida and young Lourenço with exuberant handshakes and hugs. 'May our mighty Lord guide and protect you,' Manuel said as his parting words to his viceroy. An artillery salvo thundered, and the armada weighed anchor. Rowers escorted the enthusiastic king among the fleet as they drifted with the current. Manuel embarked every vessel to give his personal farewell to every captain and leading officer. Fernão was on board the carrack *Botafogo* as it sailed behind the caravel *São Jorge,* captained by João Homem. Other vessels sailed close-by. Fernão saw the *São Jorge* veer to the left almost ramming another caravel. The pilot was yelling at the helmsman, 'I said starboard not larboard!'

The puzzled helmsman lifted his arms off the whipstaff—a steering pole located on the quarterdeck, connected below deck to a tiller which in turn was connected to the rudder. He stared back up at the pilot with a bewildered face.

The pilot pointed at the helmsman and then gestured in which direction to turn to avoid colliding into the caravel.

Captain Homem shouted to the pilot, 'Use words they understand! Instead of starboard say garlic and for larboard say onions. They must learn now! Tie up a net of garlic cloves on the starboard side and onions to the larboard.' The crew scrambled to fulfill the order. With these visible aids the entire crew could now understand their orders.

Fernão shook his head to the right and looked at Diogo. 'So many new recruits. They do not know the seaman's language yet. At least we had some training runs on the Tagus.'

'They will have to learn fast or surely perish,' Diogo said.

Fernão turned to his left and glanced at Francisco. 'You ready for this? Sleeping and eating with the crew?' Fernão pressed further. 'All sorts of crew, even slaves and convicts, up real close and personal?'

Francisco winced at the thought; 'I will manage.'

The crown had given a choice to the convicts with long sentences to serve in the new colonies with a possibility to have their sentences shortened or commuted. The Magalhães brothers and Francisco were mere supernumeraries, often dubbed a *sobresaliente*. They would eat and sleep with all sorts of crew with minimal personal space and be required to perform any menial task.

The mouth of the Tagus opened wide into the vast Atlantic. At this point, Pero de Anaia's ship, the *Sant'Iago*, sprung a leak. Fortunately, the crews were able to transfer the goods to another ship and haul back the vessel to Lisbon. It was decided to press onward. The Magalhães brothers and Francisco stood midship, starboard side, overlooking the vast ocean. Winds gusted into the armada's unfurled white sails emblazoned with red crosses. The *Botafogo* sliced through low swells. 'Do you think we will ever return to Lisbon,' Diogo asked.

'I hope so . . . nothing is certain . . . and so many never return.' Fernão's words of caution cut deep into their souls. He paused a moment then arched his back with a sly smile. 'Perilous adventure. A quest for glory and honor. Who can resist?'

All three grinned and stared off at the sea.

9

Fernão and two thirds of the crew slept on mats sprawled across the top deck. They were crowded tight, merely inches from one another. They used coats as blankets in the cool evening. Fernão could barely sleep. He watched the sails flapping in the wind and wondered what adventures would unfold in the months—perhaps years—ahead. The *Botafogo* was a large 400-ton cargo vessel. It was a three masted ship: main mast, foremast, and mizzen. To the mizzen was attached a diagonal yard which supported a triangular lateen sail. The main mast, foremast and topsails were square and supported by horizontal yards. In addition, a bowsprit was angled upward, extending past the prow. For sailing in front of the wind in calm seas, a square spritsail was attached horizontally to the bowsprit and hung before the stern.

The captain of the watch yelled out. 'To stations, to stations, mariners of the watch! Awake, awake!

Fernão looked over to his right and poked a snoring Francisco in the arm. 'It's time. Our watch begins.'

'Already? Francisco groaned. What time is it?'

'Almost three,' Fernão said.

They both ambled over to the starboard side near the forecastle where an apprentice- seamen stood near a portable galley doling out night rations of dried biscuits, cheese, garlic cloves, and pickled sardines. Fernão carried the food in his coat pocket and took a few bites of biscuit as he strolled toward the quarterdeck. Francisco remained to assist on the next cooking watch.

The crew had changes of the watch at three, seven and eleven o'clock. They were dogged watches so that on long voyages all would share in late night watches in equal times with only one exception—the officers in charge of the watches and individually referred to as—the captain of the watch. The captain took the first night watch after sundown until midnight and the pilot took the midnight to dawn watch due to the clarity of the stars for optimum navigation. The master's mate was assigned to morning watch and afternoon watch to the master.

Fernão's first task was to monitor the ship's time during his assigned watch from 3 a.m. to 7 a.m. His station was to aid the pilot. He climbed the stairs to the quarterdeck. On this upper deck was a binnacle with an attached compass and a whipstaff for steering the rudder. Fernão's mouth dropped as he laid eyes on Captain João Serrão.

'Surprised?' he said.

Fernão stared blankly. 'I thought . . . sir, you would be on the command watch.'

'I changed my watch with the pilot, decided to keep an eye on my brother, Francisco, by taking same duty.' Serrão stared up at the starry night. 'I always loved to navigate—served as pilot in the fourth armada under Da Gama.' He pointed to a fragile *ampolleta* (sand clock) that was seated within a short square wooden base to keep it secure. 'Almost three. Time for your watch and turn the clock. This is a nice device, crafted in Venice. You need to turn the clock every 30 minutes and record it.'

Fernão observed the last grains of sand falling through the glass. 'Now?'

'Yes, now! Do not be late in turning the glass,' Serrão said.

Fernão turned the clock over and watched the sand funnel down to the lower end. He scribbled a mark in a logbook to note the time. Serrão stepped behind the binnacle and observed the compass. He aimed a marine quadrant to the night sky and held one corner near his eye to line up the sights to the pole star. A plummet weight was attached to the apex by a silk cord.

'Ready to assist?' Serrão asked.

'Ready sir.'

Fernão struggled to line up the sites for the waves made it difficult to line up the star.

'Now, what's the degree altitude?'

At last, Fernão lined up the sites and took a careful reading of where the silk cord intersected the degree marks on the triangular quadrant. 'Exactly 37 degrees,' Fernão replied.

'Perfect. Good work! I see Sagres Point in the distance, and that matches our charts precisely.'

Fernão grinned. He wanted to impress his superior and advance. This was a good start. Mariners in Portugal knew of the famous Sagres Point. Along with Cape Vincent these two promontories were the most southwestern points of Europe. Legends spread about how Prince Henry the Navigator gathered in Sagres a school of experienced mariners and astronomical scientists. Much of Henry's voyages and marine knowledge was top secret. Nobody knew for certain if any guild or school really existed. Nevertheless, many exploratory voyages were sent from the nearby port of Lagos.

Captain Serrão spread out some marine charts, nautical tables, and an astrolabe upon a small wood table. He held up the astrolabe. 'I hear you have had some experience with Behaim's modified astrolabe. Unfortunately, the best time for taking a reading is mid-day. Maybe later we take some day watch readings to train ourselves with this unique tool. Agreed?'

Fernão's eyes opened wide. He was stunned that such an experienced pilot would ask advice from a mere supernumerary. However, Fernão knew a teachable spirit was a sign of wisdom. 'Fantastic. Perhaps we can also discuss your travels and experience at sea.'

'How about minding the clock for a start?' Serrão chided.

Fernão scrambled to the sand clock and just barely turned it in time before all the sand flowed through. 'Sorry sir.'

The two stared off into the starry night while minding their navigational tasks.

Dawn had arrived and the change of watch at seven o'clock was near. From the quarterdeck, Fernão could see Francisco standing near the portable galley with an iron rod poking some coals in a firebox set over sand. He was cooking fresh fish on a rack above. An apprentice seaman was adding a heavy dose of spices. Francisco scowled. 'Easy, easy! Do not over spice. You need to let it breathe.'

'Huh?' the seaman asked.

'Do not smother. Let it breathe.' Francisco was losing his patience. 'Here, look.' He took a spice jar and gently tapped some spice in his hand then sprinkled a light dusting across the fish. 'There now. That is how you season.'

The seaman stared blankly, uncaring for such subtle culinary tasks.

Francisco was about to lecture on another recipe but suddenly halted. He clutched his stomach as a loud rumble sounded.

The seaman raised an eyebrow.

'Excuse me,' Francisco said as he rushed across the main deck to the stairs at the ship's head.

Fernão observed the activities below and noticed Francisco grimacing as he climbed the stairs leading up to the prow.

Fernão yelled out, 'What's the rush?'

Francisco dared not even speak in fear it would exacerbate the situation. He simply gave a wave and continued in haste. On the prow, near the bowsprit, there was a wooden seat secured with a hole cut out on top. The seat was secured to the wooden planking. The flooring had evenly spaced gaps between the planks and allowed one to view the sea below. Hurriedly, Francisco stripped down his pantaloons just in time from soiling himself as a gut-wrenching diarrhea exploded. He watched through the floor gaps at the excrement blowing out in the wind. After a few minutes he grabbed a coiled rope on the deck. One end draped between the wooden deck beams. Francisco gradually pulled the rope upward, and once he found the frayed end, he looked in disgust. It was still filthy from the last user. 'Ah nooo,' he muttered. 'Some clown never lowered it all the way into the water.' Just then Francisco heard the captain of the watch calling the men for the morning vespers. 'Great, now they will make a search for me.' He looked left and right, frenzied, and panicked, then his eye caught a bucket, behind him, filled with saltwater, and a brush. Unfortunately, it was beyond his reach. But he found a wood handle fastened along the deck wall, and with some effort was able to pull it off. Carefully, he hooked it under the bucket handle and pulled it carefully toward him. Francisco cringed as he used the brush to clean the stinky rope. 'Lovely,' he said. 'Sail for adventure and treasure. Sure, sure. What have I got myself into?'

'You all right?' Fernão asked Francisco as they filed in line with the mariners for the morning vespers.

'I will be,' Francisco said.

'Must have been some bad cheese.'

'Stop. You do *not* want to know the details . . . trust me.'

With great reverence, a young seaman saluted the dawn and recited a blessing in front of the crew:

Blessed be the light of day
And the Holy Trinity.
Protect us this day
From all perils at sea.
The Lord shines his light
Upon those with faith and truth.

The seaman then led the crews in reciting the *Pater Noster* and singing the *Salve Regina*. In conclusion, he added another blessing:

Lord give us a good voyage and safe passage of our ship.

Give our captain and pilot guidance and grace.

Lord, aid us all in our daily tasks for a successful mission.

All the crew shouted, 'amen' then dispersed to their duties.

After several days at sea, Fernão awoke from his allotted four hours of sleep and assumed the eleven o' clock a.m. watch. He joined Captain João Serrão on the quarterdeck and guided the ship along their course.

'As we sail south the pole star will fall below the horizon, and we will need the astrolabe,' Serrão said.

Fernão watched the last sand granules run through the *ampolleta* and then turned it over.

'Noon. Ready to take an astrolabe reading?' Serrão asked.

Fernão grinned. 'A fine clear day and calm sea? Of course.'

Serrão unwrapped a cloth from around a heavy mariner's astrolabe. Fernão tied a fine rope from its metal ring and hung it from a wooden tripod. On a bench, Serrão spread open a book of Zacuto's ephemeride tables with its solar declinations.

Fernão set the date and time on the astrolabe and adjusted the movable pinhole site to line up the sun. He looked at the front of the astrolabe to figure the coordinates and compared them with the ephemeride tables. Serrão carefully observed Fernão's procedure for astrolabe computations.

'Approximately 26 degrees,' Fernão said. 'Difficult to make any closer reading with the sway of ship.'

'Yes, sounds correct,' Serrão said. 'We already passed the Canaries.' He pointed off to his left. 'Now there is Cape Bojador to our larboard side.'

'The same dreaded cape no sailor dare pass?' Fernão asked.

'Indeed. I believe it was 72 years ago when Prince Henry sent his squire Gil Eanes to discover the cape and explore beyond.'

'It must have taken a lot of courage,' Fernão said. 'All seamen feared to venture that far. Many claimed white men would turn black when they entered a green sea of darkness. Giant sea monsters would capsize ships or snatch men from the deck. Some even say that rocks would turn into serpents.'

'Yes. And what about the perilous reefs? Serrão asked.

'I have heard of the dangerous currents and heavy mists that would destroy ships,' Fernão replied.

'And the sun sending down sheets of liquid flame,' Serrão said with a grin.

'How did Eanes find the courage?'

'Prince Henry told his squire that no peril was so great that the hope of reward would not be greater. He ordered Eanes not to pay attention to myths and not to come back until he sailed past the cape. After they finally passed the dreaded cape and returned to Portugal, Eanes was knighted by the prince.'

Serrão untied the astrolabe and stored it away and the two navigators stared off to their left as they passed the infamous Cape Bojador. Fernão's eyes panned from the cape back to the deck below. His eyes squinted as he focused upon a red six-pointed star affixed upon the shirt of a seaman below. 'Who is that?' Fernão asked.

'Ah, the man with the star. A *degregado*. This one, a converso and sentenced to serve in the armada in exchange for the possibility of a pardon.'

'How did he become a convict?'

'They often call these conversos, New Christians. They are expected to follow the religion of Portugal. He was ordered to wear the star, because he was found guilty of practicing Jewish rites in secret—a high crime.' Serrão scratched his beard.

'So how do they receive a pardon?'

'If they serve well, some will receive a pardon—if they survive. A dangerous mission they have. But they are expected to do the dirty and dangerous work.'

'What work is this?'

'They are the first ones out to meet the natives; and they work as mediators between ship command and local rulers. Some are stationed as labor for outposts or sent to explore inland. Many will die or go native. But a few others will achieve some fame and receive pardon.' Serrão rubbed the back of his neck. 'You know King Manuel had been sympathetic to their cause, until he decided to court the Spanish Princess.'

Fernão noticed the last sand granules drain down the glass and turned the *ampolleta*. He gazed down upon the thin man wearing the six-pointed red star and reflected. Due to his access to the court and India House, Fernão had been informed on Portugal's political activity. His mind recounted the events over the years.

Since the days of Prince Henry, Jewish mapmakers and mathematicians had been greatly sought after. Abraham Zacuto had improved the astronomical tables under King John II's scientific council, *"Junto dos Matematicos"* and was King Manuel's personal physician. Jewish printers were pioneers in the art of movable type and many of the first books of Portugal were in Hebrew.

But during the late fifteenth century, a tidal wave of animosity came against the Jews in Spain, bringing a flood of talented refugees across the border to Portugal in 1492. At first, Manuel was generous to the new Jewish refugees. However, in 1496 he wished to marry Princess Isabella, the daughter of Ferdinand and Isabella. But there was one stipulation before the marriage could proceed. Princess Isabella had demanded the expulsion of all Jews from Portugal. Manuel gave in to her demands and issued a decree for all Jews to leave by the following October. Some estimated the Jewish population at 10 percent of all Portugal. This put Manuel in a predicament. Many of those ordered to leave were a considerable number of Portugal's greatest talent. As a result, he issued another decree. All children under 14 of Jewish or Moorish descent who refused baptism were to be taken and educated at the king's expense. Of course, no enforcement upon the Moors was made, out of fear the Christians in Morocco would suffer a vengeful recompense. An exodus of 20,000 Jews made their way to Portugal's main port in Lisbon. It was a setup. The Portuguese officials anticipated they would attempt to escape and awaited their arrival at the main exit port of Lisbon. All efforts of persuasion were offered for them to convert. Those who would not accept were forcibly baptized. Those who refused were imprisoned. In defiance, many Jewish families opted for suicide.

In such a wave of persecution, significant numbers undertook a great exodus via other routes to foreign lands, especially to France and Netherlands, where there was religious toleration. Manuel was panic stricken from the great drain of talent leaving Portugal. Therefore, in 1499 he ordered that all Jews were forbidden to leave the country. Only those with a special permit and justified commercial reasons could travel abroad. If they were granted leave, their wives and children were held as ransom during their absence. Manuel was hoping to play a middle role, pleasing Spain while keeping his skilled resources. But the seeds of unrest escalated. The crop failures in 1503—and resulting inflated prices of food supplies— were blamed on the Jews. Some were even stoned in the streets of Lisbon.

Fernão continued his watch, glancing curiously at the thin man with the red star swabbing the deck in precise patterns with diligent care.

As the *Botafogo* sailed south, tension and agitation began to vex the crew. Francisco and Fernão queued up for their ration of food just before taking the 11 o' clock a.m. watch. A commotion broke out in the front of the line. A red-sashed fidalgo—the same one Fernão had encountered on the king's hunting expedition—had shoved the Jewish converso with the red star patch to the ground and kicked him in the ribs. 'You dog! We don't want your kind here!'

Those in the food line and on deck formed a circle to watch. Fernão and Francisco pushed their way through the crowd.

'What? What have I done?' the converso said.

'You devil. You know very well, exactly what.' The fidalgo grabbed the thin man by the throat and lifted him from the ground. The converso's face began to turn blue as he gasped for air.

Fernão's veins bulged in his neck as he rushed forward, shoving sailors to the side as he advanced. 'You're choking him. Let off!'

The fidalgo's muscled arm bulged as he tightened his hold and barked at Fernão, 'You! I remember you from the king's galley. Get out of my way. He endangers the ship with his forbidden devil's magic.'

Captain João Serrão observed the events from the quarterdeck—hoping it was some short-lived outburst, due, perhaps, to the heat and discomfort of the crew. But with the escalation it appeared he would have to intervene. Serrão rushed down the steps. The men created a path as he made his way to the conflict. 'Release him, Dom Braga!' Serrão ordered.

Braga kept his hold. 'He is a traitor. Caught him myself.'

'Release him, then we talk.'

He unhooked his arm from the thin man's neck. The converso gasped for air. Braga then ripped away a satchel fastened around the man's waist. From the pouch he retrieved two dark-colored miniature square boxes made of animal hide with leather straps attached and threw them onto the deck. The crew stared curiously upon the strange devices.

The converso snatched one of the boxes and retrieved a small parchment with Hebrew letters and held it in the air for all to see. 'Look, look. Bible verses. From the Torah. No magic! No magic!'

Braga snatched the parchment from his hand. He looked it over in puzzled angst. 'Not our language. What trickery is this?'

'Hebrew. It is written in Hebrew,' the converso said.

'What is your name?' Serrão asked.

'Samuel Levi.'

'So, you know Hebrew? And what other languages?'

'Yes, I know Hebrew very well. I also am fluent in Portuguese, Spanish, Italian, and Arabic—I also have some learning in African dialects.'

Serrão scratched his beard. 'Well then. It seems our heretic may be of some use.' He then looked at Braga and said, 'Agreed?'

'But he is a heretic.'

'Yes, if found guilty in the homeland. But what if he stays on foreign soil in a land far away—performs his own rituals—away from us? Would that be of any consequence to you? Would it not be better to use his skills now, in service of the king?'

'Then what about on the ship?'

Captain Serrão looked over the crowd and finally at Samuel. 'Only Christian rites will be permitted in public view on this ship. Understood?'

Samuel gave a slow nod.

Braga stared at Samuel, and then Fernão. Then he turned and walked away.

Francisco rejoined Fernão and said, 'Careful my friend. Those fidalgos can be vindictive and deadly. Watch your back. This is our second encounter with him. You made a move on him, and he may not forget.'

Later in the evening, Fernão was deep in sleep but felt a constant nudging at his lower leg. The nudging turned to a kicking force. He sat up abruptly to see who or what was disturbing his rest. 'Diogo, what are you doing? Have I overslept?

Diogo smiled. 'Only 10:30 in the evening. But you need to see this.'

Fernão followed his brother across the main deck. They arrived under the forecastle, the bow storeroom used for keeping of ropes, sails, tools, and spare parts. During periods of bad weather crew would cast lots to sleep here. Diogo pointed to a thin man crouched in the corner, partially hidden behind swaying ropes. Fernão squinted his eyes trying to make out his facial features. Diogo crouched and then stepped over a wooden crate as he entered the storeroom. Fernão followed. The thin man glanced over his shoulder and hastily unwrapped some leather straps from his head and arm. He soon found the two Magalhães brothers looming over him.

Diogo whispered to his brother, 'I found him chanting in a strange tongue. But then I recognized it from our studies as pages of the court. It was Hebrew.'

'Ah, so now you have met Samuel Levi,' Fernão said.

Diogo looked at his brother in confusion. 'What?'

'Your shift was over. You were asleep and maybe did not hear the commotion. But Samuel here has been forbidden to practice his rites in public. Am I not correct, Samuel?' Fernão asked.

'Yes, but I was concealed here. Please do not inform the captain.'

'You are fortunate that Captain Serrão is a tolerant man.' Fernão stared at the same two strange objects he had witnessed earlier in the day. Samuel held, in each hand, two miniature boxes made of animal hide with leather straps dangling from each. Fernão's eyebrows furled. 'So, what is this contraption of yours?'

'Tefillin. Our prayers are focused and thus magnified by our tefillin.' The two brothers stared at the mysterious boxes. 'May I demonstrate their use?'

Fernão gave a slow nod.

Samuel held forward a tiny box. 'Notice here,' he said.

Fernão and Diogo took a knee to observe closer. Samuel continued. 'The tefillin used for one's head have the Hebrew letter *shin* molded into each side, and the knot affixed on top is the letter *dalet*.' He then displayed the other box. 'And here we have the tefillin for one's arm with the knot formed as the letter *yud*. Can you guess what these letters spell?'

The two Magalhães brothers looked at one another and shrugged.

Samuel smiled. '*Shaddai*, one of the names for the one true God.'

'Clever,' Diogo said. 'How does it work?'

'If you are right-handed, you take the arm-tefillin and lay it on the inner side of the bare left arm, two finger breadths above the elbow. Make sure that when the arm is bent it still faces the heart.' Samuel placed the tiny box upon his arm as described. 'Then tighten it with the thumb, say the blessing and wrap the strap around the upper arm in the opposite direction so you need not hold it anymore.' Samuel demonstrated the procedure. 'Then finish by wrapping around your arm seven times. It is a holy number.' The two brothers nodded, understanding.

'What of the other box?' Diogo asked.

'This is the easy procedure. Place the head-tefillin just above your forehead, above the hairline and the knot sits at the back of the head like this.' Samuel fastened the box to his forehead and tied the knot. 'Then bring the straps across your shoulders with blackened side facing outwards.'

'Is that it?' Fernão asked.

'Not quite. You need to finish by wrapping the arm strap three times around the middle finger and around the hand to form the shape of the letter *dalet.*' Samuel looked up, smiling.

'What about the blessing? And what was written on those parchments you pulled out earlier today?' Fernão asked.

'Four scriptures for four parchments. In summary, they remind us to love our God, obey his commandments and remember how he brought us out of slavery from Egypt.'

Fernão placed his hand on his chin. 'All people have been slaves at one time.'

'Our people were slaves for 400 years until we were delivered,' Samuel said.

'Yes. But the Moors had enslaved most of our homeland for over *500* years. Those of us who refused to convert to Islam were regarded as second-class citizens and forced to pay extra taxes. It took many bloody battles to reconquer our lands.' Fernão's face contorted in anger as he reflected upon his nation's long history of servile bondage under Moor rule. 'I see you are a slave of sorts now by refusing a forced conversion.

Samuel, perceiving an understanding and wise spirit, stared into Fernão's eyes. 'My family was taken from me. They cannot join me until I receive a pardon.'

'Maybe one day you will gain your freedom by serving the king.' Fernão said.

Diogo placed his arm around Samuel's shoulder with a reassuring smile.

10

Senegal – April, 1505

The *Botafogo* had sailed southeast past a jutting promontory called Cabo Verde, then continued south, along with the 21-vessel armada. The Magalhães brothers and Francisco stood together on the main deck. 'It is time now to take on provisions in Port d'Ale in the Senegal territory,' Francisco said.

Fernão put his hands on the ship rail as he leaned forward to view the water depth. 'Good thing Almeida pre-planned a strategy to re-supply. The smaller caravels will transport most of our goods to and from shore. They can enter closer, but we must anchor out here in deeper waters.'

They all knew that caravels were exploratory vessels; designed for navigating coastlines, beaches, and rivers. The men watched several of the smaller vessels approach the beaches as their crews scrambled to drop sails and secure them.

Further off the coast, the carracks dropped their massive black iron anchors and lowered their sails. Along the sandy beach, palm trees swayed in the wind. The weather was pleasant and mostly sunny.

Francisco placed his hands along the ship rail and remarked, 'Orders were given prior. We stay until our trading is completed and take turns on shore leave. One of the three watches will always guard and maintain the ship.' He turned to Diogo and smiled. 'I asked my brother to let your watch join ours on the first landing.'

'Good, I need to stretch my legs.' Diogo slapped Francisco on the shoulder and walked away to prepare for landing.

The Magalhães brothers, Francisco Serrão, Samuel Levi, and 12 sailors rowed their longboat to the beach. They disembarked and heaved the rowboat far on shore. Each ship of the armada had dispatched one third of their crew and were led by their respective captains. Once all craft were secured, the captains gathered near Almeida—captain-major of the fleet, and the king's appointed viceroy of India. The crewmen stood facing them in straight columns, attired in light armor—weapons of black swords, halberds, pikes, and crossbows.

Almeida addressed the men: 'My prior orders remain unchanged. Our mission here is to take on provisions of food, water, and firewood. We continue in our task until we cannot store anymore aboard our vessels. Shore duty will follow the same routine as the ship watch. This includes captains, pilots, and masters. From previous reports, we have been informed about this region. It is ruled by the Teny of Baol, a vassal state of the mighty Jolof kingdom. Men, always maintain your weapons training. Stay alert and inform your superiors if you witness anything suspicious. I will convene with my senior officers before returning to the flagship.' He paused and looked over his men. 'Oh yes, one more thing, enjoy your time on shore!'

After Almeida returned to the *São Jerônimo*, a middle-aged black African dressed in a colorful robe approached, riding a horse accompanied by a cavalry of 60 other riders. The tall and well-built ebony-skinned warriors wore cross-strapped hides across their chests and carried an assortment of weaponry: iron-tipped spears, metal hooks, swords, and iron-plated shields. They rode with leather saddles and stirrups. Their horses wore metal chamfrons over their heads and chain mail over the body. Captain João Serrão's

40-man squadron had the lead point for the Portuguese shore excursion. Samuel stood near his commander. The Magalhães brothers and Francisco remained a short distance from the captain, but within earshot.

The leader and three other warriors dismounted. He spoke in a booming voice and with authority.

Captain Serrão nudged Samuel. 'You understand any of this?'

'A little. I learned some from the slaves brought through Lisbon. It is a dialect of the Jolof peoples. He gives us greetings and wants to know if we wish to buy slaves or gold.'

'Who is he?'

'He is Tumar, a viceroy of the King of Baol. The viceroy maintains the king's divine rule along the coast for trade and security.'

'Inform him we come to trade for water and food. But today, we do not need slaves or gold.'

Samuel translated for the captain and then for the viceroy's reply, 'He wishes to know what we have to trade.'

Serrão turned and hand gestured for the crew in the rear to bring forward a large crate. Four men carried the wooden crate in between Serrão and Viceroy Tumar. The men pried the top off the crate. Samuel reached inside to retrieve some silver cups and dishes. He held them up for all to see.

Tumar seemed unimpressed.

Samuel then retrieved a fine red cloth and dangled it in the air.

Tumar still balked, then gestured to his horse, signaling that he wished to acquire more horses.

Serrão shook his head indicating he had no horses for trade.

Tumar scowled in return.

Serrão gestured again for the crew to bring forth another crate. They pried it open. Samuel grinned as he retrieved iron weaponry and gear for cavalry.

Tumar's scowl turned into a wide smile and his warriors edged forward in attention upon the goods.

Francisco whispered to Fernão, 'Good foresight to bring the iron weaponry. Horses and iron seem to be of high value in this region.'

Fernão whispered back, 'I heard that many of these vassal states, such as the kingdom of Baol and others in the region, grow impatient with the Jolof overlord and are weary of paying tribute. They are preparing for a revolution.'

Tumar beckoned for them to follow him eastward. Four crates full of cavalry gear were placed on sleds made of palm timbers and secured to two teams of horses with heavy ropes for transport. They journeyed inland through a scrubby land full of baobab trees with their odd bulb-shaped base and sparsely leafed branches spread out at the very top. The branches resembled roots and gave the appearance of an upside-down tree.

'Amazing! Diogo said. 'I bet it would take 30 men to encircle that tree!'

After nearly a mile trek along a wide dirt path, the entourage came upon a small path which sliced through a wall of thickets. An elaborate curtain of sharp branches fastened together walled-in the entire village, which was really a complex of living areas. In the first courtyard, the crates of goods were delivered to a group of thin dry-skinned mulatto merchants.

Captain Serrão grabbed Samuel. 'What is this? Moors? We cannot trust them!'

Samuel gestured to speak with Tumar. After a brief conversation in a Jolof dialect Samuel translated the message to the crew. 'He says they are Moor traders from the caravan routes across the great northern desert. But they can be trusted. He has traded often with them; many slaves and gold, in exchange for horses and other fine objects.'

'Well then. I see we have little choice. We need supplies and Viceroy Tumar trusts them.' Serrão winced at the thought of dealing with Moors. 'All right then. We will assign a squadron of men to take responsibility for the transactions, others will bring the supplies to the ships.'

One of Tumar's messengers spoke to Samuel who in turn translated to the men. 'He says, we must wait here until later summoned.'

The viceroy and his warrior escorts continued onward through another pathway and disappeared.

About two hours before dusk, Captain Serrão's men and some other crews had been taking a rest near a tall Mahogany tree in the outer courtyard. The tree's large bushy crown cast a wide shadow which offered the men some relief from the afternoon sun. A messenger approached Samuel, spoke briefly and then departed. Samuel rushed over to Serrão who had been reclined against the tree. 'Captain. The viceroy invites us to dine with him this evening.'

'What time?'

'An hour before dusk.'

'Well men, let us prepare ourselves for dinner,' Serrão ordered.

An hour later, the messenger returned. The crew followed him through the outer courtyard and past the straw huts of lower caste Africans. Captain João Serrão's men stood before another circular wall enclosure made of thickets. The messenger gestured for the crew to follow him into a narrow entrance. They emerged into another courtyard with another Mahogany tree and more straw huts. Here were craft artisans producing sculpted animals from mahogany and ivory. Others were creating fine pottery pieces. The crew followed the messenger through the middle courtyard, onto a narrow path into a third courtyard.

Samuel had been speaking with the messenger along the way. He came near the captain and reported. 'He says the first courtyard was for the low caste. The second courtyard for the skilled citizens and the third we have now entered is where the nobility and viceroy's wives live. He has seven wives and many children.' Samuel nodded toward some Moors near one of the huts who were busily counting beads on a bamboo abacus. 'And traders from the north are often given privileged access here. The viceroy desires their goods.'

They next approached a massive rectangular structure of hardened mud with a thatched roof. Arriving at the entrance, a contingent of warrior sentries exited and lined up on both sides of the crew, which alarmed and agitated them.

The messenger slowly waved his hand up and down to signal calm. The crew cautiously entered the royal hall. Torches on tall sticks lined the interior. Flames created dancing shadows upon the walls. The messenger illustrated the appropriate bowed posture the men should take upon entering the residence, and once inside, pointed for them to take their seats upon straw mats along the mud-walled interior. The Portuguese followed the messenger's lead, took their seats, and sat cross-legged.

Viceroy Tumar reclined on a carved throne from a baobab tree. It was covered with pillows finely embroidered in red and purple. The viceroy appeared to ignore the crew on purpose. Finally, after a long uncomfortable pause, Tumar addressed the men through a Moor interpreter. 'I am so pleased you have joined me this evening. We shall dine until our hearts rejoice.' Tumar bellowed a deep resounding laugh, then gestured for servant girls to commence the feast. They filed out of the hall to attend to their duties.

Tumar addressed the men, 'So tell me. Why do you not trade as other Portuguese have done? Why no horses? Why no desire for slaves or gold?' Tumar paused after asking his question. 'But I am glad, so glad you have brought iron weaponry. As you may already know, our king and our people grow weary of paying tribute to the Jolof overlord. We wish to trade and keep our profits. One day we will have the horses and the weapons to forge our own path. We shall have our freedom.'

'We are on a trade mission of other sorts to other lands,' Serrão said. 'We will sail far and cannot carry horses for trade.'

'And where do you sail?'

'India and maybe further.'

'Ah, I see. I have heard of these lands from the caravan traders.' Tumar pondered a moment. 'A trade mission to India you say. What do you seek?'

Serrão hesitated, not sure how much to divulge. 'Spices, spices of all sorts. We plan to establish a trading network. We could use your port as a supply stop.'

'You are welcome here,' Tumar said. 'Perhaps we forge an alliance. You can assist us in overthrowing our overlords.'

'You mention the Jolof overlords. What size of an army do they command?'

'It is extensive but if you supply us with iron weapons we will prevail and independently rule this land.'

'I will relay your request to our viceroy, Dom Almeida.'

'Please do so. Inform him I wish to meet before you depart.'

'I will do so.'

Tumar smiled then asked, "You carry no horses but can you all ride? Do you have any cavalry skills?'

'Yes, we have used cavalry in our countless wars against the Moors,' Serrão replied. The Moor interpreter frowned in discomfort upon the thought. Serrão and the crew gave a hard stare at the Moor.

Taking notice of the tension Tumar interjected, 'Oh yes. This is my trusted interpreter, Ahmad Ramzy. I expect his skills are sufficient, no?'

'Serrão simply nodded.

'Perfect!' Tumar said. 'Perfect! Then you shall participate in our games, tomorrow. Splendid!'

'I do not understand,' Serrão said.

'You shall see, you shall see my friend.' A sly grin crossed Tumar's face.

Just then, the conversation was interrupted by the entrance of menservants who handed clay bowls and cups to the guests. Servant girls walked by each hungry soldier with platters of dates, mangos, coconut slices, and baobab fruit. The main course was seasoned fish and rice mixed with an assortment of vegetables. The hungry men refused nothing. Viceroy Tumar had a manservant taste a sample from his fish platter and waited to see if there was any ill effect. After a minute, Tumar took a bite of fish. He whispered to his Moor interpreter, Ahmad Ramzy, and gestured for him to speak on his behalf.

Ahmad arose and spoke: 'The viceroy says to enjoy. His servants with the red jugs carry palm wine, and those with blue jugs contain the precious *buy bi* juice mixed with water and a little sugar. It is a fruit from the baobab tree. Excellent for the health. Oil from the seeds will deaden pain in the mouth and its leaves reduce fever. The Magalhães brothers and Samuel chose the *buy bi* juice. They each took a sip and smiled at the pleasant taste. 'Very good,' Samuel said.

'We should take more of this fruit with us to the ships, for the voyage,' Fernão said.

Francisco took a glass of palm wine and sipped at it. 'Interesting blend. A little bitter but seems potent. Maybe I will fare better taking the wine.' The others looked at Francisco quizzically. 'You know, nobody has yet tested to see if the water is good in this land. At least the palm wine has fermented and should be safe.'

The others looked at their cups of water mixed with *buy bi* juice, now in doubt.

'Well, I guess we will know by morning,' Fernão said. 'Pray for the best.'

Tumar stood up and held up a glass to initiate a toast. 'To the honor of our ancestors.'

Several Moors looked at one another. Ahmad then held his glass high and said, 'There is no god but Allah, and Muhammad is the messenger of God.'

Fernão looked around to see if anyone would retort, but with no response given, he raised his glass and said, 'Go therefore and make disciples of all nations, baptizing them in the name of the Father, and of the Son, and of the Holy Spirit.'

Ahmad and the Moors stared down Fernão.

Tumar perceived the tension of religious disagreement building. He held up his glass again and said, 'To new alliances and vanquishing our enemies!'

The guests cheered in support.

Ahmad held up his glass and added, 'To trade and prosper. To retire as wealthy men!'

An escalation of revelry erupted. The men clanked their cups with those near them.

Captain João Serrão raised his glass and loudly exclaimed, 'To daring adventures and glorious deeds!'

The cheers rose to a crescendo.

During mid feast, the royal messenger approached with great caution toward the viceroy's entourage. He whispered something to an advisor which was relayed in turn to the viceroy. After a long pause, Tumar wiped his mouth and whispered back to the advisor who in turn signaled the messenger to bring in the visitor. The messenger went outside for a minute then walked back inside with bowed head and sat near Samuel.

Meanwhile, a black African man entered and fell upon his knees and placed his head on the ground. Completely naked, he crawled slowly while using two hands to throw dirt on his back and upon his head. The messenger whispered to Samuel who in turn informed Serrão and the men.

Samuel whispered, 'This is one of the villagers. He has brought news of Moor traders coming from south of the River Gambia. They bring many slaves and gold to our markets for auction.'

Crawling almost prostrate and throwing dirt all over himself, the man finally came near Viceroy Tumar. With head bowed, he spoke with a low respectful voice. Tumar appeared to ignore.

Samuel told the men in a subdued voice. 'He is afraid the viceroy will anger. Some of our people who venture out of the village and near the bordering regions have been ousted as spies. Any slight or offense against the viceroy will cause ruin. For any reason, he may sell him and his entire family as slaves for profit. All fear Tumar greatly.' After some moments, the viceroy signaled for a warrior to escort the man away. 'It appears he has brought good news and will remain free.'

Fernão had heard of the slave trading ventures and culture of West Africa. The Venetian explorer and trader Cadamosta encountered similar cultures and had written his accounts over 50 years earlier when he ventured into another Jolof vassal state called Cajor, to the north. Slaves in the Senegambia region were most often captives taken in regional wars. Sometimes local rulers enslaved their own people strictly for profit. It was a brutal market across West Africa, with nation states pitted against one another in a vicious cycle of war and profit. The Moors and the Portuguese had made some raids for slaves in the past, but now they simply played middlemen in the increasing global trade of slaves. An insatiable desire for slave labor grew in Europe and the New World to the west which enticed African rulers to subdue their enemies for war booty, namely slaves. Fernão knew it was a reality, unlikely to end any time soon.

A warrior escorted the visitor away. Tumar smiled and spoke through his interpreter, Ahmad. 'In two days, we will have visitors bringing treasure to our lands. Of course, they must pay a duty of slaves and gold to trade in our market. We will use this levy to trade for more horses and weapons. So, it is a night to rejoice!' Tumar gestured toward a warrior near the entrance who in turn departed.

In a few moments, the warrior returned, now accompanied by an entourage of beautiful and topless African girls. They wore thin animal hides slung suggestively low across their hips. From outside, rhythmed drumbeats permeated the chamber inside. They danced sensually in front of the men.

Soon, the drum tempo increased and became more frenzied. The girls began to shake and jiggle their breasts. Some bent down to reveal their back side up close and personal. Francisco leaned forward in rapt attention. He stared in awe at the dancer in front of him. She seemed like a lioness, about to attack a cornered prey. The Magalhães brothers and Samuel all felt uneasy. Fernão was captivated but had vowed abstinence until marriage from his youth. Diogo was the same. But in this moment, in a faraway land with exotic girls, the temptation was intoxicating. Samuel was a devout Jew and married—yet, as most men—enticed. After the sensual dancing seemed to go on too long for Fernão's liking, the viceroy signaled for the dancers to depart. Fernão stared at his brother Diogo in relief.

Francisco shook his head. 'Oh yes. Now this is life. Never seen that in Portugal. Incredible!'

Tumar stood up, as did his interpreter. 'I hope you enjoyed the food and our dancers. Please join me tomorrow—midmorning—outside the compound. We will enjoy our games.' The viceroy's advisors and warriors exited the compound and the Portuguese followed suit. The crews made their way back out to the first courtyard and into the guest huts.

Fernão lay down on a thick straw mat, an arm's length away from his brother. Diogo turned his head to face Fernão. 'What games did he mean? He mentioned horsemanship.'

'I have no idea brother. We shall see . . . we shall see.' After an eventful day they drifted off to sleep.

11

Fernão awakened to a cacophony of snoring. He arose and stumbled around in the dark to find his clothes. Fernão left the hut, put on his shirt and shoes in the faint morning light, and left his brother and Francisco to their snoring contest. He made his way outside the outer courtyard and found a well. Fernão snatched the bucket tied to a crank above the well and lowered it. He raised it back up full of clean water. Fernão washed his upper body and then dunked his head in the bucket. It was cold but left him refreshed and invigorated. He climbed a small hill to view the sunrise and watched the rays of light crossing the eastern savannah. The peculiar baobab trees scattered across the plain created a surreal landscape. Fernão prayed and gave thanks for the blessed opportunity to witness such a unique feature of the Creator's handiwork. He made his personal requests for divine courage to fulfill his tasks well and bring honor to his family name.

Later, Fernão devoured his morning breakfast of eggs and fruits, and gathered with the crews near an open field, outside the compound. The Portuguese joked and bantered among themselves. A distant rumbling interrupted their conversations as they beheld the viceroy and his cavalry approach with a full gallop. They came to a sudden halt near the Portuguese, kicking up a cloud of dust. The Magalhães brothers stood near Captain João Serrão and his brother Francisco. The four stood in the frontline of the squad. Viceroy Tumar grinned and then laughed with a deep resonance as he rode up and down the line of armed Portuguese sailors. He spoke as usual in his native Baol tongue.

Samuel had moved forward to interpret the viceroy's words for Serrão and those nearby: 'It is a glorious day! A fine day for a tournament. Today we shall reward the victors. Let us prepare for *Chovqan*! Choose four—.'

Captain Serrão and the men stood baffled. Ahmad noticed the confused look on the men due to Samuel's limited vocabulary. He approached and completed Tumar's message, 'You must choose four of your best cavalry warriors. We will inform you of the rules—the few we have.'

The game was of Persian origin, adopted by the Mamluks and Moor traders, and a predecessor of polo. The Moors on the West African coast played with four riders per team on a large, wide, open field of grass and sand. At each end of the field was a frame of wood beams, 8 feet tall by 23 feet wide. The riders used long hockey sticks with small, curved blades to hit a leather-covered wooden ball into goals at either end of the field. The game was timed by a double-sided wooden funnel with tiny beans loaded on top.

After Ahmad's exposition of the rules, the Portuguese commanders on shore called the men together on their side of the playing field. Captain João da Nova, of the 400-ton *Flor de la Mar*, and veteran commander of the third Portuguese armada to India, addressed the men: 'We need to select four of our best riders. Any suggestions?'

Several crewmen yelled out, 'Dom Braga! Dom Braga!'

Others cried out, 'Dom Mendez!'

'Very well,' said Captain Nova. 'We need two more.'

'I suggest the Magalhaes brothers,' Captain Serrão said. 'They have excellent riding skills, trained since youths in the north-woods. Also studied the martial skills of stick-fighting as pages in the court. Useful in this competition, don't you think?'

'I trust your judgment,' Captain Nova replied.

The men spread out along the sidelines for optimal viewing. Meanwhile, the Magalhães brothers retrieved two stallions from Viceroy Tumar's stables nearby. As they fastened their saddles and personal leg braces, two Portuguese approached them on horseback, one with a red sash—Dom Braga and the other with a purple sash—Dom Mendez. The two were the same fidalgos who had caused the confrontation on the king's galley back in Lisbon.

Dom Braga stared down at Fernão with a sneer. 'Expect you will carry your weight. We represent the crown and never lose.'

Fernão glared back, 'We hold our own. But remember, this is a team sport.'

Dom Mendez in the purple sash nudged forward, 'Just move the ball forward and do not let them score.' He turned his horse and galloped off to center field. A massive crowd from numerous surrounding villages converged upon the tournament. Warriors pounded war-rhythmed beats on drums, all made of mahogany and covered with animal hides.

Ahmad smiled as the Magalhães brothers rode toward him midfield on the Portuguese sidelines. 'You should know the viceroy has selected his finest riders,' he said, and then pointed off to the far side of the field. 'You see that one with the shaved head and branded arm? He is their captain and most skilled player. Remember, this is a match that wounds many and death is possible.'

Fernão turned to Diogo and said with a grin. 'A noble competition, worthy of a true warrior.'

Ahmad shook his head at their lack of concern and walked off to Tumar's royal seating midfield, located on the opposite side of the field. The viceroy gave a slow deliberate nod of approval for the games to begin. A referee mounted a steed and trotted off to center field with a leather-covered wooden ball in his arm. Two more referees positioned themselves at the opposing two-halves of the field. The Magalhães brothers and the two Portuguese nobles faced off against four well-built African cavalrymen dressed in their warrior skins. The drumbeats grew to a crescendo and so did the crowd cheers from the sidelines.

Dom Braga turned his head to Fernão and sneered. 'No mercy to the enemy and no defeat.'

Fernão gave him a hard stare, and then turned his attention to the opposition.

On the sideline, a huge native, nearly seven feet in height, sounded a giant ivory horn. The referee near midfield tossed the ball into the center of the field for play to commence. Braga and Mendez charged their steeds forward converging upon the ball. Simultaneously, two of the African warriors also charged. Braga took early control of the ball and pushed forward. Meanwhile, the remaining two from each team dropped back into defensive positions. The Portuguese stumbled in their saddles. The Baol warriors saw this and seized the advantage. One of them made a charge against Braga. The warrior made a sharp turn in time to strike the ball in the opposite direction toward midfield. Another warrior eluded Mendez and hit the ball into the Portuguese defensive end. Fernão tried to intercept; but failed. Another pass toward the warrior's captain drove the attack further into the Portuguese field. Diogo was the last hope for any defensive stop. He charged toward the lead horseman at an angle and maneuvered alongside. Both horses raced toward the goal while both riders tried to hit the rolling ball in opposite directions. The horses banged against one another. As Diogo's mount tripped and stumbled, the warrior captain threw his forearm into him. He was thrown into the dirt and nearly trampled by his own horse. With the last defensive hope removed, the warrior captain swatted the ball neatly into the goal. A loud cheer erupted from the throngs of villagers. The drums were beat in a frenzy and men along the perimeter sounded their ivory horns. Both teams trotted off to their own sidelines.

The Portuguese crews stared in disbelief at their team. Dom Braga shook his head, and his face flushed the color of his sash. 'What the devil?'

Diogo brushed the dirt off his riding vest. 'Do not concern yourself. The match is early.'

'Hold the line!' Dom Mendez barked. 'You need to hold the line!'

The two fidalgos glared icy stares upon the Magalhães brothers.

'We are losing . . . against heathens!' Braga exclaimed.

The Magalhães brothers looked at one another and rolled their eyes.

Both teams rode back to their positions and the starter blew his horn. The Portuguese had begun to get a feel for their unfamiliar horses and made several impressive plays on both offense and defense, but they trailed four to two at half-time.

Over the next 30 minutes the two sides battled with neither side taking advantage. As the match progressed, Diogo had made two incredible saves, throttling the warrior's offense. Yet, they were also unable to score, and still needed two to tie, and a third to pull ahead on the scoreboard. But on the very next play, Fernão hooked the other rider's stick and deftly swiped the ball with his own, then smashed the ball forward to Mendez who in turn passed it to Braga already positioned in the African zone. Braga rushed ahead full gallop. He stretched half-way off his horse to connect with the bouncing ball. With precise timing, Braga connected the ball against the middle of the curved head and sent it soaring between the goal posts. The ivory horns sounded, and cheers went up from the Portuguese sailors. The two fidalgos rode back to midfield for the next toss. Braga turned to look stoically at the Magalhães brothers and gave a slight nod in recognition of the assist. The score was now, four to three, in favor of the African riders, with only minutes left remaining.

Hope was fleeting for the Portuguese. Fernão knew he must make a move now, because the fidalgos seemed stalemated by the strong drive of the warriors. He gritted his teeth. The warrior captain had the ball in his control and was charging from midfield into the Portuguese zone. Fernão charged to cut him off. He closed in just ahead. Then, at the last possible second Fernão pulled the reigns and with an uncanny stick maneuver flicked the ball away from the warrior captain and sent it the opposite direction. He timed its bounce and while hanging far off to the right of his saddle, hit it again forward. He ducked a shoulder to dodge another rider and struck the ball forward to the waiting fidalgos. Braga and Mendez passed it back and forth as they raced toward the goal. Finally, Braga slammed the ball into the goal. A cheer erupted from the Portuguese spectators. The score was tied, and there was still over a minute left in the game.

Diogo trotted up near Braga at midfield. 'A minute is a long time.'

Braga smiled and nodded.

The riders again took their positions. The midfield referee pulled out a white satin handkerchief as signal for the last regulation toss. The riders gasped for breath as they waited. The ball was thrown into the field and the riders pursued. Neither team could gain an advantage. But, with seconds left, one of the warriors made a pass deep into the Portuguese zone. Diogo rushed to intercept the rider rushing toward the goal. He swung his stick to deflect the ball away but missed. The Portuguese were filled with desperation as Diogo pursued. He struck his stick in a second attempt and deflected the ball just enough to go out of bounds as the clock ran out. The tall African sounded the ivory horn ending the game. The Portuguese sailors sounded off a cheer for their mates.

It was now overtime and the first team to score would claim victory. The exhausted opponents took their positions. The referee tossed the ball as drums beat to a fever-pitch. The horn blew, and the crowd cheered. All riders drove hard for the ball. When out of sight of the referees, sticks pounded at shins as much as at the ball. Half the regulation passed with no side taking control. Fernão rushed forward, intercepted a pass, and drove toward the goal. The warrior captain came along side. Fernão was within range to score and cocked back his stick to strike. Just then, the warrior captain slammed his stick into Fernão's jaw. Blood trickled from his mouth and onto his shirt. A referee stood on the sideline in clear view, but never called the blatant foul. He only threw a black-satin sash as a signal for an injury timeout. The Portuguese riders drew close to Fernão. Diogo hurriedly leaped off his horse to check on his brother. 'You all right?'

The two fidalgos galloped up to them. Fernão rubbed his jaw and felt for loose teeth. He stood up, dusted himself off, and smiled. 'Never been a finer day for victory.'

The fidalgos grinned. 'Blood,' Braga said. 'A badge of honor. Wear it well.'

Fernão climbed back on his horse and fell back to his position to resume the match.

With only two minutes left, the ball was tossed back into play. Riders jockeyed for advantage jabbing and hacking each other with their sticks, as horses careened together. Fernão forced an opening between two opponents and steered through before they collided back together. He spun his stick and smashed the ball ahead. Braga knocked the ball down with his stick and then hit it forward. He twirled his horse around and maneuvered past an oncoming charge by the last defensive warrior. With time only seconds before expiration, Braga lined up for a last shot and sent the ball reeling toward the goal. The crowd watched in quiet anticipation. A pause . . . then the victory horn sounded off and drummers went into a frenzied beat. Cheers erupted and victory was given to the Portuguese for their game winning goal in extended period. The Portuguese sailors rushed the field and snatched the winning team from their horses and carried them off to the sidelines in celebratory revelry.

Fernão and Diogo drank from buckets of water then poured the remaining over their heads. They watched Tumar paying off some Moors. 'I would wager he also paid the referees,' Diogo said. 'You took an obvious hard shot and no call.'

'True. But we overcame anyway.'

Later in the evening, the Portuguese were invited to dine with the viceroy in the royal hall. Near the end of the sumptuous feast, Tumar called over a sentry and whispered in his ear. The sentry nodded and walked away.

Tumar then gestured with his hand for Ahmad to translate for him. 'It has been a long time since my warriors have lost in *Chovqan*. It is customary for the

144

victors to be rewarded. Please honor me by receiving my gift to enjoy during your stay with us.'

Fernão turned his face toward Diogo. 'Gift?'

Diogo shrugged his shoulders.

Drums and pipes filled the royal hall. The guests murmured as four attractive slave girls entered. They were topless with only tiny animal skins hanging over their hips. Two girls slowly approached the victorious fidalgos and snuggled up next to them real tight and sensual. The fidalgos grinned and nodded to the viceroy. Meanwhile, the remaining two slave girls found the Magalhães brothers and draped their arms over them. Fernão gulped. A bead of sweat appeared on Diogo's forehead.

Francisco chuckled. 'You two monks would not want to offend the viceroy now, would you?'

Fernão's girl smiled and brought her finger across his ear and then down his chest.

'What can we do?' Fernão asked.

'Accept the gifts,' Francisco said. 'Perhaps I can relieve you of your burdens.' He smiled broadly.

The Magalhães brothers looked at one another and considered Francisco's proposal. They nodded.

The crews filed out looking toward the victors with admiration and envy. The Magalhães brothers, their two slave girls and Francisco made their way to the outer court. Fernão waved for the girls to depart with Francisco. The two girls, confused, looked at one another, but when they eyed the dashing young Francisco, they both smiled and embraced him, one on each side. Francisco wrapped one arm around each girl, turned his head for a moment and winked at the Magalhães brothers.

Early the next morning, the Magalhães brothers had queued up at the back of the line for breakfast.

Servants offered platters full of fruits and eggs. A few moments later, Francisco snuck up behind the brothers and tapped them both on the shoulder. 'A fine morning is it not?' Francisco said cheerfully. 'You would not believe—I mean these girls are so incredible. You would never—.'

The two brothers stared blankly at Francisco. They turned back forward and folded their arms across their chests.

'All right, all right. I thank you both from every part of my body.'

The brothers rolled their eyes. Diogo looked at the ground and shook his head.

'You know,' Francisco said. 'I could find this place quite appealing, with all the special treatment and—.' Francisco caught the reticence of the brothers, and his conversation tapered off. They took their food, found a place to sit, and ate quietly.

12

Two days after the viceroy's initial feast, Fernão, as usual, had risen early to watch the sunrise across the savannah plains. He had just finished his daily prayers when he noticed clouds of dust. Fernão squinted and stared in the distance. Some minutes passed before he recognized a contingent of Moors on horseback escorting a long line of African slaves. Fernão rushed down the hillside toward the village compound.

The Serrão brothers, Diogo, and Samuel were in the middle courtyard unloading crates of iron weaponry. Every item was carefully inventoried by the viceroy's Moor accountant and then stored under guard in a stone-built armory. In exchange, servants carried supplies to the shore: salted and cured fish, vegetables, fruits, jugs of fresh water, and wood. The fresh items were packed in crates and would soon be eaten after leaving the coast. But the salted fish and other cured food were sealed in barrels to last further into the voyage. Fernão breathed heavy as he arrived at the middle courtyard.

'What's the rush brother,' Diogo asked.

Fernão caught his breath as he replied. 'The Moor traders . . . they have arrived.'

Captain Serrão stood up. 'How far?'

'Maybe 30 minutes by foot,' Fernão replied.

A few minutes later, a clamor went up across the village. One of the viceroy's cavalry scouts sidled up to the Portuguese sailors. 'Tumar requests your presence at our market. Your men were the victors in the games and the viceroy would be honored by your presence. I can escort you.'

Captain Serrão thought for a moment then nodded his assent. Twenty-five sailors from Captain Serrão's crew accompanied the scout along a trail through scrubs and baobab trees. It was just as Fernão estimated, 30 minutes by foot. They emerged from the thickets into an open clearing, approximately 50 yards in diameter. In the center of the field, a large hollowed out baobab tree loomed behind a wooden platform. Four tall heavy wood poles, all spaced evenly apart, had been driven through the platform and inserted deep into the ground. Large circular iron hoops were inserted through the middle of each pole. The men gasped when they noticed the blood-stained platform.

The men stood 10 yards in front of the platform in columns. They stared silently upon an eerie shadow cast upon the platform by the odd-shaped baobab tree. From the opposite end of the field, in the direction of the interior country, a rustling began and grew louder. The scrub parted and a calvary of Moor traders emerged. As they neared the platform, they revealed a retinue of black slaves dragging themselves along under the weight of the iron chains around their feet and hands. They were kept in line by other black Africans. The Moors slavers gestured for the slaves to proceed toward the platform. Fernão counted 40 slaves in total.

Four slaves were brought onto the platform and shackled to iron hoops, hanging from the posts. It was a young family: father, mother, a young son, and pre-teen daughter. All were clad in animal skins. They stood with grim faces and their eyes lowered to the ground. From another path, more eager traders of the different factions arrived and gathered close to the platform. Drummers thumped a celebratory beat as they accompanied Viceroy Tumar into the trading zone. He grinned at the Portuguese and nodded a greeting, then took his place front and center on the platform as the royal guards surrounded him. The Portuguese moved closer to observe. Samuel stood near Captain Serrão and his entourage.

A Moor from the slaving expedition walked across the platform and bowed to the viceroy and commenced to display his merchandise. The Moor forcefully grabbed the chained male adult slave by the jaw. He pushed up his lips to show the specimen's healthy teeth and gums. The Moor had a two-foot-long wooden paddle attached to his belt. He unfastened it and held it firm. For dramatic effect, he slowly moved the paddle over the rippled abdomen of the slave. The Moor then demonstrated his property's potential to buyers by repeatedly slapping it into the slave's gut; and followed up with several hard blows to the arms, legs, and rear end. The slave grimaced but never cried out. The Moor continued his procedure with the son, but less forceful paddle strikes. The slaver turned to the females and grinned. He glanced at Viceroy Tumar and then ripped off their animal skins. Both squirmed in their futile attempts to avoid any further exposure. The Moor slapped each one hard on their bare bottoms to show how muscled they were and lifted their breasts to accentuate their size and firmness. The viceroy smiled and nodded. The Moor spoke the local Jolof tongue to Viceroy Tumar.

Samuel listened and then whispered to the men. 'These first four were Mandinka slaves. These will be given as tribute for allowing them to trade in his realm.'

The Mandinka slave family was unclamped from the iron hoops and led to the royal guard's custody. They were now slaves of the Baol kingdom. Another group of male slaves were fastened to the posts.

Samuel listened closely to Viceroy Tumar and the Moor, and then translated for Captain Serrão. 'The Moor claims these slaves are Jolof tribes from the interior and wishes to trade to anyone interested. He will trade to representatives from the kingdom of Cajor, Baol, or any other Moor traders present.'

The captain nodded as a lively flurry of auction activity erupted from the merchants. Slaves fastened to the poles were bid for. One by one, slaves were fastened to the poles and bid upon. Once a price was agreed, they were released to the buyer. More prisoners were tied to posts and sold in quick succession, all due to the high demands for slave labor.

An hour into the trading, only 10 slaves were left. As these last captives were led toward the platform, they squirmed to break free. The crowds gaped as the slaves bared their fang-shaped teeth, filed sharp, like canines. All had tattoos over their bodies.

Samuel pried some information from one of the merchants and relayed it to the captain. 'These are from the Mountains of Bafoor. The Moors say these mountains are in Bulom, what we call Serra Lyoa.'

'They are sorcerers, witches and follow all sorts of omens,' Dom Braga added. 'A dangerous breed with their poisoned arrows.' He spit on the ground. 'These devil worshipers eat the dead!'

Fernão gazed in wonder.

Francisco looked at Samuel with a puzzled look. 'Why would anyone want to buy such a foul creature?'

'Could be formidable warriors,' Samuel replied.

'If one can control them,' Braga said.'

Fernão's eagle-like eyes spotted commotion in the distance. He noticed two slaves snatching keys from two slumped over bodies and then opened their chains. Fernão pointed in the direction of the escaping slaves to alert his crew. Suddenly, all the merchant activity halted as the victims groaned out and the slaves fled.

Tumar fumed and barked an order in his Jolof tongue. The viceroy's warrior elite leaped upon their horses and charged off.

It was not long before the cavalrymen reemerged from the bush. The escaped cannibal slaves were dragged by ropes across the scrub covered savannah, bleeding and cursing in their native tongue.

The viceroy looked at Captain Serrão and spoke as Samuel translated. 'Two slaves had concealed poisoned arrow heads and stabbed two of my guards. They will be punished severely.' Tumar then bellowed out: 'To the tree!'

The slaves were thrown into the hollowed entrance of the massive baobab tree. Guards stood beside it with raised spears. Fernão noticed movement in the sand along the entrance. The curious Portuguese moved in closer to view the spectacle. Looking closer, Fernão could make out numerous snakes begin to stir. They were about one foot or so in length, cylindrical stout-bodied and with small tails. The heads were broad and flat with a short-rounded snout. Small white spots ran down in regular intervals along their backs. Fernão had heard of these desert serpents from returning explorers and soldiers to North Africa and India. These vipers were aggressive and extremely deadly.

One of the cannibal slaves was on his knees in front of two vipers. He bared his sharpened teeth and growled at the serpents. The vipers formed into a series of parallel S-shaped coils and rubbed them together causing a sizzling sound like water on a hot plate. As the slave backed away, the vipers rubbed their coils faster and faster with the sizzling noise increasing in measure. The slave tried to pull away, but a viper struck out at him, biting deep into his neck. A second viper clamped its fangs onto his foot. The serpents

151

attacked repeatedly. The second slave bared his teeth in a frightening manner but was attacked by other vipers repeatedly. Both men screamed in pain and fear. The snakes enveloped the two wounded slaves. Finally, the guards raised their spears and allowed the wounded prisoners to crawl to safety. Once they were away from the vipers, the guards hauled the slaves to the platform and fastened them to the iron hoops.

As the two slaves from Bulom writhed in pain from the blistering bite wounds, more cannibal slaves were tied to the remaining poles and the auction continued, unabated. No one else dared to escape after they saw the horrific punishment meted out by the viceroy.

A good hour passed before the venom truly began to take its toll. Blisters rose on the skin and the swelling from the wounds increased. Blood trickled from the mouth and eyes of both men, and one of the slaves vomited blood and bile. As the last slaves were auctioned off, the Portuguese and everyone present took a final look at the envenomed slaves on the platform. The one who had vomited now began to convulse before finally dropping limp, dead. The second slave bled profusely from mouth, eyes, and ears. He was moaning, near death and would not last long.

'These two were bitten many times,' Fernão said to Diogo. 'I suspect the second will not last much longer.'

Diogo grinned. 'Remember the story of the Apostle Paul? How it was when he was shipwrecked upon the Island of Melita?'

'I remember brother. The natives of the land had welcomed Paul. Due to the cold and rain, they built him a fire. But as Paul added a bundle of sticks to increase the flames, a poisonous viper leapt out of the fire and fastened upon his hand.'

Diogo looked toward the platform, to the envenomed barbarian slaves and their doom. 'The natives of the land thought Paul must have been a murderer who escaped the sea only to be punished by a deadly viper. But our Lord had other plans. Paul shook off the viper into the fire and no harm came to him at all. They watched him for a long time carefully observing no ill effects. They soon changed their minds and regarded Paul as a god.'

Fernão turned his head toward Diogo. 'Indeed. Remember our Lord said that serpents will not harm his disciples in their mission. But as for the heathens—.'

Just then Francisco approached and said, 'I pray we are counted worthy, then.'

After nine days in Port d'Ale for their re-supply mission, the ships were all prepared to leave. Viceroy Tumar had prepared a fantastic meal on the eve before departure and entertained Dom Almeida while they discussed matters of trade, war, and peace.

On the following morning, Almeida returned to shore with his special guard and with outstretched arms presented an engraved Portuguese sword to Viceroy Tumar. He accepted the gift and held it high with pride. Samuel served as interpreter for this last conversation.

'Ah, the famous Portuguese black sword and accompanied by the mighty fleet of black ships. I do admire such power. Please, let us remain allies and we shall prosper together.'

Almeida gave a nod. 'We shall. Thank you for your cooperation and continued alliance. We must now sail onward.'

The two viceroys, Tumar and Almeida, made a slight bow of recognition before parting.

The crews loaded the remaining gifts of food for their mates and rowed back to their vessels. Fernão climbed back aboard the *Botafogo* and took position on the quarterdeck near the binnacle and compass. Captain Serrão ambled his way toward Fernão.

'Are we ready to set sail?' Fernão asked.

'Not yet. Almeida has decided to split the armada into two squadrons. He has given Manuel Paçanha command over our fastest ships; two naus, and five caravels. We remain under Almeida's fleet.'

Fernão began scratching his beard.

'You must be wondering why,' Serrão smiled. 'No reasons have been given, only the order.'

'Why do you think the order given?' Fernão asked.

'Well, I would venture it is to increase the odds for the mission. We still must pass the dreaded Cape, and storms can sink an entire squadron.'

Fernão's mouth fell open at the thought.

'Remember Dias?' Serrão asked rhetorically. 'He named it, the Cape of Storms.'

After the crews had all re-joined their assigned ships, Almeida ordered a short salvo of cannon fire. It was a salute to Tumar's hospitality, and display of Portuguese power, meant to leave an impression. The armada set its sails to the wind.

13

Rounding the Cape to Kilwah – June, 1505

Fernão Magalhães assumed his watch on the quarterdeck as the *Botafogo* sailed south. Francisco climbed up to join him. Both wore heavy fur coats and shivered from the cold damp night air.

'Only a month ago we were sweltering in the equator's heat. Now we freeze,' Francisco said as he rubbed his exposed hands together.

The armada indeed suffered, for the doldrums had stalled their progress in the tropic zones. Finally, the winds picked up and the fleet steered for the *volta do mar*, a current flowing southwest into the South Atlantic gyre—a large system of circulating ocean currents and winds, like a vortex.

'The Southern Cross,' Fernão said, pointing to the night sky. 'It grows brighter ever since we passed the equator.'

Francisco gazed up. 'We may have to suffer heat and cold but at least we have this view.'

Fernão moved toward the binnacle; a rectangular box secured to the deck with wooden pins. A hood protected it from foul weather. Both men peered into the contraption. Fernão lit a small copper lamp within the enclosure, revealing the compass mechanism; a 32-pointed compass card marked with colored diamond shapes and lines mounted upon a pivot in a circular bowl. It turned in response to any motion of the ship by the force of a magnetized needle fixed underneath. The bowl was mounted by a gimble to prevent the card from jamming by every pitch and roll of the ship. The two young navigators both knew the eight points to signify the main winds (N, NE, E, SE, S, SW, W, NW) and divisional points for the half winds and quarter winds. A quarter wind signified 11.25 degrees. Therefore, 32 cardinal points equaled a full 360 degrees.

Fernão then pointed to the compass card. 'The pilot caravel runs further south.' He retrieved a chart marked on sheepskin and pointed to a rough etching depicting the southern equatorial current. 'Look, according to my calculations we have first sailed to the southwest.' Fernão traced his finger across the chart southwest to the Tropic of Capricorn. 'About 23 degrees south latitude we caught the westerlies and have turned due east.' Fernão then moved his finger eastward but with a sudden turn to the south.

Francisco looked over the charts and realized something was wrong. With a worried look he stared at Fernão. 'Why?'

'Unusually strong winds from the east,' Fernão surmised. 'Maybe they want to avoid the dreaded cape storms or pilot error—I am not sure. Already, we are well over 40 degrees to the southern latitude. I only hope they turn east . . . and soon.'

But the fleet did not turn east.

Almeida's squadron forged ahead, due south. At midday of the second day, as the carrack, *Botafogo,* followed the lead caravel, storm clouds formed in the distance. Heavy wind gusts churned up enormous waves. Fernão stood on the quarterdeck, holding firm to the whipstaff to maintain their course. Captain João Serrão positioned himself on the center of the top deck and yelled: 'All hands-on deck!' The weather had turned from cold discomfort to a biting chill and frigid squall. Few of the men slept much during these cold days of sailing. By this time all were becoming weary, and dangerously weak from the incessant toil of the sea. 'Men! We have a task ahead of us. We must secure the vessel and ride out this coming storm.'

Several men on deck pointed toward the lead caravel as it turned to the east. The storm began to swirl from the south and joined an eastern front, the skies growing more ominous by the minute.

João took notice of their fearful looks. 'Many of you may have wondered, why the long delay to turn east. Many of you have never sailed this far—or never sailed. The sea is unpredictable, merciless at times. By the winds from the east, our lead vessel may have judged it a good gamble to steer around from the south. Unfortunately, they were wrong.'

The men stared off to the coming storm in dread.

Deep into the southern hemisphere the winter season was near its peak and the sun had begun to wane by late afternoon. As the storm front approached, freezing sleet blew across the top deck. Waves swept over the bow drenching the sailors. Those who climbed the masts to secure the sails were frozen. Diogo met his brother Fernão in the soup line during the change of watch. But the fire below the cooking cauldron could not stay lit due to the blowing sleet and crewmen grimaced with each spoonful of cold soup.

'How long do you think we will have to endure this storm?' Diogo asked his brother.

'We are at the Lord's mercy,' Fernão replied. 'Could be many days if we are destined to survive.' Fernão looked to the heavens. 'This will be a trial by ice.'

'In that case I will triple my prayers,' Diogo said. The two brothers clenched arms in agreement to persevere in faith.

Days of turbulent seas continued to pummel the fleet. Snow blanketed the ship and icicles formed on the yards. The crews slept in cold wet clothes and suffered exposure when they were topside. Their skin cracked as they manned the ropes. Several came down with cold and fever. In desperation, a large group of men gathered under the forecastle, in the bow storeroom. Francisco was officiating a lottery. He cut a cross in a chickpea and threw it into a basket of unmarked chickpeas. He covered the basket and shook it well. From their position on the quarterdeck, Fernão and Captain Serrão could see more men going to the forecastle, including Samuel Levi.

'Magalhães,' Serrão said. 'Go see what that is all about. I will keep our course steady here.'

'Yes sir.' Fernão gave a nod and left.

Francisco shook the basket more. 'Remember, the one who draws the cross must make the pilgrimage to the shrine of Santa Maria de Belem upon return to Portugal, hold vigil every night for one week and pay for one mass.'

One of the sailors asked, 'What happens if the one drawing the lot does not survive?'

Francisco panned over the crowd and smiled. 'Simple, we have another draw.'

Fernão had circled around to the perimeter of the men and joined Samuel Levi as a spectator. 'Sir Magalhães,' Samuel said, in discreet confidence. 'What is your opinion? Will God save the ship if the group sends one man on a pilgrimage?'

Fernão looked over the men's faces. 'The men seem solid in their faith.'

'You know, my Jewish ancestors had a similar custom during moments of serious inquiry. They called it the Urim and Thummim. The high priest had two special stones with writings embedded into his breast-piece. Under the divine Shekinah presence, the priest would pose an either-or question and wait for the divine light to illumine, either the Urim or Thummim, to give an answer.'

Fernaõ gave Samuel a look of curiosity.

Suddenly, the foremast creaked loudly, as if the strain would cause it to snap in two. The men panicked and cried out to pledge their vow if they drew the lot. Francisco shook the basket once more then passed it around as each man drew. Each held their chickpea with closed hands until everyone drew.

'All right now. Who drew the cross?' Francisco asked.

One of the sailors near the front showed his chickpea with the inscribed cross. The men hugged him. Some of the literate mates gave him written parchments with personal vows to lay upon the altar in their stead. The crew clambered back to their stations with renewed faith and determination. If one man slipped on deck or fell from the yards two more picked him back up and continued their duties.

Fernão had rejoined the quarterdeck. Captain João observed with surprise and approval. 'The men look renewed.'

''Yes sir. They have come together quite well now.' Fernão said with a smile.

Days of unrelenting waves crashed into the *Botafogo*. Captain Serrão and Fernão took turns steering the vessel through frigid gusts of wind and torrential sleet. A helmsman and two sailors assisted as they tried to maneuver through the monstrous waves. Icy pelts wreaked havoc upon their exposed faces and hands. Fernão's cheeks cracked from the penetrating weather. A colossal wave rolled toward their starboard side.

Captain Serrão yelled to the men below: 'Secure yourselves! Do it now!'

Fernão and the captain both grabbed the whipstaff to steer away from a broadside collision. They had just managed to veer off 45 degrees when the vessel was slammed by the monstrous tidal wave. The ship dipped its yardarms into the sea and men hung on for their lives by anything they could hold. Fernão watched from the quarterdeck as Diogo was swept across the main deck and over the rails. In midair, Diogo snatched a swinging rope from the yardarm and desperately held on as he splashed into the sea. Miraculously, the ship tilted back upright, and the momentum pulled Diogo back out of the sea. He gasped for breath. The force of the waves slammed him against the hull as he franticly climbed the rope. Diogo summoned all his strength as he slowly made his way up the ship's side to the rail and flopped himself onto the top deck.

Fernão sighed in relief as he watched his brother reappear.

But the perilous voyage was not over, for the waves continued to pummel the fleet.

'Captain. We have lost sight of the last ship in the fleet,' the helmsman desperately remarked. 'We are now, alone.'

An elder ship surgeon with blood-stained clothes and hands struggled up the iced stairs leading to the quarterdeck. 'Captain! I need you to come below deck.'

'What is it doctor?'

'The men sir, they could use your presence. We had an incident.'

'Magalhães, come with me. Helmsman, maintain course. We will return shortly.'

Fernão Magalhães and Captain Serrão followed the doctor down the slippery steps into a cramped storage hold below, used as a makeshift ward. Fernão looked on with horror at the scene before him. Men were coughing and wheezing. They shivered under their overcoats with influenza and exposure. Several had frostbite. But his attention riveted upon a sailor screaming in agony. He was pinned against the hull's wall under a row of barrels that had broken loose from the cargo hold. He screamed and wheezed with blood dripping from his mouth. Several of his shipmates attended to him.

'His lungs are crushed with internal bleeding,' the surgeon said quietly to Captain Serrão. 'The barrels must be moved for his lungs cannot bear the weight anymore, but I am afraid in doing so, the bleeding may increase. We have no priest on this vessel.'

The captain scratched his beard. 'Magalhães, I heard you know some verses, some rites of our church. Is this not so?'

'Yes sir, but I—'

'No objections. You will remain to assist as needed.'

'Yes sir.' Fernão answered quietly, dreading the thought.

The ship was bobbing in the waves and every movement pressed the barrels into the sailor's chest. Blood flowed from his mouth and nose as he uttered pitiful gurgles.

'Proceed to remove the barrels,' the captain ordered. 'I must aid the helmsman.' He turned and left.

Fernão looked over the men, and the storage hold. He unfastened two halberds that were secured by ropes to a wood beam. 'We can use these to brace the lower barrel and then push the others aside. But we must hold firm and act with perfect timing to the pitch of the ship. These are heavy, so stand clear once we make our move.'

Fernão and another crewman held the halberds firm against the barrel for opposing leverage. They fixed their shoulders into the load.

'Now!' Fernão yelled.

The two sailors shoved the barrels aside as they jumped clear. Six barrels of wine rolled away, and one crashed, breaking open near the injured seaman. Crewmen rushed to secure the barrels.

'Well done, well done,' Fernão said.

The wounded sailor wiped blood from his mouth and held it near the wine-stained floor—nearly a perfect match. He wheezed and gasped for air as he bled out more. His skin turned a purplish hue.

'I know you cannot speak,' Fernão quietly said. 'But can you nod for yes?'

The man winced as he gave a slow painful nod.

'You have bleeding, on the inside.'

The sailor looked at him, understanding.

'There is no priest on this vessel,' Fernão said. 'Do you want me to pray with you? I know some verses.'

The man looked at his bruised and discolored chest. He nodded yes, while his eyes rolled with fear.

'You are a believer?'

The gasping sailor gave a firm nod.

'Good, good.' Fernão, from memory, carefully recited the 23rd Psalm. He then laid his hand lightly on the sailor's shoulder. 'Remember in this storm, *He* will lead you beside *still* waters and *you will* dwell in the house of the Lord . . . *forever.*' Fernão was thinking about another scripture, another prayer, but the sailor gasped, smiled, and was dead.

The ship surgeon looked for a pulse or any sign of breathing then shook his head. He said quietly to Fernão, 'I will wrap the body as best I can. We can bury him on first landing.'

There was nothing more to be done. Fernão and the crew bowed their heads before departing. Fernão's legs were almost as heavy as his heart as he climbed back up to the deck.

Several more days of heavy storms continued to batter the *Botafogo* as they rounded the Cape in late June. Finally, the weather abated, and the sun shone again.

Captain Serrão stood on the quarterdeck with Fernão as they neared a small uncharted island. 'Steer for that harbor,' Serrão said. 'It looks like a suitable place to bury our comrade. Fortunately, we lost only one. Almost lost your brother Diogo and others.'

'Yes sir,' Fernão said. 'We were indeed fortunate.'

The vessel anchored off the island and once on shore, buried their mate. The island was heavy with coconut palms, and the crew took advantage of the situation by stocking up as many as they could carry back to the ship. The coconuts would provide not only food, but a bit of fresh liquid in the form of coconut milk.

They put back out to sea and sailed north along the southeastern coast of Africa. From their extreme latitude of 40 degrees south in rounding the Cape, to their current position of 9 degrees south, was a slow journey and the temperatures gradually changed from frigid cold to an agreeable warmth.

Fernão and Captain João Serrão were near the binnacle looking at a nautical chart.

'I know Almeida had planned to port at Kilwa,' Serrão said. 'We should be close.'

The ship entered a strait between the mainland to their left and a coral island off to their right. The island was nearly four miles long and two miles across the middle.

A sailor high up the foremast had been repairing a torn sail with a stitching needle and thread when he suddenly yelled: 'Black ships, black ships!'

Fernão squinted his eyes toward a harbor situated along the northwest side of the island. 'Black ships—Must be ours—This must be Kilwa.'

Captain Serrão slapped Fernão hard on the back. 'At last! Adjust the whipstaff Magalhães. Take her to port.' Serrão yelled to the men on deck: 'Ready at the anchors and prepare the longboat.'

Fernão and Serrão grinned as they watched the crew bustle with an excited frenzy in a renewed hope to join their brothers in arms.

It was many days ago since the *Botafogo* had passed between the African mainland and the island of Madagascar, and now they were entering the harbor of Kilwa Island—located in an estuary off the coast of modern Tanzania. Cheers from Portuguese soldiers on shore erupted as they discovered they had regained their lost vessel.

'It has been over four weeks since we lost the fleet,' Serrão said. 'I expect they must have thought we capsized.'

'It is a good day sir,' Fernão said.

'Indeed. Stay here and guide us in,' Serrão ordered. 'I will go down to check on the longboat.' He climbed down the stairs of the quarterdeck.

From his elevated position on the quarterdeck, Fernão marveled at the harbor city with its modern elegance. Houses were built of stone and mortar with flat roofs and terraces. Very narrow streets separated the town structures. Minarets atop mosques gave an elegant appearance to this cosmopolitan complex. The Moors who ruled Kilwa were dusky in color with various shades between black and white. Men were dressed in fine clothes of silk, cotton, and gold. The women displayed necklaces, bracelets, and earrings of silver and gold. Outside town were large vegetable gardens planted along with fields of palm and citrus trees. In front of the town, near the harbor was a walled fortress, with towers and turrets. Almeida's Portuguese soldiers on shore escorted native black slaves laden with baskets of fresh fruits and ceramic jugs of fresh water.

All the captains had been briefed on the history of Kilwa before departing Lisbon, for orders had been given to construct a fort and establish the city as a Portuguese trading hub. Captain Serrão had explained the details to Fernão while at sea.

The people of Kilwa had divided into two; those who followed a well-liked merchant named Mohamed Ankoni and those who made allegiance to a Persian named Ibrahim bin Sulaiman. The result was 20 years of strife in Kilwa. Powerful and rich elders deposed rightful hereditary kings at their pleasure. Ibrahim was a tyrant. He was so despised that many refused to call him king, only the title—Emir Ibrahim. He had murdered the legitimate king and set himself up as ruler. The next in hereditary line was a young child, the rightful king's heir. The people feared for his life and so immediately hid the young boy away on another island.

Ibrahim had always made empty promises to meet with every Portuguese expedition since the year 1500. Da Gama paid a visit in 1502 and was met with the customary pretexts to meet but did not. But Da Gama was not a man of much patience. Only by a display of military force was the king persuaded to meet and pledge allegiance to Portugal. But when a yearly tribute was required, the king balked. Da Gama escalated his threats. Ibrahim was told the city would be burned to the ground, and that he would be pursued by dogs and carried off to India. Ibrahim would be displayed to all with an iron collar and chain as an example of what happens to those who refuse Portuguese rule. Knowing Da Gama was a man of his word, Ibrahim became filled with dread.

Ankoni, a leading merchant of the rival faction, convinced Ibrahim that he was powerless against the Portuguese forces and should agree to meet with them. Ibrahim reluctantly acquiesced and boarded Da Gama's ship. Ankoni and two Arab traders accompanied him. Da Gama informed Ibrahim that he was to pay an annual tribute of 1,500 meticals of gold and declare himself a vassal of the king of Portugal. In return, he would receive protection against all enemies. Ibrahim claimed he would retrieve the requested tribute but needed to go on shore to order the disbursement. As surety for the payment, he left Ankoni and the two Arab merchants in their custody.

Once on shore, Ibrahim plotted his revenge on his rival—Ankoni. Ibrahim suspected that Ankoni had persuaded him to board the vessel so that the Portuguese would capture him as a slave or kill him. Ibrahim delayed the payment. The hostages summoned their own personal messengers from a small boat waiting below. They ordered them to retrieve the gold tribute from Ibrahim so they could be freed. Every messenger dispatched was denied by Ibrahim and given a message: 'Ankoni can pay the tribute as reparations for his treachery.'

After two days, Da Gama lost his patience. On the main deck of the ship, Ankoni and the Arabs were stripped naked, bound, and flogged. They were then left exposed under the burning sun. Near death, Ankoni was released. He returned to his house and retrieved an expensive necklace worth 10,000 cruzados to buy their freedom. Driven by his hatred of the king, Ankoni decided to aid the Portuguese, regardless of the harsh treatment at their hands. Kilwa's tribute of gold was eventually brought to Lisbon and used for Gil Vicente's monstrance of Bélem.

Once the *Botafogo* was anchored, Fernão joined Captain Serrão, Francisco, and Diogo in the longboat squadron sent to shore. A Portuguese soldier ran toward them as they landed on shore. He saluted Captain Serrão. 'Viceroy Almeida requests to see you. You can follow me.'

The captain nodded in assent.

The crew walked along the beach. Fernão stared in awe at a massive palace situated on a high bluff ahead. The walled complex of fortification extended all the way down to the shore. Approaching closer to the lower entrance of the palace, they were saluted by two Portuguese sentries. The ornately engraved gates were opened, and the crew entered the palace grounds.

Inside the complex, Kilwa residents and Portuguese soldiers took part in strengthening fortifications. The viceroy and the highest ranked nobility in the fleet assisted, spurning on the crews with motivational admonitions and jesting. He was pushing a wheel barrel full of coral when he noticed their approach.

Almeida joked, 'So kind of you to finally join us. Now that we are nearing completion—after 16 days of hard labor. What were you doing all this time? Fishing?'

Almeida and everyone else bellowed with laughter.

He pulled a handkerchief out of his pocket and wiped sweat from his brow. As he folded the handkerchief and put it back in his pocket, the viceroy's countenance turned serious. 'The *Sao Gabriel* has not arrived. But with your ship, we now have 11 of my 12-ship squadron intact. Unfortunately, we have not heard news from any of Paçanha's squadron, leaving our entire fleet cut in half—so it's very good to see you have arrived.'

Almeida and captain clasped arms in greeting.

He waved his arm at the expanse of the fortress. 'The locals call this "Husuni Kubwa" or to us—the Great Fort.' Almeida then pointed at a large house within the palace. 'As you are aware, Dom Manuel has ordered us to build a fort. We chose the emir's residence as a base, but we had to level seven surrounding houses to create open space and use the materials for construction.'

Fernão looked over the military complex. Twenty heavy cannons were installed along the four bastions. The walls had been constructed to shelter the falconets and crossbows. Within the fortress were quarters for the men, along with the necessary storehouses for their equipment as well as storage for future commercial trade. The viceroy and men climbed up to one of the crenellated towers.

Almeida stood tall, chest out, and legs spread wide. 'Portugal's first fort in East Africa! I believe this position will give us a secure harbor.'

The men observed the walled structure and nodded with approval.

From their elevated vantage point, the men could now see the entire city of Kilwa. Looking closer they noticed damaged walls and burnt buildings.

'What happened to the city?' Captain Serrão asked.

'We had to take the city by force,' Almeida replied. 'I will brief you in my quarters in the royal house. Follow me.'

Along the way, they discovered a pavilion used as a reception hall. It featured an octagonal swimming pool, a mosque, a commercial court, and a large residential section for housing 100 people. Much of the structure was built of coral. The rooms had nine-foot ceilings and the floors were made of a white plaster. Roofs were built by laying limestone blocks across timbers. Finally, they entered what had been the sultan's quarters. The rooms were furnished with ornate luxurious furniture, and exotic silks and fabrics decorated the bed. Chinese celadon were displayed in carved niches along the coral walls. The viceroy took a seat behind a desk made of teak and ivory.

Almeida gestured for the men to take seats in stately chairs. He faced them while seated in his own regal chair. 'We had arrived here on July 22 with eight ships and were not received well,' Almeida said. 'The problematic ruler, Emir Ibrahim had once again chosen to ignore our presence and refused to display our flag. We sent a messenger to demand the two years of overdue tribute.' Almeida shook his head. 'He refused to meet me and offered only excuses and pretenses. He even claimed a black cat crossed his path and said any treaty made that day would never last.'

'Superstitious people,' Serrão said.

The two commanders nodded.

'Fortunately, we have an ally in a rival leader named Ankoni. He informed us Ibrahim would never meet us and that he had already positioned 1,500 armed men in the city and summoned Bantu archers from the mainland. This Ibrahim is an infidel. He has proven to be a deceiver. He has refused any cooperation with our great captains: Cabral, da Nova, da Gama—and just last spring—Soares. I had enough and ordered us to battle.'

Almeida arose and retrieved a map from a cabinet. He spread it out across the teak table. The men all stood up for a better view.

'At dawn, I had sent a landing party in 2 separate points, 300 under my command and 200 under my son's, Dom Lourenço.' He traced his finger on the map during his briefing. 'My squadron moved along the narrow streets at this point in the city. Here we encountered a heavy barrage of stones and arrows. We were forced to break into the houses and fight our way across the terraced roofs.'

Almeida then moved his finger to another point. 'Lourenço's squadron approached the palace from the city. From the palace roof, 300 defenders attacked his men with projectiles of arrows and spears. Lourenço's men returned fire with crossbows and arquebuses which forced the enemy to retreat. They stormed the palace and disposed of the last resistance. Once they entered the gates, they found the palace evacuated. Ibrahim had escaped out a side door and fled to the harbor where a waiting boat took him to the mainland.'

The viceroy rolled up the map. 'Once we secured the city, we made an orderly plunder of its treasures. Ankoni's house was given a dedicated guard, the palace loot was reserved for the King of Portugal, and all other goods divided equally among the men.' He pulled an arrowhead out of his pocket and showed the men. 'I only took this, as a souvenir.'

Almeida paused a moment. 'You know this Ankoni had befriended our captains in the past and is beloved by the people of Kilwa. I decided to support his ambitions. Anconi was crowned as king with great ceremonial pomp. He accepted his new position as ruler of Kilwa pending one condition. Even though he had many sons, Anconi demanded upon his death that the rule shall pass back to the rightful hereditary heir. I was quite impressed by such a noble promise and agreed to his terms.'

Almeida stored the map back in the cabinet and returned to face the men. 'Well, there you have your briefing. We must leave soon, and timing the monsoon is crucial. I have ordered Pero Ferreira Fogaça to command the garrison. We will leave 150 men. Our itinerary will be left here in case the missing vessels arrive. Take on fresh provisions for your vessel before departure. You are dismissed.

The following day, Fernão, Diogo, and Francisco wandered down to the beach harbor to search for provisions. Two men were speaking German and pointing to numerous watercrafts of various types.

'Those vessels look unique,' Fernão said. 'Maybe we should investigate. I am curious.'

Upon approaching the men, Francisco cleared his throat to acknowledge their presence. He smiled and made a hand gesture toward the Magalhães brothers. 'Fernão and Diogo Magalhães, part of our navigation team. I am Francisco Serrão.'

The two Germans glanced at one another. One replied with a German accented Portuguese. 'Wunderbahr! I am Hans Mayr, and this is my colleague; Balthasar Sprenger.'

'And what is your mission?' Fernão asked.

'We are here to oversee the commercial transactions. Three vessels of our fleet have been financed by the German banks out of Lisbon. But we have also been interested in the construction of these Moor vessels.' Hans Mayr pointed to some local craftsmen working with cords. 'They use every part of the coconut, even the fibers for cords to bind the ships together. They call the fibers coir. We have watched this construction for two days.'

'Your assessment?' Diogo asked.

'Well, they use no iron, only cord and wooden treenails to sew or bind the parts together. No saws are used. It is all very inefficient. They must split the logs into planks then trim them with an axe. So much precious wood is lost with this process. Such a pity.'

'What of the sails?' Fernão asked.

'Sails are impressive, made of a strong matting of fiber,' Sprenger replied. 'All the running gear is constructed of the durable coir.'

Francisco pointed to three different types of marine vessels. 'What's the difference between those? Some for greater distances?'

'Precisely,' Hans replied. 'The largest are called dhows—used for crossing oceans to Arabia, Persia, India, and the Far East. Next, we have pangayos—used for the trade along the coast. Last, we have the small zambucos and luzios—used for communications between towns, bringing cargo up and down the Zambesi and other like tasks. On these smaller craft, they often have awnings for shade and use poles to propel their craft through the shallows.'

Francisco rolled his eyes. 'All this is interesting I am sure, but what of the trade? What of the gold? King Manuel ordered we take interest in the gold trade from Sofala.'

'Yes, of course. The gold trade flourished from the foundation of Kilwa. It has been said: Hundreds of years ago, a man named Ali, from Persia, sailed to this island. The native Bantu tribes sold him their island for cloth and agreed to leave to the mainland.' Hans shook his head and then smiled. 'They sold their birthright out, a valuable piece of land for a pittance, mere cloth.'

The men joined in laughter upon such a foolhardy trade.

Hans looked out to sea. 'The new sheik or ruler—Ali, immediately fortified the island and began to institute a major global trading network. The trade has increased ever since. The entire coast of Africa pays homage to the king of Kilwa, from Mogadishu in the north to Sofala in the south.'

'You say a global trade hub?' Francisco's eyes glowed as he winked at the Magalhães brothers. 'What goods?'

Hans paused. 'Well, from what we have learned so far—From India: anything from silks and spices to glassware, and even luxury furniture. From Arabia and Persia: exquisite fabrics, dates, blades, and scimitars. From the African interior: gold, slaves, ivory, and animal hides. Of course, they also traded for common provisions such as: rice, cattle, and honey.' Hans paused a moment. 'You know the ruling class here all live like kings—a happy condition gained by trade and heavy duties on imports. Anyone trading with Sofala must pay 70 percent of the value of goods before leaving port.'

'What?' Diogo balked.

'True,' Sprenger said. 'Upon arrival at one's destination an additional seventh of the value must be paid. If one returned with gold or ivory, even more tariffs were paid.'

'Quite a monopoly,' Fernão said.

The men's attention soon turned to a group of black men tending the vegetable gardens and some cotton fields in the distance. 'Who are they? I thought the blacks removed themselves from the island?' Francisco asked.

'They did. But these are slaves traded from the interior. The Arabs call them "kaffirs"—infidels. You will also notice many mixed breeds of the Arab and Bantu. You see, most of the citizens of Kilwa have no issue with taking wives from the natives into their harems. Only the strictest Muhammadans retain their original bloodlines.'

'It seems everyone is an infidel these days,' Francisco quipped.

Fernão noticed Hans had an arquebus by his side. 'I have seen those fired before but never loaded?'

Hans picked up his weapon. 'It is quite simple, designed in Germany. I can demonstrate.'

He then explained its usage in detail. The latest models had incorporated a matchlock firing mechanism divided in two parts, the match, and the lock. The lock device included a clamp which held a dangling rope about two to three feet long and soaked in potassium nitrate which would keep the match lit for extended periods of time. A trigger was attached to the lever. Once the trigger was pulled it would lower the match into the priming pan, ignite the powder, create a flash to shoot through a touch hole and ignite the gunpowder. An internal explosion would then propel the bullet or projectile out the barrel. Fernão had also observed how the trigger unit was almost identical to the crossbow, a curved lever pointed backward and running parallel with the stock.

Hans finished loading the arquebus and handed it to Fernão. 'Take a shot. See if you can hit that palm tree over there.'

Fernão aimed the weapon and fired off a round and tore off a piece of the tree.

'*Das ist gut.*' Hans and Sprenger both exclaimed.

Fernão turned to the Germans and gave a slight head bow. 'It has been a pleasure to make your acquaintance.'

'Likewise, sirs,' Hans said with a bow.

On August 8, the fleet had readied to depart Kilwa. Francisco and the Magalhães brothers were reacquainting themselves to the deck of the *Botafogo*.

'You think the lost ships will catch up?' Diogo asked.

'I pray they do,' Fernão replied.

Francisco spit some betel nut out to sea. He smiled and displayed his bright red teeth.

'What the devil?' Diogo gasped.

'You must try it. They call it betel.'

'I think you need to see your reflection.' Fernão chided. Diogo and Fernão then burst out with a laugh.

'What? What?' Francisco uttered, now worried. He found a bucket of water and looked at his image. His teeth were stained red. 'Oh my, oh my, this is not good.' He desperately tried to clean his mouth with his fingers but was unable to remove the stain. The Magalhães brothers clutched their bellies and laughed uncontrollably.

14

Mombasa – August 13, 1505

The Portuguese armada of eleven ships had sailed north along the African coast for 60 leagues. After six days sailing, they anchored outside the coral reef bar of Mombasa. Ahead lay, an imposing island three miles long by almost two in width and centered in an estuary. Two winding waterways encircled the island. Steep coral cliffs, 60 feet high in some places, provided a natural defensive barrier along the seaward side.

The Magalhães brothers and Francisco Serrão stood along the top deck of the *Botafogo*.

Fernão pointed. 'Look. Mombasa.'

The three stared off at the great city built along the steep eastern seashore and with its port on the northern channel. The buildings and houses, some three stories tall, were built of stone upon the higher parts of the rocky island. A massive stone defensive wall and fortress had been constructed along the land side.

A red flag was then hoisted above the 400-ton flagship, *São Jerónimo*. Captain João Serrão climbed down from the quarterdeck. 'The viceroy's signal flag,' he said. 'He is convening his commanders. I will need a rowing crew.' He looked them over, expecting a response.

Both Magalhães brothers nodded.

'Yes sir,' Francisco said in compliance.

'And bring Levi,' Serrão added. 'We may need a translator.'

Aboard the *São Jerónimo,* the leadership from each vessel gathered with Viceroy Dom Francisco

Almeida. 'Gentlemen, we have a dilemma. The pilots taken on from Kilwa assure us the depth of the channel can accommodate our largest vessels.' Almeida crossed his arms and looked ahead at the narrow channel. He shot distrustful glances at two dusky-skinned men standing nearby. 'How can we be certain.'

Everyone turned their gaze to the native pilots. One captain exclaimed, 'Can we really trust a—'

'Moor?' The commanders and fidalgos murmured.

A Portuguese pilot took a step forward. 'I served on Da Gama's first voyage through this channel. We had three vessels, two of them crashed into the shoals. Need to be careful. Now we have vessels much larger, requiring deeper waters.'

'It will cost us more time, but I do not wish to risk any more of our vessels,' Almeida replied. 'We verify before proceeding.' He looked over his captains. 'Gonçalo de Paiva. Take two vessels for a sounding of the passage.'

'Yes sir.'

All the commanders aboard the *São Jerónimo* and the entire armada watched the two caravels led by Gonçalo de Paiva sail slowly up to the narrow channel entrance. The two ships split away from each other and began to take equal distant soundings. They accomplished this by lowering ropes with markings for every two fathoms and with lead plummets attached on the end. Only a few depth measurement readings were taken before thunderous booms sounded from shore. The fortress along the shore fired from eight mounted cannons upon the two vessels. A cannon ball slammed into Gonçalo's caravel from stem to stern. Miraculously, no serious harm ensued.

'What the devil?' exclaimed Gonçalo. 'Load the cannons!'

The crew scrambled to battle stations.

Meanwhile, on board the *São Jerónimo*, commanders and crew stared in disbelief.

Fernão turned to Captain Serrão. 'The Moors have cannon?'

'We knew there was a fortress, but we did not expect them to have any cannons,' Serrão replied. 'Maybe they retrieved them from a shipwreck.'

A heavy bearded fidalgo's face reddened and yelled, 'Infidels! The dogs need chains.'

Another comrade unsheathed a dagger and slammed it into the ship rail. 'They will surely pay in blood—and fire!'

'And the Moors themselves shall be made slaves,' the heavy bearded fidalgo added.

Fernão pondered their words a moment. The Muslims had dominated as both slave-takers and middlemen for the slave trade since the days of Muhammad in the seventh century. Now the Portuguese had inserted themselves into their dominions and threatened their hegemony in all areas of trade, including slaves.

On board his caravel, Gonçalo de Paiva ordered gunners to return fire. A salvo of cannon shots pummeled the fort. Likewise, the second caravel drew near to fire their arsenal at the enemy. An intense bombardment hammered the fort causing great damage. At last, a well-placed shot exploded the powder magazine with a deafening roar. The Moor guns fell silent. The crewmen aboard all the vessels cheered.

The soundings were resumed, and after an eventful hour passed, the task was completed. Gonçalo de Paiva rowed back to the *São Jerónimo* and climbed on board. The viceroy and commanders eagerly awaited his report on the top deck.

Paiva stood before the officers. 'Gentlemen. The sounding is completed. With care, we can sail any vessel through the channel.'

'Excellent—excellent,' Almeida said.

'One more thing sir. We sighted three enemy vessels in the harbor. I have seen these before, from Cambay.'

'Good to know,' Almeida said as he stared out at the burning fort. He turned to face Captain de Paiva. 'You took out their entire battery.'

'Lucky strike, sir.'

'I think not captain. We watched your unrelenting bombardment on their stronghold.' The viceroy looked over his hardened commanders. 'What say all of you? A lucky shot? Or steel resolve—steel nerves—steel fortitude.'

Rasps of steel swords and daggers from the commanders and crew mixed with their chants, 'steel . . . steel . . . steel . . . steel—'

Almeida grinned. 'These infidels have enslaved our homes since our early forefathers, generations upon generations with their offers of submission, forced tribute, or death. Now they shall have the same choice.'

They stared, suddenly stoic, but ready for retribution. Almeida's eyes narrowed with suspicion upon the Moor pilot they had acquired from Kilwa. 'We need to send a message to the ruler of this city. This pilot knows the best route and speaks Arabic.' Almeida observed his men sneer. Nobody trusted a Moor, especially now. 'Any other options?'

'Perhaps, I may suggest one sir,' Captain Serrão replied.

Almeida seemed surprised and gave a slight nod.

'We have here a trusted linguist,' Serrão said. 'He knows Arabic and other languages. Perhaps he can act as witness for any dialogue, confirm messages sent and received.' Captain Serrão gestured toward his own crew. Samuel slowly stepped forward.

'Your name?' Almeida asked.

'Samuel. Samuel Levi, sir'

'A Jew? Interesting.' The viceroy turned to Captain Serrão. 'You can trust him?'

Serrão and Samuel looked at one another. 'Yes sir,' Serrão said. 'I do.'

'Very well. We will leave our cargo ships here. Transfer all non-essential crews to the smaller vessels. Split our divisions into two as we anchor off the harbor.'

Almeida then crafted contingent plans in expectation the king of Mombasa should refuse his offer of peace. It was decided; Captain Serrão was to lead a raiding party to the harbor and burn the three Cambay vessels, while another squad was to perform reconnaissance further upriver. If Almeida launched a salvo, it was a signal to attack, and all were to proceed with their orders.

Fernão met Samuel on the deck of the *Botafogo* just before disembarking on his mission and inquired. 'You have a weapon?'

'Never had much time for soldiery, but I have spent a good amount of time with knives in the kitchen,' Samuel replied with a twinkle in his eyes.

Fernão chuckled at this and retrieved a dagger from his belt. 'Here, take this.'

Samuel slowly took the blade and turned it over back and forth, observing its characteristic design and weight. He nodded in appreciation and strapped it into his belt.

At dusk, the Kilwa pilot, Samuel, and four crewmen rowed a small launch craft toward the shoreline. A contingent of Moor and African soldiers lined the beachhead. They raised spears and aimed bows to prevent any safe landing. The rowers kept their vessel a safe distance.

The pilot from Kilwa stood up as Samuel kept him balanced against the rocking boat. The pilot spoke in Arabic: 'We come with a message from the Portuguese commander. He offers a peaceful friendship and an alliance against any enemies of your king. He only asks your obedience to the great and mighty King of Portugal. Only a yearly tribute is required, and you shall have protection and a sure alliance. If not, then you shall have war. You will surely have—.'

The speech was interrupted by shouts in Arabic from shore. The crowd parted, and a white man marched through to the beach. He was dressed in white garments of the Moors but armed with the signature black sword of the Portuguese militia. 'Go away!' he yelled in Portuguese. 'The king refuses any of your traitorous peace offers. The king says the Prophet Muhammad will aid him against you infidels and the city streets will flow red with your blood.'

Samuel turned to the crew. 'He speaks with an Arabic accent.'

One of the crew snarled, 'Traitor, turned Muslim.'

The Portuguese renegade continued his harangue from the shore. 'Inform your commander, the warriors of Mombasa are not the hens of Kilwa to be frightened by the sound of cannon. You will not find here chickens to have their necks wrung, but only 20,000 warriors. If you shall come ashore the people of Mombasa shall dine on your flesh for supper.'

He then snatched a spear from another Moor and threw it at their craft. It splashed in front of them. Jeers and taunts in Arabic grew as they hurled spears and shot arrows at the retreating vessel.

Once Almeida heard the report from the returning craft, he vented his rage with a series of salvos upon the center of town. With this signal, pre-planned attacks were to commence.

After sunset, the night was a moonless night, and pitch dark. Captain Serrão led his contingent of 12 men in a longboat which they rowed upriver. The Magalhães brothers and Francisco were among the small squadron. They maneuvered the craft into the harbor near the Indian vessels. Fernão held up three bamboo sticks with tightly wound rags attached on the ends. Diogo retrieved a flask of oil and doused the rags. Two men remained with the craft while the others clambered out into the waist-high waters. The Magalhães brothers and Captain Serrão led the way with the torches still unlit, while the others carried jugs of oil. Francisco grasped a peg from the outer hull of the closest of three Cambay dhows. Others quietly made their way to the other two vessels. Francisco waited for them to position themselves and then gestured toward a sailor below who passed him a jug of oil. Meanwhile, his brother, Captain Serrão was drawing near the last ship. But a Moor sailor saw them and yelled in Arabic to alarm the guards. Back at the first Cambay vessel, Francisco poured out oil over the top deck. He retrieved a long dry cannon match from his shirt, lit the torch, and set fire to the oiled deck.

The Magalhães brothers had reached the second ship but were unable to proceed—for enemy reinforcements had arrived; hurling stones, spears, and arrows. Likewise, Captain Serrão was under a major assault. They were all unaware that Bantu warriors had been summoned from the mainland by the King of Mombasa to fight alongside the Moors against the Portuguese aggressors. The natives were highly skilled in the use of the assegai: a weapon much like a javelin, with a long wood shaft and sharp iron head. The defenders positioned their assegai above their shoulders, and then, by skilled technique, they induced an oscillating motion in the shaft until it began to whirr and hum, and with its enhanced physical state, were launched with high velocity. The moonless night had given the Portuguese some cover, but now, the flames from the burning Cambay vessel had exposed them, and the sheer number of attackers forced them into a hasty retreat.

The Bantu defenders shot arrows with poisoned wood tips and managed to strike two Portuguese seamen. Then, without warning, an assegai pierced the shoulder of Captain Serrão, severely wounding him. He was forced to retreat with the assegai protruding. Every step through the water shot intense pain into the wound. The men escorted the wounded back to the two sailors guarding the longboat and rowed towards the nearest caravel. The Magalhães brothers held the captain steady in the boat. They leaned him against the rail so that the lodged spear was rested against the edge of the hull. Francisco drew his black sword and slammed it across the assegai, snapping the iron blade tip off. 'Sorry brother, brace yourself,' Francisco said, as he quickly pulled the javelin from his brother's shoulder.

Captain Serrão grimaced but never cried out.

The two crew members wounded by arrows started to convulse and blood seeped out their mouth, nose, and eyes. It was a horrid sight to behold.

'We cannot help them,' Fernão said. 'Wooden tips.'

'Why?' Diogo asked.

'I spoke with a local in Kilwa who claimed he could heal iron-tipped wounds with repeated applications of fat upon the wound. But apparently, wood retains more of the poison.'

Everyone looked with empathy upon the poisoned men nearing their end.

Captain Serrão winced in pain as he was helped back aboard the caravel. Sweat poured from his brow. Francisco carried him below deck. There was no doctor on this vessel but several on board knew basic field dressings. The poisoned men who died en route to the caravel were carried aboard for proper burial when time would allow. Messengers carried the news of the failed attack to the viceroy, who immediately called a council of war to be convened upon his vessel. Captain Serrão was in no condition to be moved, so he ordered Fernão and Francisco to go in his stead.

All available commanders gathered with the viceroy for a plan of attack. As they were discussing strategy, a prisoner was brought on board. He was brought to Almeida by a soldier.

'Sir, on our expedition upriver we captured this Moor, a member of the royal household. He knows Portuguese.'

'Indeed,' Almeida answered with a raised eyebrow.

The prisoner, terrified, sweated profusely, and his eyes bulged. 'I beg you sir. Do not treat me as Da Gama would.'

Those in the region knew of the wrath that Da Gama had inflicted upon many of those he captured.

Anyone who dared resist his questioning was tortured and sometimes mutilated. Da Gama's reputation for vengeance had spread across the trading ports. The prisoner was more than willing to volunteer information to avoid any similar fate.

Fernão had arrived late with his brother and Francisco. All eyes turned to their hasty entrance and bloodied clothing.

Almeida noticed also but turned his attention back to the prisoner. 'Tell me. What are the king's plans?'

'The king ordered his slaves from the mainland to fight with him. He brought in 1,500 Bantu warriors to Mombasa and many more expected. The king has ordered all in Mombasa to fight to the death. If anyone tries to flee, they will be put to death. The town has over 20,000 men armed and ready.'

Almeida paced the deck.

Francisco stepped forward. 'Sir, we can verify this. We were in the raiding party to the Indian ships and encountered heavy assault from natives. We lost two men, and almost my brother João.'

'Ah, Captain Serrão's crew! This is good information. Take good care of the captain. We need more with his spirit.'

Francisco nodded, then stepped back in line.

Almeida reflected a moment. 'Now we know what we face. Our numbers have been reduced since we lost some vessels around the Cape. But perhaps 1,000 of ours against nearly 22,000 of theirs seems fair, at least to me.' Almeida smirked and the men raised their chins in stoic fortitude. Almeida noted this, and said, 'We shall outwit them. I propose an attack tonight to draw their forces away from our main landing point. My son, Dom Lourenço shall lead the strike. Burn down the customs house and anything near it, then return.'

Dom Lourenço led a large force to a main landing ashore near the customs house. His men quietly moved into the narrow city streets. Houses spread out across Mombasa, all thatched with palm leaves. Between the stone houses there were wood outbuildings with porches and stables for cattle. Once the crews began setting fire to these, they blazed all night and caused widespread destruction. This did not come without cost, enemy forces swarmed upon the Portuguese, hurling stones, and shooting poisoned arrows. The damage had been done to the city, but Dom Lourenço's raid came with a price; two dead and many wounded. They made a rapid retreat to the boats, dragging the wounded along as best they could. The ploy was effective, for most of the island forces had expected further engagement and were now stationed at the customs house.

The following morning of August 15, before dawn, the priests gave absolution to the Portuguese forces. A flag was raised as signal to attack. One small attachment was sent to burn the Indian ships in the harbor. They were to create a ruse by blowing trumpets and draw the enemy away from the main point of attack. In addition, two vessels were sent to the far side of the island to watch the fjord which formed a passage to the mainland at low tide. The Portuguese did not want a repeat such as in Kilwa where the enemy escaped. A second detachment was led by Dom Lourenço near the front of town, close to where they had made a feint attack the evening before. But this time they would choose to enter a part of the town where the bank was steep and high, an unsuspecting approach. Finally, a third detachment was deployed under the leadership of Dom Francisco Almeida himself. His fleet was the main attack force and would land on the other end of town, around a promontory opposite the landing zone of his son's.

The Magalhães brothers, Francisco, and Samuel Levi were deployed with Dom Lourenço's squadron. Two of the lighter vessels were steered near the steep cliffs. A loud boom echoed across the channel from one of the big cannons.

Upon hearing the signal to attack, planks were set across from the upper decks of the ships and straight over the cliffs onto land. Dom Lourenço raised his sword and made sure he was first to run across the makeshift bridge. The arquebusiers and crossbowmen rushed across behind, followed by auxiliaries. Diogo lost his balance about midway across the plank. He looked down at the rocky cliff below and froze. Fernão was about to cross and noticed his hesitation. Diogo caught his balance, and glanced back at Fernão, who in turn gave his brother a stern look, and pointed toward shore. Diogo smiled and focused his attention ahead. Francisco and Samuel followed next. Once all were across, the squadron marched up the steep hill toward town.

The first houses were deserted due to the fires set on the night raid. Soon they came upon multi-storied houses. The defense of the town was strong. The streets were barricaded. Most could not allow two men side by side. Arquebusiers and crossbowmen led the way, weapons loaded and at the ready. The narrow streets allowed few sea breezes, yet all the humidity of the sea's proximity. The Magalhães brothers stood in a doorway as sweat dripped across their brows and through their shirts. They watched three defenders push a heavy boulder from the street above them. When the stone gained its own momentum, a rolling thunder echoed from the building walls as it headed directly toward two arquebusiers just ahead of them. Fernão recognized one; the German merchant, Hans Mayr, who had reactively brought his arquebus shoulder level.

Hans had taken aim at one of the defending Moors up on the hill and pulled the trigger as the boulder careened toward him. He hit the Moor square in the chest and knocked him backward off his feet. Meanwhile, the boulder ricocheted off stone walls and drew near with high velocity toward Hans. Fernão almost leaped across the street, but Hans quickly tucked himself into a doorway, just as the boulder slammed past him.

Han looked at Fernão and pointed up the hill. '*Das ist gut*,' he called. Then he shifted into Portuguese, albeit with a German accent. 'There are more.' Hans grinned, then pointed to the rooftops and windows above.

Moors and Bantu archers had gathered among the buildings on the street above them, launching rocks, projectiles, and arrows, all which gathered dangerous momentum as they fell from above. The Portuguese took cover in doorways and under overhanging balconies as they slowly advanced under a steady barrage of arrows and spears. The enemy made strategic retreats only to reappear again with heavy boulders to roll down the narrow streets, inflicting painful damage to the flesh and bone of the Portuguese.

'We need to take the high ground now!' Dom Lourenço yelled.

Two Portuguese smashed their way through a door and confronted two African women who immediately put up a spirited defense with stones. The standoff continued for a moment, until a crossbowman shot a bolt through the neck of one of them. The other ran off screaming. Once they were on the rooftops, Lourenço's men were able to push the defenders back and give some relief to the troops below.

Meanwhile, Dom Francisco Almeida led his squadron into the opposite side of town. Outside the walls there was no defense, but upon entering the narrow streets they were met with the same barrage of rocks and arrows that plagued Dom Lourenço's assault. But Almeida learned the lesson of the ambush in Kilwa. He ordered a barrage on the windows and terraces. The arquebusiers and crossbowmen took careful aim and fired repeatedly, providing cover for the troops as they pushed ahead. The prisoner taken the previous day led Almeida's men to the open courtyard in front of the king's palace. Here the Portuguese could take advantage of both formations and firearms. It was not long before they cleared the enemy from the courtyard. However, a steady barrage of stones rained down on them from the palace rooftop. The Portuguese smashed through the palace door and battled the defenders, room to room, and up the stairway to the roof. Eventually, the enemy was driven away from the palace grounds altogether.

Dom Lourenço's detachment pushed ahead but were stopped again when the defenders had pulled down an old wall, separating Fernão's contingent from the main body. Fernão saw the danger immediately.

'We are cut off,' he said. 'No communication with Dom Lourenço.'

The collapsed wall had sent up a cloud of dust and debris when it fell. Francisco rubbed his eyes with a cloth. 'We need to regroup.'

Fernão crouched down near Francisco and Diogo joined them. 'What's the plan?' Diogo asked.

'Find a way through to the other side,' Fernão said. 'Before they swarm us.'

'So be it,' Francisco said as he wiped the cloth over his bloodied sword.

The three of them rallied their contingent, and smashed their way into houses, and engaging their enemies with intense close-range sword fighting as Bantu warriors quickly flanked them. Fernão side-stepped a deadly swing from a war hammer and quickly shoved his sword deep into the warriors' chest. He had the presence of mind to snatch the fallen native's war hammer and used it to counter the attack from another assailant. Calling on his stick fighting skills, Fernão outmaneuvered the Bantu native and landed a crushing blow to his kneecap. He swung the mallet around and landed a decisive strike to the head which sent shattered teeth in the air. The warrior went limp and fell dead.

Diogo, meanwhile, found himself in a desperate duel with a warrior nearly twice his size. He blocked powerful axe strikes with his sword but seemed overwhelmed by the power of his attacker. Fernão saw him stumble backward and rushed full speed at the warrior, burying the head of the ax into his rib cage, then pulling out his dagger burying it deep into the Bantu's side. Still, the warrior turned and swung his axe, forcing Fernão to duck and dodge. Francisco appeared, crouching low, moving fast behind the Bantu warrior, and thrust his black sword through the native's back. It exited out the heart with blood spewing everywhere. They pulled Diogo off the ground and forced themselves over the rubble as their men clambered and battled behind them. At last, they broke through the perimeter to rejoin the main detachment.

Dom Lourenço, though he was unable to break away to assist in their rescue, took a keen interest in their daring mission to regroup. He smiled when Fernão and his men emerged from the rubble.

'Glad you could make it,' he chided in a rare moment of lull in the battle.

Fernão saluted with his sword. 'To the glory of Our Lord in honor of the king,' he said.

'Amen,' Dom Lourenço replied with a smile.

The moment of levity ended quickly as the men massed, and they moved forward. The defenders had entrenched themselves well, and soon again, the fighting grew as fierce as it had ever been. The outcome was in debate until a trumpet blew from the rear signaling Almeida's forces had outflanked the enemy. Fearing entrapment, the enemy fled in all directions. Dom Lourenço led a charge pushing toward the king's palace. After the remaining Moors were routed, they entered the palace, to which they discovered the friars had already erected a cross on the rooftop and the Portuguese flag had been raised. Dom Francisco Almeida smiled and hugged his beloved son.

The two-hour battle had resulted in 4 Portuguese dead and 70 wounded. Dom Lourenço's first major conflict proved his valor and inspired the armada. The king of Mombasa had sent messengers with offers of surrender and to pay tribute. These were accepted, but when it came time to sign the treaty, he never appeared to finalize it, nor did the tributes materialize. Almeida countered the rebuff by splitting his forces into two detachments, one to guard against any counterattack, and the other to begin looting Mombasa. Among the latter, each captain was assigned a separate district to avoid any disputes of the plunder. Almeida also ordered his forces to spare lives if the inhabitants offered no resistance.

Loot of all sorts was confiscated: pearls, gold, silver, ambergris and ivory, silk, cotton fabrics, and richly embroidered clothing. One exquisite tapestry was deemed so valuable it was reserved solely for the King of Portugal. The armada also took on supplies of rice, honey, butter, cattle, goats, and camels. Two elephants were taken and paraded around town to intimidate the people into obedience. Nearly 200 citizens of Mombasa were taken as prisoners earlier in the day but now they acquired 1,000 more, many of whom were light-skinned beautiful women. Very soon, the palace and the square in front of it were filled with loot. Francisco and the Magalhães brothers were stationed at the palace to guard the goods. Francisco took notice of the beautiful women prisoners. 'Quite impressive these harems,' he said. 'They really prefer the lighter complexioned women.'

'I hear the Moors acquired them from many nations,' Fernão said. 'They were stolen or traded for.'

'I doubt many will be taken on board,' Diogo said. 'No room for them and all this cargo.'

'We may all take our portions of the plunder. But you know, the nobles and those of rank take first choice.' Fernão remarked.

Francisco's eyes fixed upon the most beautiful of the women. 'Very fortunate for them indeed.'

'Perhaps. Or one night she could stab you in your sleep . . . or worse yet, take circumcision to another level.' Fernão smirked.

'That's a sobering thought my friend,' Francisco replied.

On the evening of August 16, Dom Francisco Almeida gave his orders. Of the 1,200 slaves taken, 200 were given out among the Portuguese nobles, the remaining were to be freed. Furthermore, only the most valuable of the plunder was to be taken on board since they had no room to store everything.

In addition, the Portuguese had been ordered to establish their southern bases in Kilwa and Sofala since they provided the best port calls en route to India. But it would only be a matter of time before Mombasa regrouped and would harass their cargo fleets off the east coast of Africa. Therefore, Almeida decided to burn the city to the ground. Winds were steady off the sea. When the fires were lit, they spread quickly across the narrow streets. The thatched roof stables between the stone buildings caught fire and burned all night. When the winds increased late in the afternoon, the inferno raged so intensely the Portuguese ships had to flee the harbor. When the citizens returned in the morning, they were met with the overwhelming stench of 1,500 corpses wafting on the light morning breeze. With Mombasa crushed, the Portuguese armada set sail for India.

Before reaching India, the armada stopped in the Island of Anjediva. There they constructed Fort São Miguel in just 20 days. Meanwhile, they sold the plunder taken in Mombasa at public auction and delivered the proceeds to the fleet treasurer. In addition, they had laid down keels for the assembly of two war galleys and a brigantine. Fernão remembered every facet and stage of building the galley and gleamed with pride upon a project well implemented. He volunteered to aid the carpenters to gain a better understanding of the ships. Later, they monitored the seaworthiness of the newly constructed vessels by patrolling the waters.

Anjediva was a strategic location since it lay off the border division between the warring states of Muslim Bijapur to the north and Hindu Vijayanagar to the south. Goa was the principal trade port of Bijapur while Vijayanagar held the high-volume spice ports of

Cannanore, Calicut, Cochin and Quilon. Yet, the Islamic merchants had also amassed profits in the south in the Hindu lands with construction of numerous mosques and palaces. Muslim influence upon the local Hindu rulers—including the Zamorin of Calicut—along the southern Malabar coast gave rise to temporal alliances between the Muslim and Hindu factions. The Muslim influence had been a vexing issue to the Portuguese since the first visit of Da Gama. Almeida would have to continue to navigate the political landscape and broker their own alliances.

The fleet departed Andejiva and sailed southeast for the port city of Onor (Honnovar) along the Indian coast. The local king had previously made a peace treaty with Almeida but had now become obstinate in his letters. Almeida had learned the famed Hindu pirate, Timoja, who had in the past caused issues for the Portuguese armadas, had his ship docked in Onor, along with a contingent of Arab vessels. The viceroy was certain they would endanger their new garrison on Anjediva and so he ordered an attack on the city on October 16, 1505. Dom Lourenço led the way. They burned many of the king's ships in the harbor, then broke into the palace where the king immediately surrendered. The Portuguese lost one man and Almeida was wounded. Once the truce was reaffirmed, the Portuguese fleet sailed south to Cannanore, in modern Kannur, India.

15

Cannanore – October 22, 1505

Fernão Magalhães stood with Captain João Serrão on the raised platform at the stern of a massive galley. It was one of the newly constructed ships in Anjediva and Serrão was given the command. The two white sails emblazoned with a red cross, furled as they were lowered on the approach to India's Malabar coast.

'Take the oars!' Captain Serrão called to the crew, then grabbed his shoulder and grimaced.

'The wound healing sir?' Fernão asked.

'If I do not feel it, that is when I worry,' he replied.

A blast of humid heat gusted over the ship as they slowed.

The shipmaster ordered the oarsmen, 'Pull! Pull!'

The rowers brought the galley near the coastline of Cannanore and entered Mappila Bay. Off to their port side, Fernão caught site of the Portuguese trading warehouse/factory situated upon the neck of a promontory facing the Arabian Sea. Its two sea faces were undefended except for during the monsoon months and random Portuguese sea patrols. The armada entered the port with flags raised and the artillery discharged salvos.

The Portuguese had been on good terms with the local ruler, Raja Kolathiri, since the days of da Gama. Almeida immediately secured permission from him to build a fortress to protect the existing Portuguese factory from the growing hostility of the Arab merchants. With the assistance of the natives, the walls and bastions for cannons were completed in five days. Upon completion of the walls of Fort Sant'Angelo, Almeida officially assumed the rightful rank and title—

Viceroy of the Indies. Furthermore, he appointed his son, Dom Lourenço—Captain-Major of the Indies. As the new Governor of Portuguese India, Almeida received an envoy from Narasimba Rao, the powerful ruler of the state of Viyayanagar—who controlled most of southern India. A treaty was proposed for an alliance by King Narasimba who hoped the Portuguese would continue to allow the unimpeded trade of warhorses from Arabia and Persia—crucial for his army. Almeida promised to do so and ordered the crews to begin construction of large stables within the fortress to accommodate both horses and elephants. Lourenço de Brito was given command and assigned a garrison of 150 men. On October 30, Almeida sailed south to Cochin, where he set up his residence and de facto seat of Portuguese governance in India.

In January, three separate squadrons were dispatched from Cochin loaded with spices. They stopped in Cannanore to load the remaining cargo and caught the monsoon winds on their homebound trip to Lisbon.

Fernão and his comrades had all taken part in the loading of the cargo and preparing the ships for the long journey. In addition, the construction project to complete Fort Sant' Angelo continued unabated. Fernão marveled at the design. The fortress was triangular and covered 12 acres. Its location provided natural protection on two sides by steep rocky cliffs facing the sea. The landward side facing the north was protected by a moat, wall, and three bastions. The construction material was laterite stones excavated from the moat, tanks, and wells. The moat received its water from the sea and functioned as a drainage system. Double wide ramparts provided ample room to patrol on top and allowed for construction of jail cells below. The main entrance on the north end was blocked by a moat and only passable by using a drawbridge. Once crossed, one had to navigate up a narrow zig-zag passage protected by parallel walls and bastions. The main gate had two wooden teak doors covered with sharp iron spikes. Inside the fortress and surrounded by an inner moat, an elevated structure like a citadel, was constructed, and from the ground level it resembled a ship. The structure was reserved for the senior captain. It had a domical watchtower on the eastern side and an underground passage below. The roof was tiled and provided extra cooling. The warehouse or factory was located to the rear of the captain's quarters.

It was now February 1506, and the Magalhães brothers along with the Serrão brothers had been stationed in Cannanore for over three months. The Magalhães brothers were assigned duty for inspecting arriving vessels and bartering deals with local merchants for the Portuguese factory. The harvest for pepper and other spices was reaped from January to February, ill-timed for the Portuguese fleets needing to catch the monsoon winds. Thus, the procurement and storage of the goods was necessary in the factory warehouses and would be loaded on the next fleets returning in November.

Fernão and Diogo were in the jetty of Mappila Bay inspecting the incoming merchant vessels for quality spices and were to report back to the warehouse agent their findings. Diogo was taking notes of inventories on a parchment.

Fernão observed a white man dressed as a Muslim briskly walking toward them. 'Gentlemen, where is the fortress of the Portuguese?'

Fernão caught his Italian accent. 'You are Italian?'

'Yes, praised be to God.'

'Do you live here?' Diogo asked.

'In Calicut, to the south,' he replied, then turned his head nervously toward a proa with two Moors pointing in his direction. 'Please take me to your captain.'

'Why?' Fernão asked. 'You are dressed as a Moor, and we do not know you.'

'I have news of an imminent attack on your forces.'

The Magalhães brothers looked at one another and nodded.

'Very well,' Fernão said. 'But if you are lying, you will suffer.'

The three walked up a long outdoor stairway from the beach toward the fort's northern end. The two Moors rowed toward shore and began shouting at the merchants in the harbor.

'Who are those men in the proa?' Diogo asked.

'Let me explain,' the Italian said. 'I have been living incognito as a Muslim holy man in Calicut. One day I feigned sickness and convinced my Moor host the air was bad for me and desired to visit Cannanore. He obliged and sent me here under the care of two Persian merchants. But now they must suspect I only wished to escape to your fortress.'

The trio crossed the drawbridge, then up the zig-zag path to the main gate. The guard looked curiously at the white man in Muslim clothing.

'Do not be alarmed Pedro,' Fernão said. 'This man has vital information. We need to see the captain-major now.'

'I need to get my report over to the warehouse clerk,' Diogo said. 'He has been expecting it. I will join you later.'

Fernão nodded.

Diogo turned and walked off to the factory.

In the captain's citadel, Fernão interrupted Dom Lourenço's breakfast. Captain Serrão and the garrison commander—de Brito were dining in company.

The Italian man in Muslim garb fell to his knees in front of Dom Lourenço. 'Sir, I commend myself to you to save me, for I am a Christian.'

'Magalhães, who is this?' Lourenço asked.

'I only know he claims to know of an attack,' Fernão responded.

All in the room stared at the stranger.

Meanwhile, the Arab merchants in the bay went into a loud uproar as news of his escape spread.

Hearing the shouting, Lourenço led the men up to the watchtower. He yelled to the gunners on the ramparts: 'Ready the guns!'

Bombardiers scrambled to load the artillery. After a tense standoff, the crowd finally dispersed. No harm had ensued.

'Who are you?' Lourenço asked. 'And how have you caused such a commotion?'

'I have news of an impending attack on the Portuguese armada.'

Lourenço turned to him intrigued, yet with suspicion. 'Attack? Tonight?

'Soon. An army is training as we speak. In Calicut.'

'Come with me—everyone,' Lourenço ordered.

The entourage followed the captain-major into a secret chamber in the citadel, often employed for council with senior officers and at times prisoner interrogation. Lourenço nodded at the rectangular table constructed of teak wood and everyone seated themselves in chairs around it. Lourenço himself remained standing.

'Now, who are you?'

'Lodovico di Varthema from Bologna, Italy.'

'And why the Muslim attire?'

'A disguise. I escaped captivity from Calicut and now—as you see—word has spread even to Cannanore. I know two brothers from Milan—Italian Christians—who are trapped in Calicut. They have been forced against their will to forge 500-small cannon for the Moors. These brothers João-Maria and Pedro Antonio are in your service. They have relayed to me news that a mighty armada has been assembling and I have also seen them amassing troops on shore. They are in preparation to destroy your fleet and assume control of the coast. The Zamorin of Calicut has sought aid from the Sultan of Cairo and summoned a war council of all the regional Muslim leaders. They all know very well that your fleet is depleted. They sense weakness.'

Lourenço chewed his lip, placed his hands on his hips, and turned to his men. 'He speaks the truth on this point. We recently sent three of our large cargo vessels back to Lisbon loaded with treasure and spice, and the coming monsoon season will prevent any reinforcements. We have only 11 vessels left for patrol.' He paced the floor in thought.

Lourenço stopped and looked at Varthema. 'But how can I know you are real?' He took a seat across from Varthema and stared deep into his eyes. 'Who are you, really?'

'It is a long story.'

'We have a long time,' Lourenço said with all seriousness.

Varthema squirmed in his chair for the entire afternoon but answered each of Lourenço's questions in detail. It was the details, some of which Lourenço and the others knew, that began to win their trust in the unusual stranger. The day passed quickly, as Varthema rattled off story after story. Each one piqued Lourenço's interest, and most fed Fernão's growing desire to explore the world.

He spoke to them in Italian, Portuguese, Arabic, Persian, and knew many other languages in various degrees. He also insisted he was a devout Christian. Lourenço brought in Samuel Levi to verify his linguistic veracity, and a priest to confirm any stated religious knowledge.

'I am a Christian and a soldier,' Varthema said. 'My role as a master cannon founder and bombardier have been tested in numerous wars.' He sketched a schematic for construction of a cannon, and listed exact quantities of materials needed, along with instructions for forging both iron and bronze cannons.

Captain Serrão looked over the papers then nodded to Lourenço and said, 'Looks about right.'

Varthema continued his tale, 'I left Italy near the end of 1502 in my quest of knowledge and adventure. You see—I have this insatiable drive to learn about new lands and customs—new species of animal, flora, and fauna. I have little time or patience for reading second-hand accounts from books, and less for hearsay. I need to witness with my own eyes—touch with my own hands.' Fernão's eyes met with Varthema's for just a moment, and he felt the presence of a kindred spirit.

'Of course, I must be honest,' Varthema said. 'The rewards of treasure and fame have not escaped my attention.' His demeanor soured as he reflected. 'But there is a price. I had to leave my wife and children behind for many years with no assurance of return. Yet, my desire compelled me, like a siren call.' Varthema's honesty and familiar quest of adventure, riches, and fame resonated deep with all in the room, especially a young Fernão Magalhães.

'I sailed first to Alexandria,' Varthema continued. 'Then upriver to Cairo. What a magnificent city, as big as Rome, only populated in greater numbers. The inhabitants are Moors and Mamluks. Egypt is ruled by a Grand Sultan and served by the Mamluks, who in turn, rule over the Moors. They control territories all the way up to Syria. The pyramids near Cairo are a wonder to behold—such mysterious origins.' Varthema paused to drink water from a cup.

'From Egypt I sailed to Beirut, Tripoli, Aleppo, and finally Damascus. There I remained for some weeks, and acquired a better knowledge of the local Arabic, and the tenets of Islam.' Varthema spoke some Qur'an passages to prove his proficiency. Lourenço glanced over to Samuel.

'His Arabic is adequate,' Samuel said.

Varthema smiled, and continued, 'It was in Damascus that I was able to purchase a position in a Mamluk garrison, with the help of a renegade Christian captain. He provisioned me with a horse and weapons. I called myself Yunus. It was early April of 1503 when our unit was assigned to escort a caravan to the *Hajj* in Arabia. I considered it a divine providence for this opportunity.' Varthema winked at the priest. 'We journeyed through the desert forty days encountering hostiles in the thousands. The Arabs are small in stature with dark tawny skin and long stiff black hair. Their voices to my ear, sound feminine. They come down from the mountains to rob the caravans, much like their prophet had done in the past.'

Varthema took another sip of water, then continued, 'One day we confronted an army of these nomads—we estimated 24,000 perhaps. They demanded we pay for their water. We replied water was given by God. Our answer was insufficient for them, and a fight erupted. Our unit fortified itself with a circular wall of camels, with the merchants remaining inside. We were besieged for two days and nights. Without water, our captain decided to consult with the Moor merchants in our caravan. They agreed to pay the Arabs 1,200 ducats of gold. They took the money but then replied that 10,000 ducats would not even be enough to pay for their water. We realized they wanted much more besides money, so the next morning our captain prepared us for war. The caravan went ahead and our unit of 300 Mamluk warriors remained behind. The Arabs charged bareback and naked upon their horses. Near us, they killed a woman and man with arrows. But the Mamluks are superior fighters and slew 1,600 Arabs.'

Lourenço grinned with approval. 'What you say rings true. Master your fear and implement a sound plan of attack with superior weaponry.'

Varthema smiled and continued, 'Once we got to Al Medinah, we visited the tomb of Muhammad.

The priest's jaw dropped, and he stammered. 'You—you actually visited the second holiest site of Islam? Few—if any—non-believer has ever done so.'

'Yes,' Varthema replied. 'The prophet is buried within a square mosque, about 100 paces long by 80 paces wide. The roof is arched and there are over 400 columns made of burnt stone, all whitened. On one side of the arches there are 3,000 lighted lamps burning. It is a remarkable place.'

Varthema glanced toward the priest. 'And we continued to escort the caravan for the *Hajj* and visited the holiest site of Islam, the Kabah of Mecca.'

The priest's eyes opened wide.

'Imagine this marvel,' Varthema said. 'In the center of Mecca lies an exquisite temple, as large as the

Colosseum of Rome. Likewise, it is also round, but instead of large stones it is constructed of burned brick. There are many doors and arches around the perimeter. Upon entering, one descends 10 or 12 steps of marble. The walls are covered with gold and under the arches stands at least 5,000 persons who sell all kinds of perfumes. Within the temple there is another square temple in the center, five or six paces, long. It is covered by an enormous cloth of black silk, attached on each of the four corners by large rings. The door of the temple is silver. During the *Hajj*, massive crowds rotate counter-clockwise around this temple they call "Kabah.""

Varthema scratched his long black beard. 'I found it strange how they would stop to kiss or touch a certain blackish colored stone that was imbedded into the temple's eastern corner. It resembled a meteor or piece of lava rock. As they neared the stone they would scream, Allahu Akbar then kiss and rub the black stone.'

'Why do you think they do that?' Fernão asked.

'They follow the custom that Muhammad had practiced,' Varthema replied. 'I met some of the desert Bedouin. They say that most of the Arabs used to worship stones. They would rub, touch, and speak to the god residing within the stone. They say Muhammad's father venerated a stone called Allah, and that his own name—Abdallah, meaning "Slave of Allah—represented his devotion. All acknowledge that Muhammad destroyed 360 idols, many of which were unhewn stones and others resembling living forms and represented every day of the year. *But* others claim in secret that Muhammad preserved his father's black stone in the Kabah—the high-god of Mecca—and originally a moon god. That is why Muhammad continued the custom of kissing and touching the black stone, and then addressing it with the words—Allah is greatest.'

'Pagan infidels,' de Brito, the garrison commander, remarked in disgust.

'What say you friar?' Varthema asked. 'A form of idol worship?'

'Well, I suppose one could view it that way,' the priest said. 'They also call us idolaters and infidels.'

'Whether idol worship or not, it seems peculiar, does it not?' Varthema asked.

Everyone in the room nodded.

'How did you go undiscovered?' Lourenço asked.

'I *was* discovered. One day in Mecca a Moor approached me, studied my face, and asked me where I was from. I said that I was a Moor. He replied: *In te chedeab* which is "You are not telling the truth."'

Lourenço glanced at Samuel, who nodded, indicating the Arabic was correct.

Varthema saw this, smiled, and continued, 'I insisted that I was a Moor, but he would not believe me. He took me to his house where he began to speak Italian and claimed to have visited Genoa and Venice. He provided proof of his visits and told me he was a Persian on pilgrimage for the *Hajj* and his name was Cazazionor. I confessed myself to be a Roman and said I had converted as a Mamluk in Cairo, to which he seemed pleased, and treated me with honor thereafter.' Varthema looked over the men with a sly grin. 'I feigned commonality with Cazazionor to secure safe passage to India. With an innocent query I asked why the trade goods had not arrived in the famous emporium of Mecca, such a well-known market for jewels and spices. He confided to me that the King of Portugal was to blame and detailed how the Portuguese navy had blockaded the trade routes. Naturally, I feigned disgust for such hostilities by the King of

Portugal. Furthermore, I confessed my skills as the greatest maker of mortars in the world, and stated I wished to employ my skills in service of the Moors in India. The Moor was greatly pleased and aided me to escape my unit and voyage onward to India.'

'Why did you offer service in India?' Lourenço asked?

'As I stated from the beginning my purpose,' Varthema said. 'I wished to explore the world. I mentioned to Cazazionor that the Portuguese were establishing a presence in India with new fleets and shipping warehouses. And I could assist the Moor resistance with my skills in forging weapons.'

'How did you know we were established in India?'

'I listen to the merchants. Your kingdom's reputation is known throughout the Red Sea and beyond.'

'A clever spy, enough for today,' Lourenço said. 'We will resume in the morning. Take him to the cell block. Dismissed.'

Fernão and Serrão escorted Varthema to one of the five cells below the ramparts and a guard locked him inside.

Meanwhile, de Brito followed the captain-major to his office. He asked, 'What if this Varthema is a double agent?'

'We will continue our interrogations until we know for certain,' Lourenço replied. 'I am testing him. We let him talk and take notice of any discrepancies in his story. I cannot trust his military intelligence until his honesty is verified.'

16

After breakfast the next morning, Captain Serrão approached Dom Lourenço and advised, 'I believe it could be useful that Magalhães attend another round of interrogations. He has served prior in the India House with access to all our top-secret naval operations and knowledge. He may be able to—'

'Notice any inconsistencies in Varthema's accounts,' Lourenço added, following the logic. 'Very well.'

Later, Fernão quietly entered the chamber and stood near the doorway as Ludovico di Varthema was further interrogated by Dom Lourenço.

'And you claim to have boarded a merchant vessel of the Moors at Zida eventually bound for India and Persia?' Lourenço asked.

'Yes. After I had left my host Cazazionor in Mecca I set out on my journey via Zida. And I will tell you it was a journey of peril and seduction.' Varthema's mischievous grin and animated expressions enticed his audience. 'After some time in the Red Sea we anchored in the great trading port of Aden. The capital of southern Arabia, and the strongest city that has ever been seen on level ground. Around the perimeter, there are large mountains with five castles built upon them. The two open ends are closed off by two fortified walls. Aden is about a mile or so in diameter . . . nearly a perfect circle. I have suspected it may sit on the base of a dormant volcano.'

Lourenço raised an eyebrow. 'A strong position.'

'I suppose so,' Varthema replied as he continued his tale. 'Every vessel arriving in Aden is inspected by officers of the sultan, who is the main ruler. The inspectors inquire from where the ship has come, when they have left, details of cargo and how many passengers on board. Once all relevant information has been obtained, the vessel is detained for clearance; masts, sails, rudders and anchors are removed and taken into the city until all duties are paid to the sultan.' Varthema sat back in his chair. 'I shall not tire you of mundane details. Perhaps my own story will inform and entertain.' Varthema looked over his audience. Dom Lourenço gestured with an extended hand and nod to continue.

Varthema smiled. 'On the following day after arriving to Aden, while awaiting the duties to be paid by the ship captain, I visited the port market. One of the Moors from the boat followed and eyed me with suspicion, perhaps due to my light complexion. He began shouting at me: "You are a Christian dog and son of a dog." Some Moors in the market took notice and hauled me off to the palace where the vice-sultan had taken charge. The sultan himself was off reviewing an army at Rhada in preparation for a battle. They claimed I was a Christian spy and consulted whether I should immediately be put to death. But, as the sultan never put any one to death, they held me in the Aden prison.

On my third day of captivity, an angry mob of 60 armed Moors stormed the palace claiming I was a spy and called for retribution. They were previously on two vessels that had been captured by a Portuguese fleet and had escaped by swimming. Fortunately, the guards locked the palace doors from within and the vice-sultan refused their request of execution. I remained in custody for 65 days with 18-pound weights of iron on my feet.' Varthema rubbed his ankle at the memory. 'I still feel them on a cold night.'

'After 65 days, the sultan sent for me. It was an eight-day journey by camel, and I was still bound with those iron weights. I arrived at the city of Rhada and was presented before the sultan. He asked me where I was from and what I was planning to do. My reply was that I was a Roman and had become a Mamluk in Cairo. I told him of my journeys to Medina and Mecca and that I had come to see his highness; because throughout Syria and at Mecca, and at Medina, it was said that the sultan was a saint, and if he were a saint, he must know that I was not a spy of the Christians, and that I was a good Moor and his slave. The sultan tested me. He ordered me to say their creed, *La ilah illah Allah; Muhammed Rasul Allah*. I stammered. I could not pronounce the words at all. Perhaps it was the will of God, or simply the fear which had overtaken me. I do not know. The sultan was not pleased with my response and threw me into prison with extra guards. For three months my rations were a loaf of millet in the morning and one in the evening. Six would barely suffice me!' Varthema looked around for a sympathetic response but was met with blank stares. He sat up in his chair, coughed, and changed the subject.

'You may be interested in the sultan's military. Two days after he imprisoned me, I was informed the sultan had fielded an army of 80,000 to wage war against the Sultan of Sana. Included in his army were 3,000 cavalry, sons of Christians, as black as Moors. They were purchased from Prester John and trained in arms from the age of eight or nine. These black warriors constituted the sultan's personal guard and regarded as more valuable than his army of 80,000.'

'Prester John?' Fernão asked. At the mention of his name, everyone in the room leaned forward, for any news of the enigmatic persona of Prester John was most welcome.

'What do you know of Prester John?' Lourenço pried further.

'Only what I have heard in my travels—much as yourselves. I would assume rumors and legends. At least until I visited a port of Ethiopia. I was informed of a great king living there, called Prester John.' Varthema stared each man in the eyes to enforce his veracity. 'I am certain he exists.'

Lourenço arched his back and twisted his neck. 'So, how were you finally released?'

'The sultan's wife had an unbridled lust for my body.' Varthema grinned and winked at the priest, who in turn looked at him coldly. 'I concocted a plot to feign madness. Like King David, remember?' Varthema turned to the priest and then to Samuel. 'First Book of Samuel. Chapter?'

'Twenty-one,' the priest said.

'Verses ten to fifteen,' Samuel said, smiling. He looked awkwardly at the priest, who remained expressionless, so Samuel continued. 'David found himself in the enemy territory of Gath and his identity was suspected. Thinking quickly, he feigned madness in front of King Achish by making marks on the doors of the gate and drooling saliva over his beard. It worked. The King wished nothing to do with a madman and sent him away.'

'Yes!' Varthema replied to Samuel's knowledge of the scriptures. 'Well, I created my own concoction of madness.' He seemed quite proud of this. 'It worked to some degree for they allowed me to roam about, albeit with my chains and an assigned guard. But it was an exhausting task. During the first days I played mad,

211

50 or 60 children followed and threw stones at me. They cried out, "madman" and pummeled me with stones and I reciprocated in turn.

'Now, one of the sultan's three wives was with 12 or 13 of her damsels, all black and beautiful. They enjoyed watching my antics from the royal palace overlooking the city streets below. The queen with her young ladies remained at her window from morning until evening to see me and talk with me. Merchants and other men of the city mocked and ridiculed me as daily I stripped off my shirt and pranced about. The queen took great delight to see me in this state and would not let me stray from her sight. She sent me good food and my body recovered from its feeble state. The queen had even suggested her own bizarre ideas to amplify my displays of madness. But one day, I was out acting my usual part, when I encountered one of my jailors. He was a vile man and uttered the customary local insult, "Christian dog, son of a dog." I threw some stones at him. The children and the jailor came at me again with stones, one of which was quite large and bruised my chest. I hastened to my prison, but due to the ankle weights, I was too slow to avoid another blow into my side, which caused me great pain. I could have easily avoided both stones but had to maintain the illusion of my insanity. I blocked myself in the prison by piling large stones in the doorway. For two days and nights I ate or drank nothing. The queen was quite worried by my absence and had the doors broken open. The jailors knew I was very hungry and gave me ground marble and said it was sugar. Others offered grapes filled with dirt, but they said it was salt. I ate everything and continued playing mad.' Varthema scanned the room. All were hanging upon his every word, amazed. 'That same day, some merchants of the city brought two men of some religious reputation who were highly esteemed and who dwelt in mountains. I was summoned before these men. The merchants asked the two holy men if I appeared holy or mad. One declared I was holy and the other claimed I was mad. They disputed for over an hour until it became unbearable to listen to them. I stood in front of them, raised my shirt and peed on them both. They ran away and cried loudly, "He is mad, he is mad, he is not holy." Now, the queen and her maidens had been watching from her window. They laughed hard and exclaimed, "By the good God, by the hand of Muhammad, this is the most capital fellow in the world.""

Fernão and Captain Serrão grinned at one another and tried to maintain their composure. Finally, Dom Lourenço burst out in laughter, and the whole room followed suit. Lourenço gave a slap to Varthema's shoulder 'For the heavens above sir. In the matters of acting mad, you have indeed surpassed the deeds of even King David.' The laughter in the room continued unabated. Even the stoic priest chuckled.

Varthema, with some pleasure, waited for the laughter to subside before he continued. 'The next morning, I found asleep the jailor who had injured me with the two large stones. A rage came over me and I could not resist the urge at retribution. I seized him by the hair, pushed my knees into his stomach and punched him in the face until he was covered in blood. I left him for dead. I wish—I do wish that I could have forgiven—but at the time it seemed impossible.'

'Nonsense man,' de Brita exclaimed. 'A well-deserved punishment, indeed.'

The other men in the room nodded in agreement. The Portuguese warrior caste were not averse to administer retribution.

Varthema waited a moment then continued his saga. 'Soon after this event, the queen summoned me to reside in the palace. My room was unlocked but I was still bound with chains around my ankles. It was not long at all before the queen called to me and asked if I was hungry. I was, of course, famished and replied, "yes." I rose to my feet, then went to her in my chains and shirt. She said, "Ludovico, not like in that manner. Take off your shirt." I answered, "O madam, I am not mad now." Then she answered me, "By God, I know well that you never went mad, on the contrary, that you are the best-witted man that was ever seen." In order to please her, I pulled off my shirt but always kept it in front for modesty. She could not resist me, contemplating me for over two hours as if I were a nymph. She uttered a lamentation: "Oh God, you have created this man bright like the sun. Would to God that this man was my husband. Would to God that I might have a son like this man." And after these words she wept continually and sighed. She passed her hands *all* over me. The next night the queen came to me along with two of her young ladies to entice me again. "Ludovico, would you like that I should come and stay a little while with you?" I replied, "No; and said that it was quite enough that I was in chains, without her causing me to have my head cut off." I never consented, never yielded. I knew I would be hunted down like a dog and lose both my body and soul. I wept all night, recommending myself to God.'

The priest gave a slight nod as sign of approval.

'When the sultan finally returned,' Varthema said. 'I was taken before him and questioned. The queen pleaded upon my behalf, and I was given liberty by the sultan.' Varthema looked over the Portuguese. They stared in rapt attention, hanging on his every word. 'All good?' he said. 'All settled and free? Not quite. I saw the queen in private conversation with the sultan and inherently distrusted her intentions. Later, she brought me to her chamber and kissed me all over, at least 100 times, and gave me nice foods to eat. I stopped her and demanded my freedom. Her response was: "Hold your peace, madman, you do not know what God has ordained for you." I spent the next 15 days holding off her lustful enticements.'

'Like Joseph and Potiphar's wife?' Samuel commented. 'From the Torah . . . Genesis, chapter 39. Remember? Potiphar, the captain of the guard to the mighty Pharaoh of Egypt had a lustful wife. She daily seduced and pleaded for the handsome Joseph to sleep with her. But the godly Joseph refused to betray his master.'

'But remember,' Varthema said. 'Joseph was accused by her and thrown into prison.'

Samuel, not sure how to respond, scratched his beard.

Varthema continued, 'As for myself, I was tired of prison but was still a slave of the queen. I had to find a way out. I feigned sickness for eight days and then informed the queen that I made a vow to God and Muhammad that I would visit a holy man who was at Aden, whom many claimed had the ability to perform miracles. Fortunately, the queen acquiesced, and even gave me provisions and money to journey to Aden. I pretended to be cured of my ailment by that holy man. Later, I wrote to the queen and explained how God had been so merciful to heal me and now I wished to see her entire marvelous kingdom. I spoke with a captain in the port of Aden and informed him that I could reward him well for a passage to India. He said the next ship would not leave until the next month and would first stop in Persia. That is why I wrote the letter to the queen. I needed a delay to make my escape . . . and thus I did escape.'

Dom Lourenço paused for a moment and said, 'Your tales are quite detailed and elaborate, so much so that I dare to believe they are true.' 'Please continue. Where did you escape to?'

Ludovico di Varthema scratched his beard. 'We were supposed to sail the Persian Gulf; but strong winds forced us to the coast of Africa, Zeila and Berbera. Eventually we sailed across the Arabian Sea to Diu in Gujurat and eventually back across to the Gulf and spent some time on land in Persia. Remember the merchant I had met in Mecca? Well, in Shiraz, Persia, I came across the very same Moor—Cazazionor. I do think this was a divine providence, for we forged a bond as partners and friends. He even wanted to groom me as a future son-in-law. He still called me "Yunus" and still believed I was a Muslim convert. We traveled over much of the world, as I will elaborate.'

Varthema for some time recounted his travels throughout the coast of India and into the interior regions. He discussed political structures, regional tactical warfare, religion, caste systems, yogi practitioners, and even a Christian sect claiming to originate from a visitation by Saint Thomas in the first century.

Fernão and all the men were completely taken by the world of mystery and adventure and Varthema seemed so easily to bring life to them. 'After leaving India,' he said, 'We ventured 14 days across the sea to a place called Tenasserim, ruled by the Ayutthaya Kingdom.' Varthema then presented a detailed account of the Tenasserim (Burma-Myanmar) military and economic structure, which turned out to be a valuable resource to his Portuguese audience. He further discussed the oddly dressed monks and their customs.

'Have you heard of the funeral rites called *Sati*?' Varthema asked. 'It is practiced in Tennasserim and other places.'

Everyone shook their heads.

'Let me explain,' Varthema said. 'A recent widow and her relations will accompany her to the location where her dead husband has been burnt. She is dressed in her finest clothing and jewels. Her family digs a pit about the height of a human and they plant four or five poles around its perimeter. They tie silken cloths to the poles and then set them all on fire. The wife attends a great feast and gorges herself on betel until she loses her wits. Instruments of the town sound loudly. Men clothed like devils carry fire in their mouths and offer sacrifice to a deity called, Deumo. The wife and other women dance in rapturous enticement. She entreats the said men to pray for her to be accepted by the god, Deumo, as his own. Finally, the woman reaches a state of frenzy and believes herself ready to be accepted into the heavens above. Then, of her own free will, she runs to snatch the burning cloth and leaps into the fire pit. Her own family pelts her with sticks and balls of pitch to speed her death. If the wife refuses to sacrifice herself then her family would be put to death, and she would be esteemed as a public prostitute.'

The Portuguese shook their heads and muttered in revulsion upon such paganism. Varthema noted their disgust. 'Strange indeed. But there is so much more.' A wide grin crossed Varthema's face as he dove deep into the profane to unveil taboo subjects.

'One day, in Tennaserim, we came across a large multitude gathered around, watching a cockfight. Merchants had laid down bets up to even 100 ducats.

We stayed for almost five hours watching two cocks with spurs of bone attached to their legs bludgeon themselves to a bloody death. The merchants argued among themselves as to which one died first, in order to claim their wagers. During this period, four merchants in the distance had been carefully observing us and often pointed in our direction. They approached and asked us if we were strangers. We replied to the affirmative. One of the merchants said, "come to my house, for we are great friends of strangers." We followed him to his house where he served us tea. He then spoke to us: "My friends, 15 days hence I wish to bring home my wife, and one of you shall sleep with her the first night; and shall deflower her for me."

The men gasped at this, and Varthema noticed the shock on the faces of his reserved audience. The priest blushed.

'Needless to say,' he quickly added. 'We were quite appalled and quite ashamed upon such a request. We were hesitant, not quite sure if they were mocking us and playing us as fools. But an interpreter for the merchant assured us this was the custom of his country. He explained that it was customary for a virgin wife to be deflowered by white men whether Christian or Moor. One of those in our company had affirmed this was true, and my companion, Cazazioner, offered his services for the said task. It was exactly 15 days later when the merchant brought home his young wife of 15 years and my companion performed the requested deed. But once the task was completed, he would not be allowed to return, even if the lady desired. Any violation of this custom would ensure a quick demise.'

Varthema's smile turned to a frown. 'And woe unto those who transgress in these lands. They employ the same horrors of capital punishment as they do in

Calicut, and that of the accursed Turks—impalement. I watched one such sentence of death carried out. A young man was forced to lie on his belly with his arms and legs bound securely. A long wooden stake is hammered up his buttocks by a giant club, over and over until driven through the stomach or shoulders. They raise up the stake and plant it into the dirt. If the vitals are not severed the poor wretch suffers in agonizing torment for days until finally expiring.' Fernão and the others slowly rose to their feet, and stood with mouths open at such a bizarre, sadistic custom.

'Forgive me if these digressions are too much,' Varthema said. 'I shall focus on more mundane details.'

The men sat back down in their chairs.

Varthema continued. 'We remained a few more weeks in Tenasserim, then sailed northwest to Benghalla (Bengal). Here we met some Christian merchants who said they were from a city named Sarnau in Siam (Thailand) and subjects of the great Khan of Cathay. They had brought silken goods, aloes-wood, benzoin, and musk for trade. They dressed in a jerkin made of folds, and the sleeves quilted with cotton. They wore on their heads a long cap made of red cloth. They do not wear shoes and attire themselves with breeches of silk laden with jewels. Their caps are also covered with precious jewels. They follow the same Christian rites as us. After a long conversation with these men from the east, my companion, Cazazionor, showed him his merchandise, among which were beautiful branches of coral. When they saw this precious treasure of coral, they promised they could secure for us a great trade in a far-off city. My partner was pleased and desired to depart immediately. They said in two days a ship would sail towards Pegu and we were invited to attend with them.

We embarked along with some other Persian merchants. Our friendship with these Christians from the east grew and remained steadfast throughout our journey. From Benghalla (Bengal) we sailed across a gulf to the south and after 1,000 miles arrived at the city of Pegu (Burma-Myanmar). The king of this city is a pagan, and their customs are like Tenasserim. The only merchandise of these people is jewels, which come from a city in the hills called Capellan. Upon our arrival, the King of Pegu had been away on a war campaign against the King of Ava. But 20 days later, after his victorious battle, the king returned to Pegu and we were presented before him. He wore jewels over his entire body. His legs are covered with gold rings, all full of the most precious rubies. Likewise, his arms, fingers, and toes were all clad with an assortment of beautiful stones. His earlobes hang down a half palm from the great weight of the jewels he wears there. The reflecting light off the jewels makes him shine like the sun. When the king saw our trove of precious corals, he was astonished and greatly pleased. The king confessed he had no money due to his two-year war against the King of Ava, but he said if we were willing, he could trade for rubies. However, the Christians with us advised us to offer him the corals at no cost. My Persian friend, Cazazionor, told the king we wished no recompense. Upon hearing of this generosity, the king replied: "I know that the Persians are very liberal, but I never saw one so liberal as this man." He swore by God and the devil that he would verify which would be the most liberal, he or a Persian. He summoned a servant to bring him a box, two palms in length, and covered in gold. It was full of rubies on the exterior and interior. When he opened it, there were six compartments, each full of varied rubies.'

Fernão and the Portuguese leaned forward in rapt attention. They listened carefully to every detail from an eyewitness account of the vast treasures of the far east. Varthema continued his tantalizing account. 'The king set the box before us and told us to take what we desired. My companion Cazazionor stepped forward and replied: "O, sir, you show me so much kindness, that by the faith which I show to Muhammad I make you a present of all these things. And know, sir, that I do not travel about the world to collect property, but only to see different people and different customs." The king answered: "I cannot conquer you in liberality but take this which I give you." He then reached in and took a portion of precious stones from each compartment and dropped about 200 of them into my companion's hands. The king said: "Take these for the liberality you have exercised towards me." And then he gave each of the two Christians two rubies, which were estimated at 1,000 ducats each, and those given to my Persian companion was estimated at about 100,000 ducats.'

Fernão's mind raced with the thoughts of vast treasures and exotic lands. Varthema's tales intrigued and inspired the men in like-minded thoughts. Varthema was one of the earliest witnesses of what opportunities lay ahead for those who dared to risk their lives in quest for wealth and fame.

Varthema continued recounting his epic journey. They embarked on a vessel for Malacca a major trading hub in the Malay peninsula. Soon after, they crossed the Malaccan Strait and anchored in the port city of Pedir on the northern coast of Sumatra. He described in detail the goods such as long pepper and varieties of perfumed woods. Pedir was a major commercial hub, so busy that 500 money changers occupied one whole city street. The two Christians from Sarnau wished to return to their home in Siam (Thailand)—but Cazazionor—with some cunning stories of wealth to be gained, persuaded them to continue their mission to the fabled spice islands. Two flat bottom boats were purchased with Cazazionor's rubies.

'We set sail from Pedir on a general course to the east,' Varthema said. 'We meandered through numerous islands, until after 15 days, we reached the Banda islands, the world's major source of nutmeg and mace. Varthema described the trade in precious spices from the Bandas.

'You claim to have reached the spice islands?' Fernão asked. 'Europe has no records of any travels to these islands.'

'Indeed. I may be the first European to provide an account.' Varthema opened his palms and straightened his arms and said, 'Such wonders to behold. We sailed to the north and discovered islands rich in cloves.'

'How rich?' Lourenço asked.

'The best quality cloves and nutmeg,' Varthema replied. 'Worth a fortune. The merchants trade much to the Malacca trade hub. Then they are shipped to India, Red Sea, then overland to Europe. A long route.'

'But if there were a direct route to Europe, would it not cut the cost and provide better quality of spice?' Fernão asked.

Lourenço arched his back. 'Indeed. We need to create our own shipping routes. What is the status of power in Malacca?'

'The sultan of Malacca is very powerful,' Varthema said. 'He commands a large army and has fortifications.'

'Interesting,' Lourenço said.

'Did you sail further east,' Fernão asked. 'Did you discover anything else?'

'We did not sail further east and decided to return to India. We left in June of 1505, but by another route. The two Christians aided our navigation to Borneo and then we changed to a larger vessel. We sailed onward south of Java.

Varthema arched his back. 'There was an interesting account I should mention. 'Our two Christian friends were able to translate for Cazazionor as he questioned the captain of our vessel concerning his navigational technique. The pilot used a magnetic compass with index pointing to the north. He used a chart which was all marked with lines, perpendicular and across. Something I had never seen before. My companion asked: "Now that we have lost the north star, how do we steer." The captain showed us four or five stars, among which was one he claimed was opposite to our north star. The captain also told us that on the other side of a certain large island, far to the south, there were some other races of men, who navigate by the same four or five stars. They also claimed that the day in that island does not last more than four hours, and that it was colder than in any other part of the world.'

Varthema paused and looked at the disbelief in the faces of his audience. 'I know—I know,' he said. Both Cazazionor and I thought he was crazy at first. But the captain was quite skilled and well regarded. He had no reason to tell fanciful stories.'

Dom Lourenço looked to Captain Serrão. 'You ever heard of such places?'

'Only rumors and stories of veteran captains.' Serrão said, then turned to Fernão. 'Magalhaes, ever hear of anything like this—perhaps in the India House?'

Fernão reflected a moment. 'I am not sure how much I can divulge.'

Dom Lourenço turned to Fernão and looked him in the eyes. 'A good answer, loyal to the throne. But we only need a little confirmation.'

'I—Well, I will not say how this occurred, but I did see a map once that showed something resembling what our witness has described. Lands far to the south. My memory is foggy on the details, but it very well could be.'

'I too have heard these rumors. Maybe true.' Lourenço grinned. 'We continue tomorrow. I want to know more detail about the friendly and hostile forces on the India coast. We will adjourn for now.'

As they filed out each man gave Varthema a pat on the shoulder. Even the priest had succumbed to his charm and admired his steadfast faith through great temptations and said so. Samuel had much enjoyed reciting in tandem the Hebrew scriptures as Varthema told his tales.

The next morning, Varthema focused his testimony on the India Malabar coast and specific to its militia. He had witnessed the Moor and Turk vessels amassing every day in Calicut, and Hindu auxiliaries were recruited every day from the mainland. Varthema provided estimates of the enemy armada, including types of ships, artillery, and numbers of men. He provided such candid answers that Lourenço now considered him a new ally and friend. But before any serious plans were to be finalized, he would have to have the approval of his father—Portuguese Governor of India, Dom Almeida.

Captain Serrão was given a sealed letter to deliver to Almeida concerning the intelligence delivered by Varthema. While sailing in the large galley, Varthema entertained the Magalhães brothers and Francisco Serrão with more personal accounts of exotic lands and enticements with the lure of vast treasures. At Cochin, Dom Almeida interrogated Varthema and was impressed with his detailed knowledge of the enemy Islamic fleet preparing to attack the Portuguese. Varthema's charm and candid desire for a Christian victory were enough for Almeida to send him along on the galley back to Cannanore along with a return letter to his son. Almeida agreed with his son and commended him to fight for the faith and his honor. In gratitude to Varthema, orders were also given to pay for the two Christian spies in Calicut—João-Maria and Pedro Antonio—to be freed.

17

Cannanore – March 16, 1506

A fleet of eight caravels, two war galleys, and a brigantine lie anchored in Mapilla Bay—harbor of Cannanore. Dom Lourenço stood at the rails of the flagship facing his naval force of 800 men standing at attention on the jetty below.

'Men, we have received news of an impending attack,' Lourenço said loudly. 'An armada of Moors and Turks from Ponani, Calicut, Kappatt, Pantalayini Kollam, and Darmapattanam have gathered their vessels in Calicut. In addition, the Zamorin has supplied his own forces of Hindu warriors. It is estimated, they have 100 large ships of war and nearly an equal number of large proas.'

Fernão had seen these double outrigger proas in action. With their two triangular sails, fore and aft, they could be easily rotated and tilted to efficiently tack in the wind. With such speed and agility, they could be formidable.

Lourenço grabbed the ship rail and leaned forward. 'My brothers in arms, we have news of a great injustice inflicted upon our brothers in Christ. Acts of aggression have taken place in Calicut.'

Fernão turned to Francisco and Diogo with a raised eyebrow. The two responded with a shrug, unaware of the recent news.

Lourenço continued, 'Two of our Christian spies have been betrayed for a bounty of 100 ducats. They dispatched 200 infidels to murder our brothers—João-Maria and Pedro Antonio. They fought back valiantly; killed 6 and wounded 40, before they were struck down by iron projectiles. These infidel savages cut open the throats of our brethren and with their hands drank their blood!'

The men responded with gasps and displays of shock.

'That is not all,' he said. 'Another purge ensued. More of our Christian brothers and sisters were brutally robbed of their goods and then duly slaughtered—48 souls!'

Sounds of rage emanated from the Portuguese crews.

'Our Lord was also betrayed,' Lourenço said. 'Gentlemen, brothers, now is the day that we must remember the Passion of Christ and how much pain He endured for our redemption. Now is the day when all our sins will be blotted out. For this I beseech you that we determine to go vigorously against these dogs; for I pray that God will give us this victory and will not choose that His faith should fail.'

Lourenço climbed the stairs to the quarterdeck and stood with a priest holding a large crucifix in his hand. The fleet chaplain spoke a beautiful discourse with great eloquence and exhorted for all to perform the duties they were bound to do. After giving absolution from punishment and sin, the priest exclaimed with a bold voice: 'Now, my sons, let us all go willingly, for God will be with us.' The spiritual oratory even caused men to pray that God would let them die in battle. The Magalhães brothers wiped tears from their eyes as the speech concluded.

Lourenço raised his sword and proclaimed loudly, 'God is with us! God is with us! To your stations men!'

The crews cheered and then hustled to their vessels.

The Portuguese fleet remained 10 miles off the northern end of the shore of Cannanore. Ludovico di

Varthema manned one of the large guns on Dom Lourenço's flagship. The Magalhães and Serrão brothers, along with Samuel Levi, stood at the raised stern of their assigned war galley.

In mid-afternoon, a lookout in the crow's nest of the flagship yelled, 'Sails! Sails!' Fernão held his hand over his eyebrows and squinted. Multitudes of ship masts gradually emerged like a giant forest gliding across the sea. Indeed, a mighty naval fleet approached.

He swallowed hard as countless thousands of enemy forces came into view. Many of the ships had their gunwales outfitted with cotton bales for protection against gunfire. They also had cannon and small artillery similar to the Portuguese. The Moor and Turkish crews were armed with swords, bows, lances, and shields. Many of the enemy were clad in red garments stuffed with cotton. Likewise, they had large caps, bracelets and gloves all stuffed in great pomp.

Fernão pointed to Lourenço's flagship and another caravel steering direct between the two largest Moor vessels, both flanked by their own fleet. The two enemy ships bore great ensigns and signified they carried the captains of the fleet. 'What is he doing?' Fernão asked? 'Only two of our ships attacking the entire enemy armada?'

'Testing their responses, and nerve,' Serrão said.

Just as they passed between the enemy flagships, the two Portuguese war ships saluted them with several mighty artillery discharges from their broadsides. The enemy was rattled and retreated southward.

'The captain-major scared them good,' Francisco said. 'Look at them flee.'

The men all nodded.

The fleet continued to patrol the coast along the north end of Cannanore.

Early in the morning, the enemy fleet reappeared. Captain Serrão and Fernão were at the stern of the galley.

'They have come back for more,' Fernão said.

'Perhaps the winds have forced them back or they wish to re-engage' Serrão replied. 'Let us see what the captain-major does.'

A messenger was sent to ask the captain-major for allowance to pass by on their voyage and that they did not wish to fight. Varthema whispered to Lourenço, 'The Moors often lie. They only wish to pass and take the fort.'

'I am aware,' he whispered in return. Lourenço then said to the messenger, 'Tell your commander: We know what you did to the Christians in Calicut, how they were robbed and slaughtered. Pass, if you can, but first know what sort of people Christians are.'

The Moors promptly responded: 'Our Muhammad will defend us from you Christians.'

Once the messenger returned to their fleet, the enemy armada then proceeded to sail with great fury towards Cannanore. Dom Lourenço waited and allowed them to approach eight miles offshore. On the war galley, Fernão turned to Captain João Serrão then pointed to the enemy fleet. 'Why does the captain-major allow them to sail toward Cannanore?'

Serrão grinned and replied. 'He wants the king of the city to view Portuguese bravery and power, and to instill both respect and dread for those who dare challenge our forces.'

Fernão scratched his beard while pondering the ingenious and bold strategy.

After concluding the midday meal, a propitious wind began to gather in strength.

Captain Lourenço called out: 'Now, up brothers, for now is the time; for we are all good knights!'

The fleet weighed anchor and prepared for battle. Once again, Lourenço sailed for the two largest Moor vessels. The rest of the Portuguese fleet was close behind. Kettledrums, cymbals, and bugles sounded from the enemy fleet—rising in tempo as they drew closer. Lourenço's caravel drew aside one of the two Moor flagships, and the Portuguese threw iron grappling hooks in an attempt to board. Three times the Moors threw off the hooks. The fourth try held firm. With tenacious fury the Portuguese pulled their ship against the Moor warship and the Portuguese spilled over the railings to face off against 600 Moors. Lourenço led the charge with halberd in hand. Varthema remained on board the Portuguese flagship to assist the gunners. From there he was able to witness the ferocious naval battle. With their black swords at the ready, Lourenço's men charged against the Turks and Moors. The Portuguese mariners cut down the enemy like farmers attacking a harvest, littering the deck of the enemy flagship with severed limbs and blood. The Portuguese showed no mercy and gave no quarter. Very soon there was no one else to fight and they stood looking at one another for a moment.

Meanwhile, Captain Serrão and Fernão ordered sails lowered and crews to man the oars. They maneuvered their war galley into the battle, aiming their three-gunned prow at an enemy war vessel. All three cannons fired, two missed but one hit direct into the hull. In moments, the ship began to list. Crews leapt into the sea. An initial blow to the enemy was cheered by the Portuguese crew on their galley.

The victory was short-lived, for the enemy converged upon their lone vessel, now finding themselves surrounded, on all sides, by more than 50 proas. Fernão took a deep breath and stared down the storm of violence approaching. His brother Diogo and Francisco Serrão placed their hands upon the hilts of their black swords, readied for close combat. Turks, Moors, and Hindus filled the air with grappling hooks, and the sheer number of them caught the ship's railing. The enemy crew pulled the ships together for boarding. A first wave was repelled but the onslaught continued. A relentless barrage of hooks thumped on the decks and retracted with great velocity. One grapple hook pinned a Portuguese sailor into the galley side. He winced in pain as it dug deep into his leg. Fernão and Diogo rushed to assist. They hacked their swords into the attached rope and freed their injured comrade. Francisco kicked two assailants off the ship edge, but the attackers swarmed over the railing in great numbers. He threw himself into the melee. Hundreds of Moors brandished their curve-bladed scimitars and daggers as they poured over the railing on either side and attacked the Portuguese. Francisco twirled his black sword with skillful precision and struck down one after another. Diogo grinned at Fernão as he snatched up a galley oar. They each took an end and rushed into a mass of charging infidels, sending them crashing onto the deck. Portuguese fidalgos and seamen finished them with hacking sword blows.

But just as one wave was repulsed, another would clamber over the rail to board the galley. Exhaustion began to take its toll. Fernão and Diogo found themselves surrounded by over 20 enemy insurgents as they breathed heavily and shook their tiring limbs. Fernão and Diogo summoned their courage and with resolution and faith engaged the enemy. Fernão felt the adrenaline rushing through his body and it took hold in his soul. The action on the deck seemed to move in slow motion. Every detail became crystal clear. He negotiated every obstacle without thinking. He moved his sword almost effortlessly and every slash, thrust, and parry hit exactly the mark intended.

The Portuguese fought with passion and fury, but the relentless onslaught of the enemy forces continued to pour onto the deck of the ship. The galley had some gunners with small falconets blasting 1-pound shot, but the close action made it difficult to isolate targets. Crossbowmen launched bolts from portholes and concealed areas and were more precise in their aim. Fernão flailed at the enemy alongside his comrades, determined against the formidable contingent of 50 proa vessels loaded with enemy combatants.

A small brigantine got separated from the Portuguese ships and soon found itself surrounded by four much larger war ships of the Moors. They pounded the little Portuguese vessel with a barrage of cannon fire until most of its crew were wounded or dead. Simon Martin, one of the Viceroy's most daring captains, directed his cannon fire until their powder ran out. Captain Martin feigned defeat and ordered his wounded crew below deck. The Moors took the bait and boarded with 15 warriors.

As the enemy searched for damage to the brigantine, the captain stormed up the stairs and cried out: 'O Jesus Christ, give us the victory! Help our faith!'

With indignation and adrenaline-fueled speed, he commenced to slash at the necks of seven Moors and left their heads rolling across the deck. Those remaining were consumed with fear at the sight of it and leapt off the ship. Once the four Moor vessels discovered the Portuguese had achieved the victory, they cautiously drew near to the brigantine to rescue their comrades who were flailing about in the sea.

Captain Martin quickly found a cannon with some powder left. He retrieved a piece of sail and stuffed it inside the hole of the barrel. This appeared white like a stone mortar. Immediately, he placed a handful of powder over the barrel and lit a fire in his hand as though he were to launch a mortar. The captain's clever ruse worked. The enemy turned away.

Captain Serrão's galley was engaged in heavy fighting for much of the day. The Indian coastal humidity and stifling heat wore upon the Portuguese. Fernão was drenched in sweat and wiped his forearm across his brow. In the lull of that moment, a Turk crept behind him raising his scimitar.

Diogo had just pulled his sword from an assailant and saw the menacing figure looming over his brother, but he was too far away to assist. He yelled: 'Fernão! Watch out!'

Before the words were out of his mouth a shadowed figure dropped from the mast above and rammed a dagger deep into the Turk' neck, where it joins the shoulder. Diogo rushed over. Fernão turned to witness a man writhing on the deck, scimitar laying helplessly nearby and Samuel Levi withdrawing his bloodied dagger. With composure surprising for the scene, Fernão finished the Turk. He helped Samuel up and said, 'You have played my guardian angel today.'

'Sure. An angel . . . angel of death.' Samuel grinned as he sheathed his dagger. The moment of levity was short-lived however, as both Diogo and Fernão were quickly occupied with more attackers.

Francisco, meanwhile, had been surrounded by the enemy and stood against the edge of the vessel fending off their attacks. Moors continued to climb up ropes from behind him. One of them gained the advantage and wrapped an arm around Francisco's neck. Another, on board, sliced through his puffed white shirt sleeve and into his arm. The fidalgo with the red sash, Dom Braga, nearby, was able to shove two of the attacking Moors off the ship, giving Francisco enough space to break free. At the stern of the ship, Captain Serrão was overwhelmed as he fended off five Moors. The Magalhães brothers and Samuel charged to assist and met Francisco and Braga along the way.

Just as they made the deck, Fernão felt the slash of an enemy sword grazed hard against his lower leg and was slammed in the head with a club. Braga and Francisco charged at the assailants with their swords cutting down one after another. With a lull in the action, Braga turned to Francisco with a big smile and raised his sword in victory.

Francisco smiled but then his jaw dropped, and he yelled, 'Watch out!'

His warning was too late. A lone Moor emerged from behind a large wooden crate and thrust his scimitar through Braga's back and the tip exited out his chest. Full of rage, Francisco sliced his sword across the Moor's chest and then followed with a hack across his neck. The head dangled from the torso by a single tendon and the body fell on the deck with a thud.

Meanwhile, Fernão staggered, held his head, and pulled his hand away covered in blood. He could not put his full weight on his leg and quickly pulled a blood-soaked pant leg up and was swept with nausea at the sight of his white shin bone, bright as finished ivory, protruding from the bloody gash. When he took a step forward, pain shot through his leg, and he fell to one knee.

Likewise, Braga stumbled forward while clutching his bloodied chest and fell to one knee facing Fernão. The two looked at one another's blood-stained uniforms. Braga struggled to speak, 'Blood . . . a badge of honor. You wear it well.' He smiled and collapsed dead.

Fernão looked at him helplessly. Francisco picked up Fernão and draped his arm around his shoulder. 'Come on,' he said. 'I need to get you to a safe area.' Francisco then carried his friend behind some dropped sails, wrapped the wound tightly and gave Fernão another cloth to hold against his head, and concealed him under a folded sail. 'Be back soon.' Safe, but reeling, Fernão passed out.

The battle carried on. More Portuguese were wounded, and more attackers fell to Portuguese swords. Captain Serrão, freed from his attackers by Diogo, rallied the men with a revived effort to repel the invaders from their ship and now they once again took the offensive. Wounded men, who were still able, manned the oars. The captain steered the galley into the mass of proas and fired off the large cannon in front, until the barrel glowed orange. Many vessels sank under the barrage and others were rammed by the long prow. The enemy responded with its own cannon fire, sending iron balls crashing into the hull, and across the deck. Wood shattered and men screamed as they were hit. Portuguese crossbowmen, undaunted, continued to launch bolt after bolt, and gunners fired their falconets. The galley continued to pound the enemy with cannon fire.

Meanwhile, on board the flagship, Dom Lourenço had driven his crew to a decisive victory over the 600 hundred Moors—all killed or forced into the sea. Now Lourenço had tracked down the second of the two massive flagships, along with Captain Nuño Vaz Pereira on board another caravel. Pereira's men had already secured grappling hooks on one side of the

Moor flagship. Lourenço came along the other side of it and his men quickly tied into it. Both Portuguese vessels fired their cannons into the sides of the Moor vessel, and then boarded. An intense hand to hand battle raged on the deck of the enemy flagship. The force of the combined crews was overwhelming. The Portuguese slew the Moor crew of 500 in short order. Once the Moor flagship was decimated, Lourenço's crew wasted no time in dispatching their ship, and Dom Lourenço steered into the midst of the enemy. The Portuguese sunk 10 vessels with heavy cannon fire. Taking into consideration their losses of ships, especially the two massive flag ships, the remaining Islamic invaders turned their ships around to make a hasty retreat.

Seizing the moment, Captain Lourenço exclaimed: 'Praised be Jesus Christ, let us follow up on our victory against these dogs!'

The men cheered. The Portuguese captains rallied their ships in pursuit, and soon the enemy vessels were surrounded. The last battles were quick and decisive. Those not killed dove into the sea. But even then, the Portuguese would not relent. From late afternoon onward through the night the Portuguese hunted down the enemy. Skiffs were launched in pursuit with lancers and crossbowmen, cutting down anyone swimming for shore. The sea was awash with blood, and bodies washed ashore for days.

On the following morning, Captain Lourenço ordered the two galleys, a brigantine, and some skiffs ashore to count the bodies. Fernão was recovering on board the galley, now covered in bandages, and seated among other wounded. An uneasy dizziness overcame him as he struggled to his feet. Fernão squinted his eyes to view the carnage on the nearby shore. Portuguese mariners were piling up bodies in stacks.

Most of the men onshore covered their faces with handkerchiefs to quell the stench of rotting flesh in the rising mid-morning heat. Captain Serrão approached Fernão, who was sweating and grasping the ship rail tightly to steady himself.

'You did well,' Serrão said. 'And you have the wounds to prove it.'

'Only my duty sir,' Fernão gasped, and forced a smile.

Serrão stared out toward shore at the bodies. 'A great victory. Indeed, perhaps a miracle. But it did not come without cost. We have lost many lives and have many wounded.'

'I believe, captain—.' Fernão's words tapered off as his knees buckled. Serrão took him by the arm to steady him.

'Magalhães, you look terrible. I will have Francisco escort you to the hospital in Cannanore. Perhaps this is our last time together. I will now join the fleet preparing in Cochin.'

The two looked at one another. Fernão nodded. Serrão smiled and nodded also. There was little more to be said.

In the late afternoon, the men on shore returned to the ships and the final casualty numbers were reported to the captains; 70 Portuguese had been killed, and over 200 wounded. They concealed their losses to the enemy by burying the dead far out at sea. Over 3,600 enemy forces were killed. More had been killed in the sea or drowned. It was a stunning defeat for the Islamic alliance. Later, the King of Cannanore would declare to the Portuguese and all his subjects: 'These Christians are very brave and valiant men. And truly, I have found myself in many battles in my time, but I have never seen any men braver than these Portuguese.'

The following morning, Fernão was laying on a cot in the hospital of Cannanore. Both staff and patients wore cotton clothing for keeping the body cool. Fernão knew the monsoon rains would not appear until late May or early June. It was now the middle of March, and the temperatures were nearing the yearly peak. Fernão's eyes were shut, and his body was drenched in sweat. A sudden pleasant breeze flowed over his chest and face. He opened his eyes, and a dark-skinned girl was waving a large green palm over him. Fernão scanned the room and noticed servants rotating among the patients with similar fans, alleviating the suffering and speeding recovery. His eyes turned towards the far end of a long row of cots and focused upon two Portuguese doctors clad in blood-stained cotton smocks. They pointed across the room at Fernão. A dreadful foreboding loomed over his soul. He knew his leg was damaged and had not yet been treated. The doctors began their slow walk down the aisle between the beds. Just then, a divine providence emerged— Diogo and Francisco entered the hospital. They looked across the room then pointed at Fernão. They made haste and arrived along with the doctors in front of his bed. Francisco nudged in between the two doctors and placed one arm around each. He turned his head toward the one on his right side and smiled. 'So, what do you have planned for my friend here?'

The doctor raised his eyebrow in surprise at such an absurd closeness. He cleared his throat. 'We must set the bones . . . two fractures . . . it will not be pleasant.'

Fernão swallowed hard and the dizziness returned.

Diogo stood over Fernão. 'I expect the Lord will guide these good doctors. You ready for this?'

Fernão took his brother's words as a divine utterance of encouragement. 'Get on with it then,' he said.

One doctor placed a thick leather strap between Fernão's teeth. Diogo and Francisco aided the doctors in restraining him from any sudden movements as they worked him over. Fernão grimaced and bit down on the strap as the two doctors maneuvered the bone pieces into proper position. Blood from the wound flowed across the white sheets and Fernão writhed from his bones scraping together as they were set. He blacked out. The doctors wrapped the leg in a makeshift cast to keep the bones in position as they fused together with the passage of time.

When Fernão awakened he could tell it was late morning by the sunlight through the windows. The servant girl was again waving her palm over him. She smiled and ran across the room to tap one of the Portuguese doctors on the arm. The girl went out to notify Diogo and Francisco in a waiting room and brought them to Fernão's bedside. By then, the doctor had returned to examine his head wound, as well as the leg. 'The bones set well,' he said. 'But you will have to remain still for some time, for the leg and the head wound. You will not be able to report for duty any time soon.'

'How long doctor?' Fernão asked.

'If there is no lasting trauma to your head and the leg heals normally, I expect it will take eight weeks.'

The doctor departed and Diogo stepped into his place. He had an announcement, 'I plan to return home today, on the next fleet en route from Cochin—and to settle back in Porto. I have my liberty chest full of goods and a share from the Mombasa campaign.

Francisco and Fernão stared blankly, stunned by his abrupt plans.

'You sure this is what you want?' Fernão asked. 'Remember, there are more treasures for the taking and new lands to explore.'

'I am certain. This is all I need. Enough to manage the farm.'

Fernão tried to think it through, to argue, but his mind was foggy and the pain consuming. He realized he would not be able to persuade Diogo, once his he had made up his mind.

'Very well my brother,' Fernão said. They clenched arms. Diogo said his farewell and left.

Francisco stepped forward. 'I am not leaving,' he said. 'You are stuck with me.' Both chuckled at this. Francisco pulled up a chair and began to reminisce upon the battle. Fernão knew his wounds would take time to heal, but for the moment, he was thankful for his friend's presence.

The Magellan Chronicles: Sources

Albuquerque, Afonso de. *The Commentaries of the Great Alfonso de Albuquerque*. Translated by Walter de Gray Birch. 4 vols. New York: Cambridge University Press, 2010. (London: Hakluyt Society, 1875).

Arciniegas, Germán. *Amerigo and the New World: The Life and Times of Amerigo Vespucci*. Translated by Harriet de Onís. New York: Alfred A Knoff, 1955.

Barbosa, Duarte. *A Description of the Coasts of East Africa and Malabar in the Beginning of the Sixteenth Century*. Translated by Henry E.J. Stanley. Kentucky: n.p., 2014.

Bergreen, Laurence. *Over the Edge of the World: Magellan's Terrifying Circumnavigation of the Globe*. New York: Harper Collins Publishers, 2003.

Blackburn, Graham. *The Overlook Illustrated Dictionary of Nautical Terms*. Woodstock, NY: The Overlook Press, 1981.

Bridgeman, Keith and Tahira Arsham, eds. *Magellan*. England: Viartis, 2008.

Camerota, Filippo, ed. *Museo Galileo: A Guide to the Treasures of the Collection.* Firenze, Italy: Gionti, 2010.

Caruncho, Daniel R. *Royal Alcazar of Seville: More than a Thousand Years of Art and Architecture.* Translated by Cerys Giordano Jones. Barcelona: Dos de Arte Ediciones, S.L., 2016.

Castanheda, Fernão Lopes de. *Historia do descobrimento e conquista de India pelos Portugueses.* 2 vols. Lisboa: Typographia Rollandiana, 1833.

Corrêa, Gaspar. *Lendas de India.* 2 vols. Lisboa: Academia Real das Sciencies de Lisboa, 1858.

Cliff, Nigel. *Holy War: How Vasco da Gama's Epic Voyages Turned the Tide in a Centuries-Old Clash of Civilizations.* New York: Harper Collins, 2011.

Cribb, Joe, Barrie Cook, and Ian Carradice. *A Comprehensive View of the Coins of the World Throughout History.* London: Little, Brown & Co., 1999.

Crowley, Roger. *Conquerors: How Portugal Forged the First Global Empire.* New York: Random House, 2015.

Danvers, Frederick Charles. *The Portuguese in India.* 2 vols. London: Elibron, 2007.

Delagado, Francisco Gil. *Seville Cathedral.* Spain: Escudo de Oro, n.d.

Diffie, Bailey W. and George D. Winius. *Foundations of the Portuguese Empire 1415-1580*. 10 vols. Minneapolis, MN: University of Minnesota Press, 1977.

Edwards, Charles Lester and Amerigo Vespucci. *Amerigo Vespucci*. Edited by Keith Bridgeman and Tahira Arsham. England: Viartis, 2009.

Fernándo-Armesto, Felipe. *Amerigo: The Man Who Gave his Name to America*. New York: Random House Publishing Group, 2007.

Gibbons, Tony, ed. *The Encyclopedia of Ships: Over 1,500 Military and Civilian Ships from 5000 B.C. to the Present Day*. San Diego: Thunder Bay Press, 2001.

Góis, Damião de. *Lisbon in the Renaissance*. Translated by Jeffrey S. Ruth. New York: Italica Press, 1996.

Green, Toby. *Inquistion: The Reign of Fear*. New York: St. Martin's Press, 2007.

——. *The Rise of the Trans-Atlantic Slave trade in Western Africa, 1300-1589*. New York: Cambridge University Press, 2012.

Guillemard, Francis Henry Hill. *The Life of Ferdinand Magellan and the First Circumnavigation of the Globe: 1480-1521*. London: George Philip & Son, 1890.

Hargrave, Catherine Perry. *A History of Playing Cards*. New York: Dover Publications Inc., 2014.

Hazard, Henry W. and Kenneth Setton, eds. *A History of the Crusades: Volume III: The Fourteenth and Fifteenth Centuries*. 6 vols. Madison, WI: The University of Wisconsin Press, 1975.

Johnson, Donald S., Tapio Markkanen Juha Nurminen, and Pär-Henrik Sjöström. *The History of Seafaring: Navigating the World's Oceans*. London: Conway Maritime Press, 2007.

Joyner, Tim. *Magellan*. Camden, ME: International marine Publishing, 1992.

Kemp, Peter, ed. *The Oxford Companion to Ships and the Sea*. Oxford: Oxford University Press, 1988.

Konstam, Angus. *Historical Atlas of Exploration 1492-1600*. London: Mercury Books, 2006.

Krondl, Michael. *The Taste of Conquest: The Rise and Fall of the Three Great Cities of Spice*. New York: Balantine Books, 2007.

Lavery, Brian. *Ship: The Epic Story of Maritime Adventure*. New York: DK Publishing, 2010.

Major, Richard Henry, ed. *India in the Fifteenth Century*. New York: Cambridge University Press, 2010. (London: Hakluyt Societ, 1857).

Mandeville, Sir John. *The Book of Marvels and Travels*. Translated by Anthony Bale. Oxford: Oxford University Press, 2012.

Martyr, Peter. *The Discovery of the new World in the Writings of Peter Martyr of Anghiera*. Edited by Ernesto Lunari, Elisa Magioncalda, and Rosanna Mazzacane. Rome: Istituto Poligrafica, 1992.

Menzies, Gavin. *1421 The Year China Discovered America*. New York: Harper Collins Publishers, 2003.

Monteiro, Saturnino. *Portuguese Sea Battles Volume I: The First World Sea Power 1139-1521*. 8 vols. Translated by Maria do Céu Barreto. Oeiras, Portugal: Saturnino Monteiro, 2014.

Morris, John Gottlieb. *Martin Behaim the German Astronomer and Cosmographer of the Times of Columbus*. Baltimore: John Murphy and Co., 1855.

Morrison, Samuel Eliot. *Admiral of the Ocean Sea: A Life of Christopher Columbus*. Toronto: Little, Brown & Co., 1970.

Newitt, Malyn, ed. *The Portuguese in West Africa, 1415-1670*. New York: Cambridge University Press, 2010.

Nicolle, David. *The Portuguese in the Age of Discovery c. 1340-1665*. Oxford: Osprey Publishing Ltd., 2012.

Nielsen Jr., Niels C., Norvin Hein, Frank E. Reynolds, Alan L. Miller, Samuel E. Karff, Alice C. Cochran, and Paul McClean, eds. *Religions of the World*. New York: St. Martin's Press, Inc., 1983.

O'Bryan, John. *A History of Weapons*. San Francisco: Chronicle Books, 2013.

Passos, John Dos. *The Portugal Story: Three Centuries of Exploration and Discovery*. Lexington: Doubleday, 1969.

Pearsen, Michael. *Port Cities and Invaders: The Swahili oast, India, and Portugal in the Early Modern Era*. Baltimore: The John Hopkins University Press, 1998.

Perreira, Duarte Pacheco. *Esmeraldo de Situ Orbis*. Translated and Edited by Geroge H.T. Kimble. New York: Routledge, 2016.

Pigafetta, Antonio. *Magellan's Voyage: A Narrative Account of the First Circumnavigation*. Translated and edited by R.A. Skelton. New York: Dover Publications Inc., 1969.

———. *The First Voyage Round the World by Magellan*. Edited by Henry John Stanly. New York: Cambridge University Press, 2010.

Pires, Tomé. *The Summa Oriental of Tomé Pires*. 2 vols. Surrey, UK: Ashgate Publishing Ltd., 2010.

Preto, Luis. *Jogo do Pau: The Ancient Art and Modern Science of Portuguese Stick Fighting*. n.p. 2013.

Rossfelder, André. *In Pursuit of Longitude: Magellan and the Antimeridian*. La Jolla, CA: Starboard Books, 2010.

Sanceau, Elaine. *The Reign of the Fortunate King 1495-1521*. USA: Archon Books, 1970.

Stephens, H. Morse. *Albuquerque*. Oxford: Clarendon Press, 1897.

Theal, George McCall. *History and Ethnography of Africa South of the Zambesi 1505-1795*. 3 vols. New York: Cambridge University Press, 2010. (London: Swan Sonnenschein & Co., 1910).

Thomas, Hugh. *The Slave Trade: The Story of the Atlantic Slave Trade 1440-1870*. New York: Simon and Schuster, 1997.

Webster, Roderick and Marjorie. *Western Astrololabes: Historic Scientific Instruments of the Adler Planetarium & Astronomy Museum*. 2 vols. Chicago: Adler Planetarium & Astronomy Museum, 1998.

Weinstein, Donald. *Ambassador from Venice: Pietro Pasqualigo in Lisbon, 1501*. Minneapolis, MN: University of Minnesota Press, 1960.

Whiteway, Richard Stephen. *The Rise of Portuguese Power in India. A.D. 1497-A.D. 1550*. Columbia, SC: n.p., 2018.

Varthema, Ludovico di. *The Travels of Ludovico di Varthema in Egypt, Syria, Arabia Deserta and Arabia Felix in Persia, India, and Ethiopia, 1503 to 1508*. Lexington, KY: Forgotten Books, 2014. (London: Hakluyt Society, 1863).

Vicente, Gil. *Four Plays of Gil Vicente*. Translated by Aubrey F. G. Bell. San Bernardino, CA: Forgotten Books, 2015.

Zweig, Stefen. *Magellan*. London: Pushkin Press, 2011.

About the Author

Brett Stortroen has authored the biographical novel, *Night of the Dragon: The Saga of Saint George* and the non-fiction book, now sold in over thirty countries, *Mecca, Muhammad & the Moon God: A Candid Investigation into the Origins of Islam*.

With a BA and MA in Theological and Historical Studies, he also publishes articles on his web site, bigfaithministries.com.

Traveling the world as a telecommunication engineer in the cruise industry, he has been able to incorporate his maritime experiences and historical research into the latest biographical novel series, *The Magellan Chronicles*.